THE WOMAN WHO WALKED INTO THE SEA

PHILIP R. CRAIG

A MARTHA'S VINEYARD MYSTERY

W9-ASI-787

AVON BOOKS  NEW YORK

This is a work of fiction. Names, characters, places and incidents either are the product of the author's imagination or are used fictitiously. Any resemblance to events or persons, living or dead, is entirely coincidental.

AVON BOOKS
A division of
The Hearst Corporation
1350 Avenue of the Americas
New York, New York 10019

Copyright © 1991 by Philip R. Craig
Published by arrangement with Charles Scribner's Sons
Library of Congress Catalog Card Number: 90-48283
ISBN: 0-380-71536-8

First Avon Books Printing: June 1993

AVON TRADEMARK REG. U.S. PAT. OFF. AND IN OTHER COUNTRIES, MARCA REGISTRADA, HECHO EN U.S.A.

Printed in the U.S.A.

RA 10 9 8 7 6 5 4 3 2 1

To my children,
Kimberlie and James,
fourth generation Vineyarders
whose island ancestors sailed
from the wild Azores.

~1~

WE WERE ON the clam flats at the south end of Katama Bay. The tide was out, and the flats had again risen from the waters as they had since time immemorial. Beneath the mud and sand were blissful mollusks, leading peaceful clam lives, little suspecting that above them clam hunters were coming after them. Such is the innocence of Eden. The hunted sometimes never realize that they are the prey of the hunters. Instinct may make the deer wary of the lion, or the gopher wary of the hawk, but such ancient blood knowledge seems to have eluded the clam. Perhaps because he has no blood.

I suggested as much to Zee, who was on her knees beside me, rubber gloved, her basket at hand, as we dug in search of the innocent, delicious clams.

"You're weird," said Zee. "Besides, clams may not have blood, but they do have all this oozy juice that probably amounts to the same thing. Their problem is that all they can do to escape is burrow deeper into the sand."

"Just like lots of the rest of us," I said. "I'm glad to learn that you're catching on to the secrets of the clamming trade. To capture these little guys and gals, you have to dig down to where they are and then grab them before they can catch the elevator to the next lower floor."

I came up with a clam and dropped it in my bucket. We'd been on the flats since a half hour before the tide reached low, and our buckets were filling up. Zee was a fast study and had quickly caught on to all I'd ever learned about clamming. And I'd been at it for years, too. It was a skill you were morally obliged to develop if you were going to live on Martha's Vineyard. The island was surrounded by salt water full of fish and indented by bays full of shellfish, and if you didn't learn to outfox the many sea creatures you were no true islander at all.

Here, now, on the Katama clam flats, our knees were black, our gloved hands were black, the mud beneath us was black. It was June, and already the summer folk were pouring down. Soon the clam flats would be emptied of their treasure by hordes of hungry amateur clammers. So we were getting ours while the getting was easy. Later we would be obliged to seek more obscure clamming grounds. Behind our backs, Katama Bay reached north toward Edgartown. Sailboats carrying day sailors from the Edgartown docks, moved over the blue water. To our south, beyond the flats and beyond the far sand dunes where the June people were browning in the sun, stretched the Atlantic, going "all the way to the Azores," as the local descendants of the Portuguese were inclined to say. Over us, the summer sky lifted out of the white haze to the south and curved pale blue over us and down again into the white haze of the north. The sun was hot on our backs.

"Look," said Zee. "Isn't that John Skye's Jeep?"

It was indeed John Skye's Jeep. It had come east from the end of the paved road in Katama, over the flat sands inside of the dunes, and was now stopped a hundred yards away from us beside my own ancient Toyota Landcruiser. A hand waved. We waved back in the manner of those who, doubtful about who is waving at them but fearful of appearing stupid or unsociable if they don't wave back, wave back. The hand curved back inside the door of the Jeep, the door opened, and John Skye—who else?—stepped out. Other Jeep doors opened and two other people got out: an elderly woman and a man about my age—early thirties or so, still approaching his prime.

John Skye owned most of what had once been a Vineyard farm back in the days when Vineyarders, like many folk who lived along the edge of the sea, had combined farming with fishing as they tried to make a living. The farm was only a couple of miles from my own place. He was a professor from Weststock College. I'd met him during a bluefish blitz on Wasque Point when we'd been side by side hauling in the blues and having a very fine time. After the bluefish had gone, we'd shared coffee laced with rum and talked of this and that before going off to scale and clean our fish. We'd met again now and then and learned a bit about one another—most importantly, to him, that I was a neighbor and lived on the island year round and was quite capable of closing down a house in the fall, looking after it during the winter, and opening it up again in the spring, and that I could haul, paint, and launch a catboat. He could use somebody to do all those things for him while he was busy being academic, and I could use the money he was willing to pay me to do them. Later we became almost friends and later still real friends. John was originally from out west but was now a permanent New Englander. He came to the island as soon as he could wind up his college duties in the spring and stayed until the last possible moment in the fall. He was tall and balding, about fifty years old, and taught things medieval.

And now he dug out clam buckets from the rear of his Jeep and came walking across the muddy clam flats toward us, his companions chatting cheerfully.

"I see you've come to raid our clam flat," I said. "You shifty-eyed mainlanders are all alike. You wait until hard-working, honest, but starving natives finally discover the whereabouts of the elusive clam, then move in and rape the area."

"The economic principle that made America great," said Skye. "You understand it perfectly." He peered into our clam baskets. "You've done some ruthless exploiting of your own, I see. Did you leave any for late arrivals?"

"Plenty. They're just a couple of inches deeper than you think they ought to be. We've been here about an hour. You know Zee Madieras."

He did. They exchanged how-do-you-dos and Skye's eyebrows involuntarily arched, as normal men's did when looking at her. Zee was dark and sleek as a panther and single again. Even covered with clamming mud, she reminded me of summer wind. Her black hair had blue tones in it and I had seen it fall like a tropic night over her shoulders, though now it was bundled up under a kerchief. Her eyes could be as deep as eternity.

"Allow me to introduce my companions," said Skye. "Both professors, I fear, but civilized nevertheless. Dr. Marjorie Summerharp and Dr. Ian McGregor. Marjorie, Ian, Mr. J. W. Jackson and Miss Zee Madieras."

"Mrs. Zee Madieras," said Zee, looking a bit too long, I thought, at Dr. Ian McGregor. "Zeolinda, actually . . ." Her voice trailed away, and I too looked at Dr. McGregor. He was six feet tall or so, about 190, wearing shorts and a T-shirt that said something witty and revealed him to be very fit. He had an Apollonian head topped by dark curls. His eyes and smile were brilliant.

"Mrs. Madieras," he said in a rich baritone. "Mr. Jackson." He extended a hand and I pulled off a muddy glove and took it. There were two split knuckles on his hand. His grip was strong. So was mine. His brilliant eyes hardened for an instant. Then we parted and he was looking at Zee while I gazed up at Dr. Marjorie Summerharp.

Dr. Summerharp was in her seventies, lean and leathery, with short gray hair and one of those faces that keep you in line if its owner is your schoolteacher. A nononsense face, etched with countless lines, with a bony nose and wire-rimmed glasses. Her iron-gray eyes stared out upon the world with a look half of amusement and half of general disapproval. She extended a bony hand, which I took. Her grip was surprisingly firm.

"How do you do?" she said.

"Reasonably well. And yourself?"

A fleeting smile touched her thin lips. "Reasonably well, thank you."

"These two have been my guests for a couple of weeks and are taking over our house while I take Mattie and the twins out to Colorado to introduce them to their western kinfolk. Marjorie and Ian needed a quiet place to finish up some important work, so I invited them down to the Blessed Isle. I was going to phone you, but now I don't have to—I'd appreciate it if you'll be their emergency number in case anything goes wrong. The water, electricity, anything like that. You know the place better than anybody else.''

Skye had a new family. He'd married a widow with twin teenage daughters and adored all three of his new women with ill-concealed affection. He was no doubt anxious to display them to the rest of his family, all of whom still lived in the high mountain country. I approved of his decision.

''Sure. Be glad to.''

''Fine. I'll leave your number by the phone.''

''We'll try not to disturb you, Mr. Jackson,'' said Dr. Summerharp. ''I can clean a drain or fix a leaky pipe or replace a fuse if I have to. In a pinch, I can rewire a fixture and unplug a sewer line, too.''

I looked up at her and felt my mouth turn up at one corner. ''I'll bet you can, Doctor,'' I said. ''How are your clamming skills?''

''I was born on the Maine coast. I think I can find a clam if I'm looking for one.''

''Well, down here on the Vineyard they don't just jump up into your basket for you. You have to go after them with a shovel or a fork or a bathroom plunger on the end of a stick or with your hands. Since you aren't armed, all you have is your hands, so if you want some steamers you'd better get down here in the mud and start digging. You have gloves?''

She extracted some from a hind pocket of her rolled-up jeans. ''I have. I'm a little creaky in the joints, but I can get down and I can get up again. When does the tide turn?''

An intelligent question. Not de rigueur for some academic types I've met. ''It's just turned,'' I said. ''There's an hour and a half difference between the tides in here and those out yonder beyond the sand you drove in on. Everything here happens later than out there.''

She nodded and began an arthritic old lady's careful descent to her knees. ''I've been on the island before and I've seen the maps and charts. The only way water can get in and out of here is through the gut between Edgartown and Chappaquiddick. It makes for a fast current in the gut and late tides inside.''

I was thus impressed twice in a single minute and was beginning to respect Dr. Marjorie Summerharp. ''That's right. You'll have an hour or so of dry digging here before the water gets up to you. Plenty of time for an old pro Maine clammer to get her limit.''

''John Skye's limit, that is,'' she said, grimacing then relaxing as she settled onto her heels. ''We off-islanders have to pay a fortune for our shellfish permits, so today we're all using his.''

She knelt beside me and we both began to dig. John Skye aligned himself on my other side and got to work, too. Somewhere beyond my peripheral vision I heard Ian McGregor's voice mixing with Zee's. I listened in spite of myself and noted that he had a ready wit and a pleasing tongue and that after a while Zee laughed.

''So, what are you doing down here?'' I asked Dr. Summerharp, so as not to hear that laughter or that clever voice.

''We're preparing a paper for one of those obscure but vitally important journals that we academics take terribly seriously. It will be my last such contribution to scholarship and thus is of little professional consequence to me, but for Ian it will mean great things for his career. My career, you see, is basically over, while his is just flowering.''

A touch of bitterness dwelt in her tone, I thought. I heard Zee's laughter. ''And what is the subject of your learned paper?'' I asked.

Dr. Summerharp glanced at me, and again that brief smile touched her thin, dry lips. ''Are you are another academician, Mr. Jackson?''

John Skye laughed. ''I assure you he's no academician. He may have problems, but that's not one of them. No, Marjorie, J. W. is a normal human. A fisherman, a handyman, and an ex Boston cop. And I warn you, J. W., Marjorie is a jester as well as being a genuine brain. A lot of her more solemn colleagues are confused by that. She's tweaked a few scholarly noses in her day, so watch yours."

"I'll keep my gloves up," I said.

"So you're an ex-policeman," she said.

"Retired."

"You're young to be retired."

"I'm independently poor."

"An unoriginal remark." I felt like a schoolboy as she looked at me with those steely eyes.

"J. W. was shot and is retired on a disability pension," said John Skye. "He gets a little something from Uncle Sam, too, in compensation for some shrapnel he acquired in our recent undeclared war."

How did he know about that? "How did you know about that?" I asked. I was not inclined to share such information. I looked at him.

"I have my sources," he said. "I'm an intellectual, remember? We intellectuals are paid to be smart." I looked at him some more. "I talked to George Martin," he said. "Your name came up."

George Martin and I had shared more than one flask of brandy at Wasque while waiting for the October bluefish to show up. *In vino veritas.*

"How shot are you?" asked Marjorie Summerharp.

"Just enough to loaf on Martha's Vineyard all year and pretend to fish for a living."

She looked at me with her iron eyes, waiting. I suddenly wished that I could be one of her students. "The bullet lodged near my spine," I said. "They decided to leave it there instead of trying to take it out. It doesn't hurt and it probably won't ever move. The shrapnel was mostly in my legs and they got most of it out. It's no big deal."

"I see." She dug down and extracted a large clam who had lived a long clam life but had now come near to the end of it. She dropped the almost late great clam into her bucket. "Well, for what it's worth, we're drafting a paper that maintains that a document we found a couple of years ago near London is, in fact, a fragment of a previously unknown Shakespearean play."

I thought about that as hard as I could, so as not to hear Zee's voice blending with that of D. Ian McGregor. But I had little luck. My attention was not under my control. I took it by the throat and focused it on Shakespeare.

"I thought they had all of Shakespeare's plays already."

"That's what everybody thinks but Ian and me. This paper we're writing is about how we found it and why we think it's the real thing."

"Why should anybody think it isn't?"

She raised her gray eyebrows in feigned scorn. "You, the ex-cop, should ask? Because it will be perceived as a scam! What else? We scholarly types are particularly susceptible to con men, you must know. We've believed in the Baron of Arizona, the Piltdown Man, the Cardiff Giant, and dozens of fake Rembrandts, Vermeers, and Klees. You can imagine how people will react to the announcement that an unknown Shakespeare has been unearthed. And I don't blame them. I didn't believe it myself when we found it."

"But now you do."

She hesitated. "Yes. At the moment."

"And that means something to me, at least," said John Skye, "because Marjorie, here, in spite of the jokes she's played at the expense of our stuffier colleagues, is the very Queen of Skeptics in our profession. She doubts everyone and every conclusion and every thesis. She turns scholars pale, makes ambitious intellectuals shudder when she examines their texts, sends grad students into the streets to earn their livings with tin cups and dark glasses. A veritable fiend for legitimate research." He grinned and dug up a clam. "She's a famously formidable doubter and one, I'm glad to say, who was not on the board that read *my* thesis!"

"And well you should feel that way, John Skye. Your conclusions about the language of *Gawain* are open to considerable debate."

"You see what I mean?" asked Skye. "The woman is not even talking about her own field, yet takes me to task after all these years!"

"And why not? You wrote a slick thesis and you talk a good game, but all good teachers have a bit of con in them. Why not you? Your students say you're a ham at heart."

"Sacrilege," protested Skye mildly.

"Why do you believe the document you found is real?" I asked, to hear the sound of my voice instead of McGregor's.

Dr. Summerharp had found herself a clam colony, a senior citizen retirement home, from the size of them—all big and mature. She brought up one after the other and for a while ignored my question. Quite understandable, I thought, envying her find. I like big clams; Zee, on the other hand, favors the medium to small variety and claims that the big ones make her gag.

The professor exhausted her mother lode of clams, dug a bit more, and sat back on her skinny heels. "Because we checked out everything and everything checks. The paper is the kind they used then, made out of rags. The ink is the right sort—lampblack and a solution of gums. The age of the document is right—as right as carbon dating can establish it, that is. The document was in a book bound in the seventeenth century, so if it's a fake, it's a very early fake, which seems unlikely, since nobody thought enough of Shakespeare in those days to write a play and sign his name to it. And the signature we have is a lot like the signatures we think are Shakespeare's. Ergo, we have a genuine document."

She coughed and pulled a kerchief from a pocket and wiped her lips. I saw flecks of pink on the kerchief before she tucked it away.

"What's the play about?"

"It's only a piece of a play. Part of one act. I'm not sure it was ever finished—"

"It's about King Arthur," interrupted John Skye. "That's what interests me."

"You medievalists have limited concerns," said Dr. Summerharp in what I was beginning to recognize as her Severe tone. "I assure you, Mr. Jackson, that the subject of the play is of only incidental importance."

"Nonsense," said Skye, unintimidated. "The interesting thing, J. W., is that for the last thousand years everybody and his dog, except Shakespeare, has written about King Arthur. Shakespeare wrote about Romans and Italians and about Scotsmen and Lear and the War of the Roses and about this and that, but never about Arthur. I've always wondered why not, so when Marjorie told me about this find of hers, I took to it like a crow to a dead cat."

"A wonderful image, John," said Dr. Summerharp.

Skye grinned. "Image be damned. If you're right about this manuscript, Marjorie, it'll take a load off my mind that's been there for thirty years or more."

"The load you're carrying isn't on your mind, John," said Marjorie Summerharp. To my surprise, she gave me a devilish wink.

Then, just as I was beginning to feel pretty good, the sound of Zee's voice floated back into my consciousness and pulled my eye around. ". . . There isn't a Mr. Madieras," she was saying. "There was a Dr. Madieras, but there isn't anymore . . ."

She and Ian McGregor were side by side on their muddy knees, digging in the dark sand and talking in an exploratory way that I didn't care for very much. Worse yet, McGregor's bucket was already fuller than it had any right to be. The bastard was a master clammer as well as a Greek god. I climbed to my feet.

"I think we've got enough, Zee," I said. "Between us we can feed a small army."

Zee looked at her clam bucket, her face averted from mine, then flowed up onto her feet like a dancer. "Okay, Jeff. I guess you're right." She smiled down at Ian McGregor. "Nice to meet you," she said.

"And you," he said. "Thanks for the clamming lesson."

"You're a natural." She grinned. He grinned.

"Nice to meet *you*," I said to Dr. Summerharp. I nodded to McGregor, the natural clammer. "If you two need any help around John's place, just give me a ring. See you later, John. Have a nice trip west."

I restrained an impulse to grasp Zee firmly by the arm as we walked to the Landcruiser. As we went, she glanced back and waved. Then she looked up at me and blushed a bit, I thought. I could feel McGregor's eyes following us.

~2~

WHAT COLOR IS jealousy? Envy is green, you get red with anger, white with fear, blue with cold, and spotty with fever. I felt sort of purple but remembered that it, like red, was for rage.

Not that I had any right to be angry. I didn't own Zee; I wasn't married to her; I wasn't even living with her (if only because she'd declined my invitation). I was her wooer, her friend, a lover. Only those things . . .

She wasn't too far away from a bad marriage to the jerk of a doctor I'd never met. She was beginning to feel human again and to have some fun in life, to feel attractive and worthwhile and adventuresome. And maybe I was just part of the adventure. She wasn't that to me, but maybe I was that to her. Certainly she owed me nothing.

So now here she was, meeting a handsome, successful, charming man and apparently feeling tingles she liked feeling, even if she felt guilty about feeling them because I was there.

I thought these thoughts and others like them as I prepared a bachelor lunch, Zee having gone home to West Tisbury to tend to private matters about which I, brooding as we had driven to my place from the beach, had not bothered to inquire. Zee, thinking thoughts of her own and no doubt knowing why I was saying nothing, had nothing much to say either. At my place she picked up her Jeep and left.

But even those lorn of love must eat. So I cooked and listened to a tape of Pavarotti filling my house with a sound like emeralds and diamonds. While Pavarotti sang of grand

Italian passions and I thought of Zee's attraction to Ian McGregor, my hands were preparing a salad made from fresh vegetables from my garden and leftover bluefish from yesterday's stuffed bluefish supper. My dry mouth began to water of its own accord. I got a Molson from the fridge and unbaggied a loaf of bread I'd made in the distant past, the day before yesterday, before Zee and McGregor ever met.

The Molson wasn't bad. Neither was the bread—Betty Crocker's white bread from her *old* cookbook. I bake it four loaves at a time and usually eat the first one before it's even cool. This was the last of the last batch, since I'd given a loaf to Zee and had eaten two by myself already. Betty C's bread is dynamite stuff, but lacks staying power.

I found another beer, took bread and salad outside, and sat in my yard, under the hot June sun. There, I looked out upon the blue Vineyard Sound, where the sailboats leaned in the wind and the powerboats left white lines behind them across the pale blue water. I ate for a while, got yet another beer, and ate a bit more. It was good, but not as good as it should have been. I knew why. Yesterday, Zee had been with me for lunch under the noonday sun. Today, she was not.

I went to the garden and picked weeds for a while. There, as I was on my knees between the kale and the cucumbers, I heard the phone ringing.

It's always a fifty-fifty proposition as to whether I'll get to my phone just before it stops ringing or just afterward. Still, since I don't get many calls, it's worth my time, I figure, to make the dash. After all, one never knows, do one?

So I dashed, thinking that maybe it might even be Zee calling to make things perfect again. And I got there in time. But it wasn't Zee. It was Dr. Marjorie Summerharp.

"I wonder if you will join us for supper," she said. "John's having a few people over and we'd like to add you to the group."

"Well . . ."

"Ian has already phoned Mrs. Madieras," she said with

undisguised irony, "and I'm calling you. I do hope you can come."

I felt stiff. "Well . . ."

"Roast beef and the fixings."

"Ah . . ."

"Martinis at six."

"Um . . ."

"Women love him," she said unexpectedly. "There's nothing you can do about it. The damage is done, if there is any damage. Besides, you're a big man. You can handle yourself."

I was silent.

"We have a leaky faucet," she lied.

I almost had to laugh. "Okay," I said.

After that, I didn't want to weed anymore. I rattled around the house for a while, was disgusted with myself, and thought about fishing. I checked my tide tables because my brain wasn't functioning quite as well as usual and I wasn't sure I remembered the time for low tide at Wasque. But I was, in fact, right: five P.M. on the dot. I looked at my watch—the $2.95 kind that you can get if you fill up your tank at the gas station. I had just time enough to catch the last two hours of the west tide. Fishing seemed to be a much better idea than staying home being stupid, so I got in the Landcruiser and rattled toward the beach.

The principal hindrance to this plan was navigating past the eternal summer traffic jam between the Edgartown A & P on the one side and Al's Package Store on the other. People in cars attempting left turns make this spot a leading contender, second only to the infamous Five Corners in Vineyard Haven, for the traffic jam championship of Martha's Vineyard. Eventually I crawled through, fetched Pease Point Way, and headed for Katama, where, only short hours ago, the joy of clamming had turned unexpectedly somber. At the end of the pavement, I left the parking lot, lined with parked cars and alive with walkers and bikers still headed for South Beach, ground into four-wheel drive, and turned east toward Chappaquiddick. The clam flats were now covered with water, but there were people along the south edge of Katama Bay working away with their rakes in pursuit of quahogs. My own rake was on the rack atop my truck, but I scorned the prospect of quahogging, for I was going bluefishing.

It was a chamber of commerce afternoon: warm, bright, with just enough breeze to let the kite fliers fill the sky with their brilliant-colored toys. The kites soared and looped above me as I drove down the beach. I've never been much of a kite man, myself, but there are a lot of them on the Vineyard in the summertime: fat men, thin men, men with boxer shorts, men with bikinis, young men, old men, single men, family men. Occasionally a woman. Occasionally a child. But usually men. They love their kites and play with them all day long, launching them as soon as they get to the beach and winding them down from the sky at the very end of their day. The women of the kite-flying men seem to do everything else: lay out the blankets, set up the chairs, get out the inner tubes, find the food, find the sun lotion, watch the kids; and then pack all that up again while the kite men wind down their kites. I like to watch the kites, but I can't imagine flying one for very long.

But I can fish for a very long time and not get tired of it, and one of the best places in the world to catch bluefish from shore is at Wasque Point, on the far southeast corner of Chappaquiddick, where the rip tosses up bait and the blues come to pig out and, in their greed, regularly mistake artificial lures for genuine eatables. Fish are not very smart, in spite of rumors to the contrary. A fact for which we should all go to church regularly to thank whatever gods there may be.

There were about thirty assorted four-by-fours lined up along the beach at Wasque, and I could see some people down along the shore actually casting. But I could also see that most of the rods were standing straight in their holders or were leaning against vehicles. That meant that the blues weren't really biting much at the moment. For if they were biting, none of those rods would be standing there; all of them would be working in the hands of fishermen.

I found a spot almost where I wanted to be and pulled

in. I took my rod off the rack, hooked on a three-ounce red-headed Roberts and checked both sides to see what kind of fishermen my neighbors were: were they really fishermen or were they pilgrims—summer ginks who, when they cast, were a danger to everyone within fifty yards? Al Prada's Jeep was on my left, so that was okay. He wasn't in it, but was about three cars down the line chewing the fat with some other regulars. I didn't know the guy on my right, but he had seven years' worth of Wasque Reservation stickers on his side window so I figured he must know something about fishing. Having scouted the terrain, I went down to the water.

I use an eleven-and-a-half-foot graphite rod and twenty-pound black Ande line, so with a plug like the Roberts I can get some distance in my cast most of the time. I'd added a couple extra yards by learning to use a reel without a bail, so by and large I can throw it quite a ways, a useful ability if the fish aren't close enough to shore. Now I put my back into it and really put the Roberts out there. If there was a fish there, I wanted to get it.

I didn't. I got nothing. I cast a dozen more times. Nothing a dozen times. Up and down the line of men, women, and children along the shore, nobody was catching anything. That was both good and bad—bad because nobody was catching anything, indicating that there were no bluefish to be caught right now, and good because it's really disgusting to have fished as long as I have and get nothing and then to have a child or a hundred-year-old woman who has never held a rod before catch a fish right beside you.

I tried a couple of other plugs. Nothing. Then, just in case they were feeding under the surface instead of on top of it, I put on a Hopkins with a triple hook. Normally, I knew, I'd not be doing this sort of thing; I'd be up there on the beach with all the other smart fishermen, saving my energy until there was some sign that there was a bluefish out there ready to be caught. But I was not in a normal mood and I needed something to keep me from thinking about Zee. So I put on the Hopkins and whipped it out as far as I could throw. Way out in the rip I saw it splash home, and three turns on the reel later I felt the fish hit.

Geronimo! It's really terrific to catch a fish in a crowd of people who aren't catching anything. On both sides of me, inspired fishermen were quickly lining up and casting, but only I had a fish.

Wonderful. I cranked him slowly toward shore, hoping that none of the pilgrims would cross my line and cut him off. He was a biggish fish and the current was still running pretty well, so I walked him down, ducking under rods, until he was close. I could see him in the last wave, and I waited until the moment was right and brought him onto the sand. A good fish, ten pounds or so. I got a hand in his gills and carried him to the Landcruiser. The regulars quickly noted that I'd taken him with metal and rigged up with the same. As I got the lure out of his mouth, I saw a rod bend, then another as the long casters began to reach the school. I put the fish in the shade of the truck and went back to try for another one. I fetched another on the second cast, and after that, in spite of the pilgrims, we had some good fishing until the rip flattened. I hardly had time to think about Zee at all.

But as I gutted the fish at the Herring Creek, I had time. I dropped all of the fish but one at the market on my way home, keeping the last one as a gift for John Skye and company. Then I went home and showered and shaved, wondering once again whether I should grow some hair on my face. From the looks of it, it wouldn't hurt to cover it up a bit. Maybe I'd start a beard tomorrow. It would save shaving time, if nothing else. Besides, it might serve to give me a new personality. I felt like I could use one.

I had a beer and then it was time to go to John Skye's farm. I checked my clams in their bucket of salt water, where they were dutifully spitting out sand in preparation to being eaten tomorrow. They were hard at it. Good old clams.

For my visit, I wore Vineyard cocktail party clothes: sandals, faded red shorts (it was too warm to wear my faded red pants), and a blue knit shirt with a little animal over the pocket. Very stylish and almost new from the thrift shop. I thought that I would fit right in.

I arrived fashionably late and went into the kitchen,

where I deposited the bluefish on the counter and kissed Mattie Skye, who looked lovely as usual.

"Here," I said. "I know you and John can catch all the bluefish that you can eat, but I thought maybe the learned doctors could use one. When are you guys headed west?"

"In a few days. Here." She put a tray of hors d'oeuvres in my hands. "Take this out and put it on that table beside the one with the booze. Then fix yourself a drink. We should still have some Mount Gay if you didn't drink it all the last time you were here. Dinner will be coming along later. No, I don't need any help yet."

Through a window I could see Zee talking to John Skye and Marjorie Summerharp. No Ian McGregor in sight. Hmmmmm. I went out the door as one of Mattie's twins came in.

"Hi, J. W.," she said.

"Hi, whichever one you are," I said. "Where's the other one of you?" I simply could not tell them apart, no matter how easy it is to do so, according to John, their mother, and the girls themselves.

"Oh, she's showing Ian the chicken coops. She's such a flirt, it's disgusting."

"Well, Jen, that's the way Jill is," I said.

"I'm Jill," she said.

"Well, Jill, that's the way Jen is," I said.

"Hmmmph," said Jill and went inside. I carried the hors d'oeuvres out to the table, tried a few, and found the Mount Gay. I poured a nice double slug over ice and looked around. Ian McGregor was still not in sight, but there were a couple dozen other people standing around, glasses in hand, carrying on cocktail conversations. I went over and joined Zee, John, and Marjorie Summerharp.

"Hi," I said. Zee looked terrific in a white dress that made her dark beauty even more startling than usual. "You look terrific," I said.

"Hi," she said. "Thanks. You're looking quite Vine-yardish yourself. Very stylish."

"People come from miles around to ask me my opinion of haute couture. I owe it to them to always be perfectly attired."

She smiled. Wonderful teeth. Then her glance left me and went toward John Skye's barn. I turned and saw—what else?—Ian McGregor and Jen, flirtatious and disgusting sister of Jill, coming out. Jen was smiling up at McGregor and chattering on about whatever it is that teenage girls say to handsome older men on whom they have a serious crush. I flicked a glance down at Zee. Did I detect a narrowed eye? I did. A missing smile? Yes, indeed. Zee jealous of a thirteen-year-old? Could be. Me jealous of Ian McGregor? I turned back and said to John, "Who are all of these people? I don't think I know a single one of them."

"I should hope not," said Skye. "These are all academic types. This island crawls with them in the summertime. This particular selection consists of friends, more or less, of Marjorie and Ian."

"More Ian and less me," said Marjorie Summerharp. "I know a lot of them, but I'd hardly call them friends. I don't have many friends in academia."

"And no wonder." Skye grinned. "You're not nice to them when they bungle or do shoddy work. You get on their cases in public places." He glanced at me. "In the learned journals," he explained. "Many very impolite things are said in those journals, and Marjorie has said more than her share of them."

"Not more than my share. Just my share. And rarely a misdirected barb, I fancy. You have no idea, J. W., how stupid highly educated people can sometimes be, or how vain or petty or, worse yet, how sloppy and deceiving they can be in their thinking or in the quality of their research." She allowed herself an icy smile. "I confess that I enjoy puncturing their balloons."

"And are there many such dimwits here?" I asked.

She glanced around. "Some. Not all. Hooperman there, the one looking down the front of that young woman's dress, barely got his Ph.D. Wouldn't have gotten it, if I had my way. Second rater. Mediocre thesis, mediocre exams, mediocre man."

"How'd he get by?"

"Mediocre examiners. I was outvoted. And I told him so."

"You often are outvoted, my dear," said Skye.

"Very true. And Barstone there, the woman with the bosom Hooperman is admiring. A genuinely third-rate mind. A Doctor of Education, no less. As John here knows, I maintain that no one who has been trained as an educator has ever had a single original or useful idea about education. The only interesting educators have been people trained in some other area of study. Still, Barstone commands the attention of many an institution of higher, they say, learning and is paid handsomely as a consultant on matters educational. A more sanctimonious fraud I've rarely met inside of academia. I take the whole notion of a school of education to be an oxymoron."

"Like Face Rump Roast," suggested Skye.

"Exactly so. Dr. Barstone is not here, Mr. Jackson, because of me, because she knows that whenever possible I advise institutions not to hire her. Rather, she is here because of my colleague, Ian McGregor, who collects women as honey collects insects."

I flicked an eye down toward Zee and noted a bit of a blush, which indicated she'd been listening. She was watching McGregor and Jen the disgusting flirt, who were smiling and talking as they walked up toward the house. I felt sorry for her suddenly. She was smitten, and there is no one more disconcerted than an intelligent woman surprised by such feelings. I had no wise advice for those so swept away. After all, I'd been smitten by Zee. And still was. I had no more choice about it than Zee had about her attraction to McGregor.

"You're in excellent form, Marjorie," said Skye. "Is there anyone here you do like?"

"Well, you're tolerable, John. And Mattie is a fine young woman aside from her taste in second husbands. Ian may be a womanizer and an occasionally violent hothead, but he's done sound work on this project of ours. And J. W. here knows his clams, as does Ms. Madieras. People who can dig clams are possessors of at least rudimentary virtues. I doubt if the rest of these people can find clams anywhere outside of the fish market.''

"Actually," said Skye, turning to me and smiling, "Doctors Barstone and Hooperman are perfectly legitimate academicians. But Marjorie also disapproves of them because of what they're doing down here.''

"Indeed I do," said Dr. Summerharp agreeably.

"And what are they doing?" I asked without caring.

"Working with Tristan Cooper," said Skye. "Tristan was Marjorie's predecessor as chief seventeenth-century honcho at Weststock. When he retired she got the Renaissance chair.''

Marjorie Summerharp snorted and took a gulp of her drink.

"Marjorie hasn't forgiven him for abandoning Shakespeare and company for things prehistoric," said Skye, "or Hooperman and Barstone for taking him seriously.''

"Tristan," said Marjorie Summerharp, "was the finest in his field. When he left the college to chase these prehistoric phantoms of his, legitimate scholarship suffered a terrible loss.''

"Not a fatal one, though," observed Skye. "You took over where Tristan left off and no one suffered a whit.''

"Nonsense. Everyone suffers when a great mind disappears.''

Skye arched his eyebrows. "Well, Tristan didn't exactly disappear, Marjorie.''

"He did for me.'' She emptied her glass.

I looked at her lined face, considering the passion that lay behind her voice.

"Tristan Cooper," explained John, "was always a maverick, but is even more so in his old age. He's become an advocate of some unconventional anthropological and archeological notions, to wit—that America, more particularly New England and specifically Martha's Vineyard, contain persuasive evidence of pre-Columbian contacts with European and African culture. As a matter of fact, he thinks he's got some convincing evidence right on his own farm in Chilmark.''

"Utter rubbish," said Marjorie Summerharp. "Tristan has slipped a cog. Tragic."

"Professors Barstone and Hooperman disagree with you . . ."

"Nitwits."

". . . They're here to work with Tristan, J. W. Study his work. Raise the question of whether it's legitimate . . ."

"Make some money selling nonsense to the popular press," said Marjorie Summerharp with curled lip.

". . . Give his ideas serious professional exposure."

"Those two? Ha!"

Skye grinned. "You can judge him for yourself. I think that's his pickup coming in now."

～3～

I GLANCED AT Marjorie Summerharp. She was turning her empty glass in her hand and looking toward the driveway. I followed her gaze and watched a middle-aged Chevy four-by-four pull into the yard and disgorge a brown old man. He glanced around, waved an arm at us, and came rapidly across the lawn.

There was a simian quality about him. His arms were long and his legs slightly bowed. His face was wrinkled and the hair grew thin at his temples. His ears and hands were large, and he moved with a feral grace in spite of his years. I calculated that he must be in his eighties, but when he neared us I saw that his eyes were bright and youthful. They were focused on Marjorie Summerharp. I wondered if I only imagined a hint of color on her cheek.

"Marjorie. You look wonderful." He took her hand and swiftly kissed her. He turned to Skye. "John, good of you to invite me." He released Marjorie Summerharp's hand and shook Skye's, then my own. His bright eyes met mine. "I'm Tristan Cooper. You look familiar."

"J. W. Jackson. My father used to hunt on your duck pond. He took me along sometimes. A long time ago."

"Of course. It's been years. You look like him. I read that he was dead. He was a good man. Do you shoot?"

"Yes."

"Hunt at my pond this coming season."

"Thank you."

Then he was looking at Zee and taking her hand and introducing himself and she was smiling her wonderful smile as she gave him her name.

23

"You are a great beauty," he said, studying her.

"Thank you."

He flicked his eyes to me. "You are a fortunate young man, sir. This lady has great life within her." He held her hand with both of his and looked back at her. "Gaia." He smiled. "Do you know of Gaia?"

"No," she said, looking at him with the smile still on her face.

"The earth goddess," he explained. "Mother of the titans. The Romans called her Tellus."

"I'm afraid I know nothing of mythology."

He pressed her hand and then released it. "No matter. She is the oldest of divinities, the nourisher of all that exists. You strike me as Gaia in modern dress, as it were."

"Thank you."

"You are a fortunate man, sir," he said again, looking at me.

"I'm glad you think so." Behind him I saw McGregor and Jen the disgusting flirt enter the house.

Zee, charmed by Tristan Cooper's remarks, gave him a healthy grin. "I dare say the ladies, young and old, have beat a path to your door. We're suckers for a silver tongue."

"You never change, Tristan," said Marjorie Summerharp. "Always an eye for a beautiful woman."

"More so than ever," he agreed cheerfully. "It has been one of the surprises of my growing old to discover that my libido has not aged with the rest of me. You may think me an old fool, Marjorie, but I have a young id."

"I don't consider you a fool, Tristan, I only consider your studies foolish." Marjorie Summerharp's bony face seemed softer than I'd seen it before. "Your place is in Renaissance Studies, not in these romantic prehistoric postulations."

"Your err on three counts in a single sentence, my dear," said Cooper briskly. "My work is neither romantic, prehistoric, or postulational. There is both physical and written evidence supporting it, as you've seen yourself."

I wondered how many men could get away with calling

Marjorie Summerharp "my dear" and correcting her diction at the same time. Not me, certainly.

"I've seen your evidence, Tristan," she said in a tone no more testy than usual, "and I'm not persuaded of your thesis. You are inclined, I fear, to interpret your data so as to support your presumptions. It's a common mistake, but a disappointing one."

"If you were more of a linguist, Marjorie, your criticism would bear more thought. You should not restrict yourself to modern languages, as I've often told you, but master ogham, Celtic, and Phoenician at the very least."

"I know, I know. I should also learn Algonquin, Iroquois, and Hopi if I'm to grasp your evidence. It's a circular argument, Tristan."

It seemed to be an old debate between old friends (colleagues? lovers?), but I was more interested in Zee, whose eyes were upon the two elderly academics but whose thoughts seemed elsewhere.

I said, "Zee, why don't you and I go up to the house and see if Mattie needs any help? Thanks to all I've taught you about cooking, maybe we can both lend a hand."

She gave me a quick, wondering look. I took her arm. "See you later," I said to John and Marjorie Summerharp and Tristan Cooper and led Zee away.

"Am I so obvious?" asked Zee.

I put a smile on my face and looked down at her. She shook her head and looked straight ahead. We got to the kitchen door and I drank down my rum. "Look," I said. "I'm going to get a refill. I'll see you inside." I squeezed her hand and left her and walked down to the table holding the liquor. There I poured myself another Mount Gay on ice. When I looked up at the house again, Zee was not in sight. Inside, I expected. I took a drink and walked back to join John Skye and his guests. I felt empty and thinly metallic, as if I were the Tin Woodman of Oz, without a heart, rusty in the joints.

"Back alone, I see," said Marjorie Summerharp with a crooked smile. Tristan Cooper's untamed eyes flicked between the house and me. I groped for a neutral subject of conversation.

"Tell me about your other guests," I said to John. But Marjorie Summerharp replied.

"The women are friends of Ian McGregor or wish they were. I believe a couple are ex-mistresses. He doesn't keep any woman long. The men are the mistresses' husbands or lovers or perhaps wish they were. All of them enjoy free drinks and food and no doubt meet regularly at cocktail parties all summer long exchanging gossip and partners."

"You give them too much credit," laughed Cooper. "It would take some of these folks all night long to do what they wish they could do all night long. They may think sex, but I doubt if it goes much farther than that."

"Then I imagine they fumble as much as they are allowed to," retorted Dr. Summerharp. "I'm an old woman, but even I could still fumble if I wished."

I liked the thin smile she threw at Cooper. I looked through her years and saw her as a young woman teaching at Weststock College in a Renaissance Department chaired by Dr. Tristan Cooper. She looked like she could do more than fumble. Then I was back in time present and she was again old and tough and ironic.

"Why are they really here?" I asked John Skye.

"They all have some interest in this Shakespeare project, and Bill Hooperman and Helen Barstone are also concerned with Tristan's work. Bill and Helen are both Renaissance people in addition to their other academic interests. Helen had a master's in sixteenth century before she took the Ed.D. that Marjorie so loathes, and Bill's doctorate is in seventeenth century. Something similar is true of most of the others. This is a sort of a prepublication gathering. Ian and Marjorie are putting the finishing touches on their article, and this was my last chance to get some of their colleagues together for a few best wishes and some talk about things to come once the article is printed. It'll be a big deal in literary circles."

"And these hounds will all be delighted to say they were right here on the launching pad. Celebrity by proximity, as it were." Marjorie Summerharp drank her martini. "Not that I really care. I've already tendered my resignation, effective at the end of this coming term, and once I'm gone I honestly don't give a damn about how much mileage these leeches might get from our work." She looked into her glass, then dug out the olive and nibbled at it. "Besides, as Yogi said, it ain't over till it's over. Maybe they're all wrong. Maybe we won't do the article after all. Maybe God will strike us dead first. Maybe we'll change our minds and decide we've goofed and the document isn't real after all. Who knows? Many a ship has floundered in sight of port."

Skye squinted at her. "I take it that you're not serious," he said.

She gave him a smile that was almost warm and her hand touched his arm. "Oh, I'm serious, all right, but I expect everything to proceed on schedule. I think I was just wishing there was some way to screw certain of my colleagues before I depart their company for the last time. Tristan, here, is to be our final arbitrator. In spite of his follies with prehistoric theories, he's still the best person to judge our work with the Shakespeare document. We'll give him the final draft next week at the latest. If he okays it, we'll publish in the fall."

"I'm shocked by your description of your colleagues," I said. "I always thought that the groves of academe were stocked with high-minded intellectuals who lived above all the petty passions of lesser folk."

"You don't look shocked," said Marjorie Summerharp.

"It's all inside," I said. "Truly manly men like myself are trained from youth to show no emotion."

"But behind that mask . . ."

I nodded. "Exactly."

Her eyes flicked beyond me, and I turned and saw Ian McGregor come out of the kitchen with Jen the disgusting flirt and walk with her back down toward the barn. A moment later, Jill came out and looked at them as they strolled away. Jill had a tray of hors d'oeuvres. She took them to another group of guests, then brought them to us.

"I'm afraid you're right about Jen," I said. "A really disgusting flirt."

"I'm Jen," she said, "and Jill's the disgusting flirt, not

me. I already showed him the barn and my rabbits. Now she's making him go back down there and look at the horses. I already showed him the horses.''

"He's probably just trying to be polite," said John.

"He's really strong, you know?" said Jen. "I showed him where we swing on the ropes in the loft and he swung clear across and back with just one arm, pretending to be Tarzan!''

"He certainly could manage that," agreed Marjorie Summerharp. "He brought his weights with him when we came down, and he's usually on his way out for a morning run when I go for my swim. He's very keen on being fit. The ideal advanced by Northern Indiana University, our old alma mater. Stolen from the Greeks—be sound in mind, body, and spirit. That sort of thing.''

"Karate, too, I'm told," added John mildly. "A belt of some color or other. I never could keep them straight. And that's his surfboard on top of his car over there. Surf sailing is quite the rage, I hear. Marjorie here is no athletic slouch herself, J. W. She swims every morning at six, rain or shine, winter or summer. Right now she's doing it at South Beach, at Katama. Personally, I can't imagine getting into the water when it's cooler than sixty-five degrees or so, but she's still swimming outdoors in December. Not normal, if you ask me, but then Marjorie's not your normal woman.''

Cooper looked at her admiringly. "So, Marjorie, still at your morning swim? You never change. You were a bold woman when first we met and you're a bold woman yet.''

"Swimming is the perfect sport, Tristan, as I've told you many times. You can swim at any age and keep in excellent condition thereby. No fat knees or shin splints or ripped muscles or any of the other wounds you can receive from running or pumping iron. And you don't need anyone else to help you do it as you do in tennis or any of those other games people like to play. You should take it up. Do you a world of good. Probably cure your insomnia. Healthier than that chloral hydrate you take for it, certainly.'' She pointed a bony finger at John. "You, too, John Skye. Get rid of that little pot you're developing.''

"Emergency rations in case of atomic attack," said John defensively.

Zee came out of the kitchen with Mattie, carrying trays of food to the tables on the lawn. After a while she and Mattie joined us, and I lured Zee away with me to get another drink. It was my third or fourth; I couldn't remember.

"Have a beer with me after all this is over," I said, pouring her a glass of the white wine she requested.

"I can't," she said. "I already have a date."

"Ah." So that was why she had let Jill take Ian McGregor off to see the horses. While in the house, she and McGregor had made plans to get together someplace more private than John Skye's barn.

"Why did you take me up to the house and then leave me there?" she said suddenly.

The thing women complain about more than anything else in their relationships with men is that men don't communicate. I read that in some women's magazine. It was a poll of some sort. I knew why men didn't communicate: When they did, it caused trouble. Nevertheless, I tried it.

"I took you up there because I knew you wanted to talk with him but wouldn't go because of the way you thought I'd feel. So I took you up there myself."

"You mean you wanted me to see him? I thought you wanted me to be . . . with you. You mean I was wrong? You mean you don't . . ."

"Look," I said, "I know how you feel about him. It was in your face the first time you saw him this morning on the clam flats."

"But you and I . . ."

"What's important is how you feel. I don't want you to not feel some way just because you're worried about how I feel." From the hors d'oeuvres table I captured a scallop wrapped in bacon—a most excellent goodie—and popped it into my mouth. Normally delicious, now tasteless. "I think I've just rattled off too many 'feels.' The thing is that I want you to be happy, and it's clear to me that you're taken with him. And why shouldn't you be? He's smart and good looking. You don't owe me anything. We're not tied to each other. You can go where you please and see who you please. I took you up to the door and left you there to show you that I understand that.''

"But how do *you* feel, Jeff? That means a lot to me, too. I don't think I can just . . . And what do you mean we're not tied to each other? There *are* ties between us. . . . At least I thought there were. I thought . . .''

"Don't do this to yourself,'' I said, letting my anger crawl into view. "Just take the opportunity and go. You have your own life to live, and you'll be making a bad mistake if you don't do this thing if it's important to you. Do it, if that's what you want to do. Go with him. I want you to do what you feel like doing. I don't want to be the person who holds you back. I won't be that person. I refuse.''

She put a crooked pretend-coquettish smile on her face. "You mean you won't fight for me like the heroes do in the novels and movies when a rival shows up?''

I put my big hands on her shoulders and looked down at her. "If you're ever in trouble, I'll fight for you. If this guy treats you badly, I'll do my best to make him wish he was never born. But if you want to be with him, and I can see that you think you do, then I'll not fight at all. You're a grown-up woman, and you get to decide how you're going to live your life.''

"But you don't want me to live it with you.''

"What I want has nothing to do with this.''

"Yes, it does. I feel like you're just giving me away.''

"I'm not. I can't give away something I don't own, and I don't own you. I don't keep slaves.''

"Damn you!''

"Look.'' I nodded toward the barn, and she turned and saw Ian McGregor and Jill come out, laughing and talking. While Zee watched them come up to tables of food and drink, I walked back to John Skye, who had gathered a larger crowd while I'd been gone. Looking over my shoulder, I saw Zee talking to Ian McGregor while Jill, an annoyed look on her face, stood off to one side. Girls often lose out when real women enter the game of love.

"J. W., meet some more guests.'' John Skye's tone was

carefully toneless, a sure sign that he was half amused. I turned and met four people.

"Bill Hooperman and Helen Barstone, meet J. W. Jackson."

Two of many on Marjorie Summerharp's dimwit list, I recalled. Barstone was she of the cleavage and Hooperman was he of the appreciate eyes. As I shook hands with him, those eyes seemed angry. Words apparently had been exchanged between him and someone else. I could guess who. Helen Barstone ran her tongue along her upper lip as I took her hand. Whatever her intellectual deficiencies, she revealed few physical ones. I let my eyes fall upon her famous bosom, then raised them again to meet her gaze. She smiled. Hooperman's eyes fired darts at Marjorie Summerharp and his mouth turned down at its corners.

"And meet Hans and Marie Van Dam," said John. More handshakes. "Hans and Marie are leasing Tristan's land in Chilmark," continued John. "They're running the Sanctuary program up there. Maybe you've read about it."

I reached back into my memory. "I've read things in the *Gazette,* I believe."

Hans Van Dam smiled a smile full of bright teeth. He wore expensive Vineyard casuals and was tanned and healthy looking. His wife used makeup very carefully and was vaguely ethereal in a longish dress something like a sari. A hearty voice emerged from Van Dam's bright mouth. "It's a spiritual, psychological, and physical retreat for the well-to-do, to put it simply. Our guests receive sanctuary from their everyday troubles, can receive therapy from our counseling staff if they wish, and have a chance to take healthy exercise under the guidance of professional trainers. We offer a private beach, tennis courts, sailing and motorboating, massage, swimming, and private religious services for those who prefer not to attend the regular island churches." He smiled his gleaming smile down at his wife, who answered with a mystic half smile of her own. "Have I left anything out, my dear?"

She, like her husband, looked to be early or mid fortyish, although what with modern cosmetics and all, it's hard to tell these days. Her voice was sibilant and slightly musical. "You might add that Tristan's land was the most perfect we've found for our work. That it is not only isolated and lovely but ancient and holy as well."

"Of course, my dear, I should have made that clear. Sanctuary, Mr. Jackson, takes very seriously indeed the ancient stones and temples on the land we are leasing. I believe I would be right in saying that had we taken less interest in those sites, Tristan would have hesitated to lease us his property. Am I right, Tristan?"

"You are," agreed Tristan Cooper. "A half a dozen developers were begging for the privilege of making me a rich man in exchange for my land, and one of them, as you know, was even willing to name his proposed development 'Standing Stones' and design his landscape around them. A particularly wretched prospect. But then you arrived and have proved yourself a proper tenant."

"Our religious services," explained Marie Van Dam in her dusky voice, "are not denominational in any modern sense. Rather, we attempt to orient ourselves to the cosmos, as it were, and try to treat all creation as sacred. We believe that the religious wisdom of the ancient people who built such monuments as those we find on Tristan's land was akin to our own, and thus we hold services at those sites for whomever wishes to join us in our songs and prayers." She smiled suddenly, showing small, even teeth. "We also encourage our guests to attend services in the local churches. So we are not so unconventional as you might imagine, Mr. Jackson. We use both modern and ancient methods of therapy and are quite shameless about it." She put her silken arm around her husband's. "Our guests will testify to our success, won't they, darling?"

"Indeed. Our files contain dozens of letters of appreciation, and many of our guests have returned for second, third, or even fourth visits. You should come by yourself, Mr. Jackson, and have a tour of our grounds and offerings. Call ahead and one of us may shake free from our schedules and take you around; otherwise, one of our staff will assist you." His wide, toothy grin sparkled with sincerity.

"Thanks. Maybe I'll do that."

"Good God," said Marjorie Summerharp, "next we'll be hearing about flying saucers and Mu. I think I need another drink." She had been standing beside Tristan Cooper all this time with a sour milk look on her face. To be grouped not only with Hooperman and Barstone but with the Van Dams as well was apparently more than she could bear. She looked disgustedly at Hans Van Dam. "You're an advertising brochure for a brothel, nothing more."

Hooperman's angry eyes bulged. "By God!" he cried, "you are a bitch!"

"And you are an ass!" she replied, thrusting a finger at him.

Hooperman gave a drunken bellow and plunged toward her with a raised right arm. He was a large man thirty years her junior and moved remarkably quickly. But I had been thinking about his anger and caught his arm as he went by me. He spun and swung blindly at me. I took the blow on my forearm, then held his wrists in my hands. His eyes blazed, and he wrenched in vain to free himself.

I squeezed his wrists. "Stop," I said. He swore and tried to jerk away, but I held him tighter. "Stop," I repeated.

As suddenly as his anger had caught him up, it left him. His shoulders slumped and he shook as though chilled. Then Helen Barstone was at his side, and John and Tristan Cooper stepped near and put their hands upon his shoulders. Hooperman took long breaths and his eyes closed. I released his wrists and stepped away.

"Amazing," said Marjorie Summerharp. "Now I really do want that drink." She headed for the bar while the Van Dams and Helen Barstone looked coldly after her. Skye's eyes seemed to be laughing. Tristan Cooper's were expressionless. I glanced around the yard. It had happened so fast that no one else seemed to have noticed anything.

Mattie Skye's voice announced that dinner was ready to be eaten and that if we wanted it hot we'd better dig in now. Our party moved toward the food tables, relieved murmurs indicating that some of its members at least were glad to be extracted from an awkward moment. Helen Barstone held Hooperman's arm. As she led him away, she threw me what might have been a grateful glance.

I ate roast beef beside Mattie and John and we talked of their upcoming trip to Colorado. Fifty feet away, at a table under a large oak, Jill and Jen and Zee shared the pleasure of Ian McGregor's company. The four of them seemed to be laughing a lot. When I left for home right after supper, they were still at it.

~4~

THAT NIGHT I could smell the fragrance of Zee's hair on my pillow, so I got up and went out into the living room of my house and read until I was too sleepy to know what I was looking at. My furniture is comfortable but old and sagging, mostly stuff my father bought long ago and some that I've salvaged from the world's champion discount store, the Big D., a.k.a. the Edgartown dump, where every bargain comes with an absolute money-back guarantee. Edgartown is a summer home for a lot of very wealthy people who throw away housefuls of perfectly good stuff just because they may be tired of it or too busy or lazy or unimaginative to fix some simple malfunction in it. Other year-round islanders and I take the stuff home and use it. We are dump pickers because we like finding things and fixing them up and because some of us have thin wallets. Maybe if I win the Megabucks I'll forego dump picking, but until then I won't.

After finally staggering back to bed and sleeping badly with the scent of Zee in my dreams, I was up again at three and back at Wasque Point at four to catch the last two hours of the tide as it fell away to the west. The fish were there, as were three other four-by-fours full of fishermen, and when we were not too busy reeling in bluefish to do so, we watched the red sun climb out of Nantucket Sound and bring another fair summer morning to the island. Wasque is one of the loveliest places in America from which to watch a rising sun. The sky brightens slowly, and if there are clouds they become touched with reds and yellows and whites and odd shadows; then, like

35

something out of a Japanese painting, the round sun rises, newborn once again, and the world is fresh and clean in the singing light.

And when the bluefish are in, it's even better. I have a market for my bluefish, so I do not mess around. I fished hard until, about a half hour before six, the bluefish decided to go off somewhere else. I got a final one with a diamond jig far out in the last of the rip, and then there weren't any more for us shore fishermen. Far out beyond our casts, early morning boatmen were still doing nicely, thank you. They could follow the fish wherever they went, of course, and I thought again about somehow buying myself a good, simple boat that I could use for fishing during the summer and fall and scalloping during the fall and winter. Something strong and stable that would get me out there and back again reasonably quickly. I didn't need a speedboat, but I didn't want to take forever getting out to the shoals or coming home afterward. The winds can brisk up pretty quickly around Martha's Vineyard, and I wanted to be able to get back to harbor without delay, if need be.

But right now my dinghy was the only boat I could afford, so until someone left a bigger one in the dump, I was a shore fisherman. It could be worse, I thought, as I watched the sun climb into the sky and wash light over land and sea.

While I was drinking coffee and listening to a country and western station from Rhode Island on the Landcruiser's old but good radio, John Skye drove up, took one look, and sighed.

"All gone, eh?"

"Perfect timing, Professor."

"Serves me right. Too much party last night. I overslept this morning. Oh, well. I'll pick up some quahogs instead. Sorry you had to leave so early last evening." He squinted at me and poured himself some coffee from his jug. "Woman trouble, I take it. Ian's got the touch, whatever it is. For what it's worth, his women don't normally stay with him long. He's easily bored, they say, and some say he has a temper. You might keep that in mind in case he points it at you. Still, most of his ladies keep right on thinking highly of him after they go their separate ways. It's amazing."

"Yeah, amazing." A guy on the radio was singing that he had a funny feeling that he wouldn't be feeling funny very long. I had to smile.

"He's got what they call charm," said Skye. "Even Marjorie likes him, and she doesn't like anybody very much."

"How is your sweet-tempered lady professor friend? Still as cheerful and loving as when last I saw her?"

"Marjorie? Just the same. She gets sourer every year, but I just ignore it. She's okay in my book. She may not be politic, but she's smart and she's honest and she hates a phony, and that's good enough for me." He nodded toward the west. "You'll probably see her car parked at the end of the pavement when you go back. A beat-up Chevy Nova. She'll be taking her six A.M. swim."

"People shouldn't swim alone, they say."

"I'll let you tell her that, J. W. She's been doing it for sixty years, and she's not about to change her ways now."

"In that case, you might suggest to her that South Beach may not be the safest place for solo swimming. There's a good tide there sometimes, and sometimes the breakers get pretty rough. She doesn't look too strong to me."

"I gave her that sermon when she first came down here. That's probably why she's swimming there instead of up at the bend between Edgartown and Oak Bluffs where I recommended she go. She's got a stubborn streak that's close to perverse."

The independent sort. "Tell me," I said, "is she sick?"

He cocked an eyebrow. "Why do you ask?"

"It's none of my business one way or the other, but I saw blood on her handkerchief after she coughed."

He looked thoughtful. "I don't know. She never mentioned it." He paused. "But then she wouldn't."

"She said she was retiring. Maybe her health is one of the reasons."

"It's more than that," said Skye. "She's over seventy and she's been hanging on to her job a long time past normal retirement age. There's pressure to move her out.

Young bucks want the old-timers out so they can find tenure slots for themselves. Can't blame them, really. And there's the fact that Marjorie hasn't produced much writing for quite a while. This Shakespeare thing will send her out with a bang, which will please her just because it will annoy the harpers who think she's all done as a scholar. And finally, the simple truth is that a lot of people just plain don't like Marjorie very much. She doesn't smile at administrators, she laughs at people and ideas her colleagues take seriously, she says what she means at faculty meetings, and she doesn't take to the idea that her classrooms are democracies. She figures that her job is to teach her students what she knows and test them on that whether they like it or agree with it or not.

"Oh, she'll be wined and dined and given a chair with a Weststock logo and she'll get a plaque and maybe she'll even get a bookshelf in the library named after her, compliments of some alum the president will nail for a financial contribution for her memorial. But she will be retired, no doubt about it."

I felt mean and therefore nosy. "What's with her and Tristan Cooper?"

Skye squinted at me then shrugged. "He was department chairman when she joined Weststock. Gossip has it that they had something going together before he packed it in and moved down here to protect his rocks and work on his theories of early European and African encounters with the New World. She became Renaissance chair. He was always a controversial guy, I'm told. Divorced twice, rumors about other women. The Brilliant but Decadent Professor tales. I heard them when I joined the faculty just after he resigned."

"Under pressure?"

"I've heard various stories, but you should know that academics are great gossips. Marjorie says they live such boring private lives that they have to make up tales about their colleagues just so they can continue to think of themselves as interesting people. Could be."

"You met him down here?"

"At a cocktail party. We're not friends, but we've had

some good conversations and he's showed me the stones on his property. Maybe we get along because I'm the type he expected to scoff but I didn't.''

"Speaking of gossiping, do you know why Marjorie Summerharp loathes the Van Dams? I got the impression that words had passed between them before I arrived and was introduced.''

"Ah. Well, Marjorie detests religion for profit in general and quasi-mystics in particular. As you might guess, the Van Dams are perfect targets for her arrows, and she'd fired a few just before you joined us. A few remarks equating certain religious hypocrisy with sexual perversion, as I recall. She's mentioned that theory to me before, and she's surely not the only one to advance it. The Van Dams have excellent stage presence and never batted an eye. They just tried to look lovingly sorry for her. Bill Hooperman was not so cool.'' He finished his coffee. "By the way, thanks for stopping Bill before he did something stupid. He'd been into the gin, I think, and Marjorie got to him. I'd never seen him pop his cork before. He phoned apologies this morning.''

"Passions run high within the ivy walls.''

"I think he's permanently mad at Ian McGregor, and since he can't take it out on Ian because Ian would make mincemeat out of him, Bill let loose at Marjorie. My own ten-cent psychology. You get it free.''

"Why's he mad at McGregor?''

"A woman—what else? Helen Barstone, if rumor has it right. Bill fancies himself her man when her husband's not around, but Ian took her, kept her, and only gave her back when he met a sweet young thing from up island. That was a couple of weeks ago. Bill took it hard. Helen was more realistic. Women usually are.''

"So now McGregor has an up-island girl.''

Skye's face assumed a careful expression. "I understand that she's also been returned to her previous boyfriend, who got a face full of fist when he took issue with Ian's handling of the situation. I'm told it happened right in my front yard, but I wasn't up to see it. An early morning fracas.'' He shook his cup upside down. "I guess I'll make a couple of casts, since I'm here. Then I want some big quahogs for chowder. There are a lot of littlenecks along the south end of Katama Bay, but there aren't many big ones. You have any wise advice?''

I told him to try Pocha Pond. There are some nice big growlers out there in the mud. At low tide you can see them with your bare eyeballs. As he got his rod down off his truck roof, I left. Now I understood McGregor's skinned knuckles, at least. I wondered if I should try to stop worrying about Zee.

After gutting the fish at the Herring Creek, I drove on out to the pavement, and there, sure enough, was an old blue Chevy Nova parked with its nose in the sandbank. Out of curiosity, I stopped and took out my binoculars—heavy WWI German glasses with excellent lenses, found in the Big D on a fortunate day and needing only a half turn on one of the lenses to make them good as new. I climbed a sand dune.

South of South Beach there is nothing but water for thousands of miles. I believe Puerto Rico must be about the nearest land in that direction. It's a long swim. I looked out and saw nothing for a while except the trawlers that had been working the south shore of the Vineyard since early spring. Then, a couple of hundred yards out, I saw a white dot amid the morning waves. I focused and was looking at a white bathing cap with Marjorie Summerharp's craggy face beneath it. Her thin arms were rising and falling steadily and tirelessly. She didn't look like she was in any sort of trouble. I remembered a fisherman telling me that the south shore of the Vineyard was thick with sharks. I didn't know if he was right, but if he was, all of them were leaving Marjorie Summerharp alone. Too tough a morsel to chew, perhaps.

I got back in the Landcruiser, drove to town, and sold my fish. The price wasn't too good because there were a lot of bluefish around. Then I went home and weeded in my garden until the Edgartown Library opened. I still had a bit of the hangover I'd been ignoring, so I drank a bottle of Sam Adams, America's best bottled beer, felt a bit better, washed up, and went back into town, once again surviving the A & P traffic jam and even finding a parking place on North Water Street, where Edgartown's most elegant old captain's houses look out across the outer harbor toward the sometimes island of Chappaquiddick. The library is also on North Water Street. I went in, and after fingering around in the catalog boxes, located books on Shakespeare and King Arthur. I had an hour before Edgartown's industrious summer meter maids would put a ticket on my car, so I found a table and began to read.

I didn't learn much, but at least I had something to do besides think about Zee. I had a little tickle in the back of my brain about what John Skye had said; that Shakespeare hadn't written about King Arthur. I haven't read much Shakespeare, but I have read enough to know I don't like *Lear.* And somewhere in *Lear,* I thought I'd run across something Arthurian. So I looked there first and after a while found it. It wasn't much: in act 3, scene 2, the Fool says, "This prophecy Merlin shall make."

That was all. I found no further references to the Arthurian tales. After most of an hour of scanning books about the Bard, I concluded that a lot of guesswork had somehow passed as scholarship as far as Shakespeare's private life was concerned. Nobody really seemed to know a lot, although a lot of people had opinions. I decided I wouldn't learn much about him from such books. Leaving the books on the table, I went out, saw a parking space a block down the street, drove and parked there and went back to the library, thus eluding the dread meter maid for yet another hour.

Libraries are treasuries. They're mountains of information in which you can delve for free. They have things to read and places to read them, and you can even take material home with you. And librarians are also treasuries. When you can't find something yourself, they will show you how or else find it themselves. And unlike people at the Registry of Motor Vehicles, librarians *want* to help you.

I told the librarian what I wanted to know: Did Shakespeare ever write anything based on the Arthurian stories other than that one line spoken by the Fool in *Lear?*

"Yes, he did," said the librarian.

I smiled. "That was quick. What? Where?"

"I know because my son is reading *Henry IV, Part I*. Hotspur says something about Merlin. Let me see if I can find it for you . . ."

I handed her the copy of *Complete Shakespeare* that I'd taken from the shelves, and a moment later there it was: act 3, scene 1. Hotspur says, "He angers me with telling me of the moldwarp and the ant, of the dreamer Merlin and his prophecies . . ."

It seemed likely that Shakespeare knew about more of the Arthurian tales than just the Merlin bit. "Anything else?" I asked.

She pursed her lips and thought. "Well, I'm not sure. There is one play, but . . . The problem is that though some people think it might have been written in part by Shakespeare, most of the authorities pretty much discount it as not really his work. Do you know about that?" She didn't want to suggest that I was guilty of such ignorance.

I, on the other hand, thrive on admitting ignorance. "Tell me," I said. " 'I'm a man who likes talking to a man that likes to talk.' "

"You do a bad imitation of the fat man," said the librarian.

"Sorry. Blush."

"You're forgiven. I don't know much myself about the play, I'm afraid, but I remember reading about it in a Shakespeare course I took at college. I don't think we have a copy of it in the library, but I do believe we have a reference to it somewhere. Let me see if I can find it."

She went to the files and with faster fingers than mine flipped through the cards. Then she went into the stacks and came back almost immediately with one of the numerous books I had decided not to look at.

"Here you are," She ran a finger down the table of contents. "Ah. Here it is. *The Birth of Merlin.*" She smiled as she gave me the book. Helping me made us both happy. I went back to my table wondering if Shakespeare ever wrote about anybody in Arthur's court *but* Merlin.

The Birth of Merlin was first published in 1662, long

after Shakespeare had crossed the pale, but was apparently written much earlier than it was published. Its title page said that it had been written by William Shakespeare and William Rowley. I had never heard of William Rowley. The play had been published by a Thomas Johnson, whom I'd never heard of, for two other people I'd also never heard of: Henry Marsh and Francis Kirkman.

Apparently, during the 1600s and 1700s nobody had any particular reason to doubt that Shakespeare had helped write the play. Besides, at that time, most people didn't think that he was anyone special, so it probably wouldn't have occurred to anyone to tack his name on the title page of *Merlin* unless it was believed that he really wrote it. Ergo, it would seem that Thomas Johnson, at least, thought Shakespeare had helped write it.

A hundred years or so later, on the other hand, Shakespeare forgeries were far from unknown. A guy named William Ireland wrote one called *Vortigern* and even managed to get it staged before confessing that it was his work, not Shakespeare's. At a distance of nearly two centuries I admired Ireland's gall. There's something in me that cheers when experts in the arts get conned. I wondered if Marjorie Summerharp would approve of such an attitude and decided that she might.

Most scholars, it seemed, now considered *Merlin* to be of doubtful authenticity. Apocrypha, as it were. On the other hand, other scholars held the opposite view. I wasn't surprised. What else do scholars do but disagree? As with economists, apparently, you could lay all Shakespearean scholars end to end and they could not reach a conclusion.

I didn't blame them for disagreeing. When I examined the evidence about Shakespeare, as an ex-cop I didn't see enough to make a case that would hold up in court one way or another.

I was thinking about that as I was leaving the library and so managed to bump into a woman coming in as I was going out.

"Excuse me," I said, then saw that the woman was Marie Van Dam.

"Why, Mr. Jackson," she said in her soft voice. She smiled up at me with her perfect, small white teeth.

She was wearing some sort of silky, flowing dress made of thin pastel-blue layers with some lilac and rose layers showing here and there. Not a sari, but something akin to one. She had on some sort of makeup that reminded me of pictures I had seen of Theda Bara. She was carrying books, the cover of the largest of which had a design that included zodiac signs.

"Mrs. Van Dam. We meet again."

"Kismet," she smiled. "Good fortune is mine. I had been thinking of you." She put her small hand on my brown arm. "I wanted to thank you for what you did at John Skye's party. Dr. Hooperman, I fear, momentarily lost control of himself."

She held her esses just a flicker longer than her other letters, and it gave her voice a hissing quality that made me think of a snake. A gentle hiss, like that of a small serpent.

"Glad to help," I said. "Tell me what it was all about. Something had happened before I got there."

We were in the library doorway, and she glanced inside. Then, her hand still on my arm, she led me out and to one side. Her small voice got even smaller.

"It was nothing, really. Dr. Summerharp, poor thing, made some remark about"—she looked up into my eyes—"religion being a substitute for sex." She paused. I waited, looking down into those siren eyes and remembering that "vamp" was derived from "vampire." She gave a small shrug. "That's all. It's too bad the woman is so vindictive. I understand she was a great beauty when she was younger. Now, unfortunately, she is reduced to making spiteful comments about those of us who still have faith and find life beautiful. I feel sorry for her. It's sad to hear people say cruel things."

"What did she say? She's an elderly woman, but she seems too intelligent to make foolish remarks."

Again that small, feminine shrug accompanied this time by a slight tightening of her hand on my arm. "Nothing new, I assure you, Mr. Jackson. Are you familiar with the formal religions?"

"Not as familiar as some might wish."

She smiled a forgiving and understanding smile. "I assure you that I have no intention of converting you, Mr. Jackson. Her remarks had to do with the notion that intense religious experience is a manifestation of sexual frustration. The evidence offered by people who advance that theory consists in part of writings wherein varieties of religious experiences, particularly those which are visionary or ecstatic, are described in what the theoreticians perceive as highly sexual terms. Some of Donne's poetry seems to lend itself to that interpretation, as do the words of certain saints and Catholic nuns. The religious experience is orgasmic, as it were." She raised a brow. "And if you prefer to pick on Protestants, the theorists will point out that the hymn that begins 'I come to the garden alone, while the dew is still on the roses'—do you know that one?—is actually more of a sentimental love song than anything else." She cocked her head. "Do you know what I mean? There's much more, but that will give you an idea of what she was talking about. Naturally, she directed her remarks at my husband and me."

"And you took no offense?"

She gave a small smile. "Of course not. I believe a salesman would say it comes with the territory. Besides, there may be something to the idea. Why should flesh and spirit be separate, after all? D. H. Lawrence thought that the separation of the two was the major malaise of western civilization, you know." Her fingers played on my arm and then suddenly withdrew, as if she had just become aware of them being there. "Dr. Summerharp is just an old . . . woman without a good word for anyone. She needs love and understanding, not hatred."

"Dr. Hooperman was not so generous in his feelings."

"Ah, well, he must be forgiven, too. Momentarily done in by gin, I believe. I recall that my husband invited you to visit us at Sanctuary. I echo that invitation. Please do come up." Her eyes looked up at me from beneath hooded lids.

"Thank you." I was suddenly sure that her husband would never leave her no matter how involved she might sometimes be with some other man or woman. I looked at my watch. "I'm afraid I must go and save my car," I said.

She offered her hand. "A pleasure seeing you again. Do come and visit us."

I went down the library walk. Glancing back, I saw that she was watching me. We exchanged waves. Three cars behind mine a meter maid was scribbling out a ticket. I just beat her to the Landcruiser, thus thrice escaping the clutches of the law in a single day. Not willing to press my luck, I left town and went home, where I worked at things that I'd been meaning to tend to but hadn't because I'd been occupied with Zee. Now I had the time. Too much of it, really.

That evening, I looked up "moldwarp." I learned that it was a name for the common European mole. I had now pulled even with Hotspur on one word, at least.

Precisely one week later I read that Marjorie Summerharp was dead.

~5~

I REMEMBERED MY last conversation with her.

It had been a beautiful week, with bright sun, soft winds, and a rapidly warming sea. The blue Vineyard waters were alive with fish below and boats above, graceful yachts leaning before the breeze, their sails white and gold or spinnaker bright against the pale blue sky. I had been working harder than normal in pursuit of both blues and shellfish and in getting my garden into shape. This, so I'd have less time to think of Zee and Ian McGregor off together. I'd not phoned Zee, nor had she phoned me, nor did I expect such calls, though more than once I caught myself holding my telephone in my hand; each time, I returned it to its cradle and busied myself at some task.

After first spotting Marjorie Summerharp swimming off the beach, I'd fished Wasque for two days, until the tides changed too late to make that profitable. Around Martha's Vineyard, the tides rise to the east and fall to the west an hour later each day. Generally the best times for fishing the rip are the two hours before and after the change in early morning or evening, so when the tides are wrong at Wasque, I fish other spots until they're right again. On the first morning, as I'd come off the beach shortly after six, I'd seen Marjorie Summerharp's blue Nova parked at the end of the pavement. On the second morning I met her as she was toweling herself off beside the car.

She wore an old black bathing suit that revealed a lean, bony body with ropy muscles under an aged tanned skin. As I pulled alongside and stopped the Landcruiser, she wrapped herself in a bright robe of many colors and gave a last hard rub to her short gray hair.

"Hello."

"You smell of fish, young man."

"I nailed a few at Wasque. You need one?"

"Am I robbing you of income?"

"There are more where these came from. Take your pick." I climbed out of the driver's seat and opened the back so she could see the fish box.

"A nice haul," she said approvingly. "We used to catch blues off the Maine coast when I was growing up. I like them filleted, then grilled with mayonnaise and dill." She grabbed a six-pounder and hoisted it out. "I've got a grocery bag in the back of my car. This fellow will just about fit in it."

I walked with her to her car and held the paper bag while she slid the fish into it.

"The last time I caught a Vineyard bluefish was way back when," she said. "Tris Cooper took me out in his boat to Noman's Land and we must have caught fifty of them. You've inspired me. I'll ask him to take me again while I'm down here."

"It's good fishing there. So you two were fishing buddies in spite of your arguments about this work he's been doing since he left Weststock."

"He always had a lot of interests. Very bright. Too bright, maybe. Too complicated for most people, anyway. A little off tilt, some would say. But a good fisherman and the best Renaissance man I've ever known. And yes, he used to take me fishing when I came down here years ago." She ran her hands through her hair and shook it. There was something girlish about the gesture that made me smile.

"I take it that you think he should have stayed in the Renaissance business. Just what is it that he's doing instead that you disapprove of?"

She looked irritable. "Every profession has its idiot fringe. The idiot fringe of the study of early American history is occupied by a group of people who are convinced that waves of European, African, and Asian explorers and colonists have been coming to America for the past three thousand years—Libyans, Phoenicians, Celts of various types, and apparently every other civilization that ever owned a boat. These people, including Tris Cooper, I'm sorry to say, believe they've found ancient monuments in the style of European standing stones, altars, temples, and whatnot that show transatlantic contacts from God knows when. They also think they've found epigraphical evidence that supports their theories. Ancient writings on rocks, mostly. Nonsense, mostly, if you ask me. But Tris always was a bit off the wall, even at Weststock.'' She gave me a sudden roguish grin, as she recalled those long-ago days. "No wonder the ladies love him. Who can resist a handsome, brilliant rogue whose glands occasionally get the best of his brain?''

"Modesty prevents me from pointing out that that's almost a perfect description of me. Am I safe in your presence?''

She laughed. "Tristan Cooper wasn't! I caused his second divorce! Then he left me for a graduate student. It was fair but painful. Later I chased him down here, if you want to know the truth. But when I had to choose between living with Tris here and going back to the Renaissance chair at Weststock, I chose Weststock.''

"And survived whatever regrets you might have had.''

"Yes. And Tristan no doubt found himself other adoring women. At least he's straightforward about sex, which is more than you can say about those pious pimps who run Sanctuary. I told Tris I was going to do an exposé on them and sell it to the scandal mags to help support myself in my retirement. Your friend Zeolinda is Tris's favorite type, by the way. He likes strong women with dark hair, though he never limited himself to them. Mine was black when I was young, I might add.''

"I think Zee has someone else on her mind right now," I said.

"Ah. Well, Ian is a ladies' man in his own right, so you have two rivals on your hands, I'm afraid.'' Suddenly she was ironic. "From the gleam in her eye, I suspect that you might find momentary comfort with that vacuum,

Helen Barstone. I dare say her blood circulates fast enough below her neck. It just doesn't get any higher."

"I got the impression that she and Hooperman were close."

"Hooperman!" She laughed. "What a dolt! She keeps Hooperman on the string because he's safe, like that wimp of a husband of hers, but I saw how she looked at you when you kept her boyfriend from misbehaving."

"She must drive Hooperman wild. First McGregor, now me."

"Oh, you know about her and Ian, eh? Well, I'd hardly say that Ian was her first, and as far as I know you're just the current prospect. Hooperman may feel wild, but he won't ever do anything rash unless it's to someone weaker, like me. Don't worry about Hooperman, the twit. Thanks for interfering the other day, by the way. Bill was quite in his cups."

"I hear that Ian McGregor is a bit more physical than Hooperman."

"Ah, yes. You do have big ears, Mr. Jackson. I take it you refer to the young Sanctuary lad and the lass with the copper hair. The girl and Ian met up island when he and I were visiting Tristan, and naturally she succumbed to his charms. They were an item for a couple of weeks till he got bored. The morning after he shed her, the boy showed up feeling Irish and manly. It was an interesting vignette, since I've rarely had the opportunity to personally observe the masculine rites of supremacy. I was just going for my morning swim, but I stayed to watch. I think the boy had been drinking. Possibly all night. At any rate, they exchanged words rather loudly, the boy saying he would not allow the girl to be so sorely used and Ian responding that she was only a whore anyway. Then the boy went at him and Ian knocked him down. He got up and Ian knocked him down again. Then the boy went to his car and drove away and Ian apologized to me for the scene. Actually, I thought he enjoyed it." She tilted her head. "That was a couple of days before we all met on the clam flats. I fancy Ian might have more trouble with you. I wouldn't mind having a front-row seat for that one."

"I don't like trouble," I said. Then I felt a smile on my face. "You are a tiger." She grinned, and I got into the Landcrusier and went to town to sell my fish.

During the next couple of days I motored my dinghy across to the Cape Pogue gut and fished there with some luck. Taking the dinghy from Collins Beach in Edgartown saved me the long drive out to Cape Pogue and then back down the elbow to the gut—twenty minutes by boat versus an hour by Landcruiser.

Then, for two days, I went up island, a place I rarely go, and fished Squibnocket and Lobsterville. I don't like to go to Gay Head, the island's westernmost town, because I dislike their politics and their tourist practices: pay toilets, over-priced parking lots, and not only No Parking signs but No Pausing signs on their roads. When I'm king of the world, I'm going to ban pay toilets on religious grounds as an abomination in the eyes of God. Until then, I avoid Gay Head except to fish. I do roam Gay Head's fishing grounds when I can find a place to park, since there are few better places to cast a line, especially for bass.

And when I wasn't fishing up island, during late mornings or afternoons I worked the shellfishing grounds in Edgartown, digging clams or raking for quahogs at the south end of Katama Bay. I had a market for littlenecks and sold most of what I got, but my clamming was done mostly for me; I love them steamed, fried, chowdered, any way at all except raw. Why not raw? I wondered. After all, I ate raw littlenecks and raw oysters and raw scallops; why not raw soft-shell clams? Because they looked yucky?

And I worked in my garden, weeding it more than I'd ever weeded it before, more than it needed to be weeded.

And I cooked complicated things that required much chopping and sorting and different stages of preparation; and I ate many-coursed meals with more than one wine. Alone.

And finally the weather changed. A west wind blew in a steady all-night rain from New York and I slept soundly and decided I was getting better.

The evening of the following day I opened the *Vineyard Gazette,* which was now coming out in its twice-a-week summer editions, and saw that Marjorie Summerharp's body had been brought up in the nets of a trawler fishing off South Beach south of Katama Bay. Three or four of them had been working off the beach most of the summer, their spreaders making them look like great water birds opening their wings as they swam. When the *Mary Pachico* had hauled in her catch at noon the previous day, Marjorie Summerharp, clad in her old-fashioned black bathing suit and white bathing cap, was there among the fish, quite dead.

I had a sudden sense of guilt, remembering the last time I'd seen her, thinking of the warnings I'd suggested be given to her but that I'd not given myself when we'd spoken that last morning, remembering the sight of her out in the blue waves, swimming effortlessly, her wiry arms rising and falling in a steady rhythm, remembering the wink she'd once given me and the dry, ironic voice and the tough, wrinkled face and cool eyes and her surprising laughter and frankness and how I'd liked her for no reason I could name.

What had happened to her? I read the article through. According to Ian McGregor, she had left the farm to take her morning swim just as he was starting his morning run, so he'd ridden with her to South Beach and run home from there. She had not come back at her usual time, but he had been working and had not thought much about it. Toward midmorning, when she still hadn't returned, he had phoned a friend, Mrs. Zeolinda Madieras, expressing concern, and the two of them had driven to South Beach and found Dr. Summerharp's car at the end of the Katama Road, still parked where it had been when he'd left her that morning. The lifeguard had seen nothing of the missing woman since coming on duty. McGregor had then contacted the police, who in turn contacted the coast guard. A couple of hours later, the *Mary Pachico* had hauled in the body from a point a mile straight offshore from where the victim's car was parked. There was sea water in her lungs, and every indication was that she had drowned.

I had been fishing up at Lobsterville that morning and so had missed the action: police cars, coast guard helicopters, the works. John Skye would have phoned me the news, but John and Mattie and the girls had left for Colorado earlier in the week and probably didn't know anything about it themselves, yet. Zee hadn't called either; but why should she?

I got a Molson from the fridge and took it and the paper outside and up onto the balcony, where I could look out on the Sound and watch the sailboats inch toward their night anchorages through the light evening winds. Cars drove silently along the road on the other side of Anthier's Pond, going to and from Edgartown and Oak Bluffs. Bicyclists moved along the bike path beside the road, and beyond them the bright sails of windsurfers still glided back and forth along the beach; some of the June people were taking advantage of the fine weather and were stretching their beach time as far as they could. They neither knew nor cared that Marjorie Summerharp had just drowned not five miles from where they swam so safely.

I drank my beer and read the article again. It still contained the same information; I hadn't missed a thing. I thought it was probably just as well that the people on the boats and beaches knew nothing of the fate of Marjorie Summerharp or of the other dark events of Vineyard life. For them, after all, the Vineyard was a place in the sun, a gold-rimmed green gem set in an azure sea, where they could forget for a time the realities that would confront them soon enough when their vacations ended. They were pleased to live for a time in their summer dreams, and I was not about to deny them that pleasure. Time enough for hard times; no need to seek them out. Time enough to read of the deaths of kings and the ruin of lives.

I finished my beer and drove down to the new drugstore at the triangle, where the Vineyard Haven and Oak Bluffs roads split coming out of Edgartown. There are a lot of newly built stores there, and I like them because I can reach them without having to drive through the A & P traffic jam. I bought a copy of the *Boston Globe* and read its version of the story. Marjorie Summerharp was a well-known figure in higher education circles, and the *Globe* writers had gotten considerable comment from her colleagues, all of which was tactful and complimentary and expressed regret in the proper tones, but some of which suggested that she had been ill and more than a little depressed over her health and impending retirement.

A hint of suicide, I took it, although no one actually said that. Marjorie Summerharp in death received mostly rave reviews. I wondered if she would have been amused or irritated by them.

The next edition of the *Gazette* referred to the official coroner's report: death by accidental drowning. A trace of alcohol and sleeping pills was found, but insufficient to cause coma. Another tiny hint of suicide? The *Gazette* does not emphasize the unpleasant side of local stories when it can help it.

Marjorie Summerharp had been elderly and not in good health. She had gone swimming at six in the morning as was her custom and apparently simply swam out too far and drowned before she could get back to shore. That was all. Relatives had taken the body to Maine for burial. Dr. Ian McGregor, greatly upset by the death of his colleague, had concluded his work on the paper he and Dr. Summerharp had been working on and intended to publish it as scheduled in both of their names. The paper would be dedicated to her memory.

Touching. Annoyed that the word had come into my mind, I examined the photo of him that accompanied the story. Broad shoulders slumped. Apollonian face drawn in sorrow, the picture of formal grief. Behind him, a bit out of focus, stood Zee and the chief of the Edgartown police, both solemn.

Marjorie Summerharp had been dead for almost a week when I saw the photo, and I had spoken to no one about the matter. I had, however, been reading the *Globe* every day, looking for a detail I never found. And now I read the *Gazette* from end to end and didn't find it there either. I thought about it as I watched the day dim into evening and the distant beach-goers gather their umbrellas and pull in their kites and reluctantly depart for their vacation homes. It occurred to me that I was probably making something out of nothing, that others would have asked the question in my mind, and having asked it, must have gotten a satisfactory answer in reply.

I climbed down off the balcony and made myself a refrigerator soup: all of the leftover vegetables and meats in the fridge mixed together, simmered in a bit of bouillon and wine, and served with homemade white bread. Delicious! I had seconds and then drank two Cognacs while I listened to the news and heard about a lot of things, but didn't hear anything of the detail I hadn't found in the papers.

Later, reading in bed, I somehow got to thinking about ice cubes, about how, when I saw that the ice cube container in the freezer was getting low, I would break the ice cube trays into it until it was full, so I wouldn't have to do it again for a while, but that Zee would only put in as many cubes as she needed right then.

The next morning, I was up at three and at Wasque at four and back home again by seven and downtown by nine, looking for the chief of police.

~6~

THE CHIEF WAS, typically, not in his office. When a town of 2,500 winter souls becomes a town ten times that big in the summer, nobody in the police department has much time to sit in the office except, in this case, Kit Goulart, ace woman-of-all-work, who was there five days a week making sure the system worked as well as possible.

"Nice badge," I said, eying it appreciatively.

"If there was a law against leering, you'd be a lifer," said Kit.

"Chief in?"

"He's on Main Street someplace," said Kit.

"If I was chief, I'd stay right here," I said, staring at her badge with wide eyes.

"Get out of here!"

"Will you marry me?"

"I already have one more husband than I can manage."

"I doubt that," I said as I left. I liked Kit. She and her husband Joe looked like twins, both six feet tall and weighing 250 or so. A matched team.

The chief was at the corner of Main and Water Street, watching a young summer rent-a-cop directing traffic. She wasn't doing too badly, either, and so the chief had time for me. We leaned against the wall of the bank and watched the cars creep by.

"Why they're here on a day like this, instead of at the beach, I'll never know," he said. He'd been saying that as long as I'd known him.

I didn't know either. "They're city people," I said. "They're uncomfortable unless they're in traffic jams.

They feel unnatural at the beach because there's so much room there and so much clean air. They like exhaust fumes and horns honking and so they drive around Edgartown all day, down Main, back out past the A & P, around the Square Rigger and back past the A & P to Main Street again. It gives them a sense of using their vacations in a meaningful way. Everybody knows that.''

"Now that we've cleared that up," said the chief, "we come to a tougher question. What are *you* doing here? You hide out in the woods all summer and only come into civilization for booze."

"You wound me. Only last week I was at the library . . ."

"Astonishing. I didn't know that you could read."

"You're confusing me with Edgartown policemen. I'm famous for my comic book collection, and when they're off work, all your crew come by to look at the pictures and ask me what the little letters say. I'm thinking of charging tuition."

"Not a bad idea," said the chief. "From the look of some of their reports, they could use some help along literary lines. You have a pained expression on your face. Have you been thinking of something?"

"As a matter of fact."

"And . . ."

"And maybe you know the answer to a question."

"We policemen are encyclopedias of information. Why, only this morning I was able to tell a woman from New York that there is no bridge between the Vineyard and the mainland. She seemed shocked."

"I dare say she was. My question is also well within your scope, I'm sure. If Marjorie Summerharp went swimming at six in the morning, how come her body was found six hours later a mile straight out from where she entered the water?"

The chief thought. "You got me. What's the answer?"

"I don't know."

"Maybe because that's where the *Mary Pachico* was trawling. If the boat hadn't been there, it wouldn't have collected her in its nets."

"Very sharp. Now I know why they made you chief.

The thing is, if Marjorie Summerharp drowned off the end of the Katama Road where they found her car, she shouldn't have been a mile straight out from the spot six hours later.''

"Why not?"

"Because the tide was dead low at six o'clock that morning and ran east for the next six hours. If she went in at six o'clock like the papers said, and if she drowned like the papers said, her body should have washed way off toward Wasque Point by the time the *Mary Pachico* picked her up. But the *Mary Pachico* netted her straight out from the end of the road.''

The chief watched his rent-a-cop traffic for a batch of tourists in sunglasses, shorts, and wild shirts who wanted to go from where they were to the other side of the street. Traffic backed up beyond the town hall. Then the rent-a-cop waved the cars ahead and the long line inched forward.

The chief looked up and down the street. Cops' eyes are always moving. "Maybe the *Mary Pachico* netted her down that way but didn't haul in until she was back off Katama."

"Yeah. Maybe so. I didn't see anything about it in the papers. Did anybody ask?"

"I imagine somebody did. I didn't." He looked at me. "I'll call the coast guard. It should be in their report."

"Will you let me know?"

"No."

"Not even if I kiss your foot right here on Main Street?"

His eyebrows went up. "Well, maybe if you kiss my ass." He pushed away from the wall and went to help his rent-a-cop, who had gotten herself into a problem she couldn't solve, a complex jam of cars and pedestrians that had created a kind of gridlock. "I'll let you know," he said as the horns began to honk.

The next morning, as I was going into the station to find out where he was, he arrived in the cruiser and stepped out. He gestured toward his office. " ' "Step into my parlor," said the spider to the fly.' "

I ogled Kit Goulart as we passed her and she clutched her heart in feigned passion.

The only soft chair in the chief's office is his. The rest are hard. I took one.

"According to the coast guard, the *Mary Pachico* was trawling west of Katama. She'd come east along the south shore and hauled just after making her turn to go west again."

We looked at each other.

"There's no way Marjorie Summerharp's body should have been out west of Katama," I said.

"So, maybe she just swam straight out for a mile. People do things like that. They just swim out so far that they can't get back. They do it on purpose."

"You mean she may have committed suicide?"

He shrugged. "There was some talk. It could be. She was a good swimmer, they say, and maybe she could have gotten out a mile."

"So she swam out a mile, then swam against the tide for six hours until she drowned. That's what she'd have had to do in order to get gathered into the *Mary Pachico*'s nets."

He got out his pipe, and I enviously watched him stuff tobacco into it. Except for an occasional cigar, I have given up smoking but will never, never stop missing my pipe. Knowing this, the chief lit up anyway, but gave me a look not totally devoid of sympathy.

"So how did she get out there?"

"She could have gotten there if she went into the water several miles to the west. The tides could have carried her there in six hours. I don't know how far a body would drift in six hours, but the coast guard can probably figure it out."

"Maybe I'll ask them to do that."

"Another possibility is that she went into the water earlier than six o'clock and washed first west, then east. I figure that's what could have happened if, say, she went into the water about midnight. She'd have washed west for six hours, then east for six hours, and ended up about where the *Mary Pachico* picked her up."

"But she didn't go into the water at midnight. She went in at six o'clock, as she usually did."

"How do you know?"

"It was no secret. She always went swimming then. Everybody who knew her testified to it."

"If she wanted to commit suicide, maybe she went in at midnight instead so nobody would stop her."

He nodded, puffing. "That makes sense, but it didn't happen. Ian McGregor was with her at the beach at six A.M. So she was alive then, which means that whatever happened to her happened afterward."

"Maybe."

"Unless somebody's wrong about something," said the chief.

"Or lying," I said.

"Or that," said the chief, nodding and puffing. I inhaled the lovely fumes and wondered why a pipe made a man look more intelligent. I could really use one on those grounds alone.

"Maybe some fisherman saw her down there that morning. Maybe somebody saw her driving there. I'll ask around. If I don't come up with anything, we can put out a request for information over the radio station and through the papers. We might come up with a witness—the roads aren't busy that early in the morning, but there are people around. Somebody might have seen something."

"You'll talk again with the crewmen on the *Mary Pachico?*"

He nodded. "Or the coast guard will."

"And Ian McGregor?"

The chief blew a smoke ring and looked at me. "I thought I saw him in town a couple of times with Zee Madieras."

"Could be." Even I could hear the sourness in my voice.

"I'll talk to him again about when he saw Marjorie Summerharp that morning. I can't see him changing his story at this late date, but I suppose he might. Anybody else you can think of? Any other advice to us dumb cops?"

"You think you're smart just because you've got a pipe

and I don't. No, unless there's somebody that we don't know about, the crew of the *Mary Pachico* and McGregor are the only ones who gave information about when the woman went swimming and when and where her body was found. Theirs are the only stories we have to check.''

'' 'We'?''

''You.''

''That's right,'' said the chief. ''Me, not you.''

I inhaled a last lungful of his pipe smoke and left.

I was smoking bluefish a couple of days later when I heard the car coming down my driveway. I'd caught the fish the day before, soaked them in a brine and sugar solution overnight, rinsed them and air dried them this morning, and now was smoking them over hickory chips out behind my shed in the smoker I made out of a refrigerator and some electric stove parts I'd salvaged from the Big D. I have an illegal sales agreement with a certain elegant island eating establishment for my smoked bluefish. I get top dollar in cash and my client gets the Vineyard's best smoked bluefish. The Health Board, which would stop this free enterprise if it knew of it, on grounds that my fish preparation facilities do not meet government standards, has not been informed. Nor has the IRS.

Cars rarely come down my driveway, so each one that does is of interest. A few are cars driven by people who just like to know where roads go. I like to do that myself sometimes. I have not put up No Trespassing or Private Property signs, since I don't like them, so nobody has any reason to think they can't come down my driveway if they want to. The explorers, seeing that they've arrived at a private house, sometimes with a naked man sunbathing on the lawn, beer near at hand, all turn around and leave.

This car stopped in front of the house and two doors opened and closed. I shook some more hickory chips into the skillet on the hot plate at the base of the smoker and shut the door. I heard a voice hallo and recognized it and went toward the house just as Zee and Ian McGregor came walking around it toward the back yard.

''Hi,'' said McGregor, putting out a hand. I took it. Our grips were firm as ever. He squeezed. I squeezed. He noticed Zee watching and released his grip. "I hope we're not interrupting," he said. "I wanted to see you, but didn't know where you lived, so I prevailed on Zee, here, to show me the way. I phoned a couple times first, but nobody answered."

"I was probably out back." I looked at Zee.

"Hi," she said. "My nose tells me you're smoking fish."

"Yes." She looked wonderful in tan shorts and a greenish shirt tied in a knot at her waist. She wore sandals, and her thick dark hair was pulled back by a bright ribbon. Her skin was smooth and browned by the summer sun, some of that browning having been accomplished right here in this yard. "I'm about to have a beer," I said. "Would you care to join me?"

McGregor cast a quick eye at the sky. "Somewhere the sun is over the yardarm," he said. "Sure. A beer would be good."

"You two go out to the front yard," I said. "I'll bring out the beer."

They did and I did and we sat in the fast-warming sunlight and looked across the garden at the distant sea. The beer felt cool and slick as I drank it down.

McGregor was in shorts, sandals, and an animal-on-the-pocket knit shirt. He looked very fit. He caught my glance and lifted his beer. "Cheers. Thanks for the beer. You have a terrific view. Zee told me it was great and it is. I like your place, too. It's just the right size and just the right age and it has a good feel about it."

"It's good enough for me," I said.

"Maybe you can show Ian your dad's decoys before we leave," said Zee, looking a bit ill at ease. "Ian does some woodcarving himself, and I think he'd like to see your dad's work."

"I do some hunting," he said, "and I do like hand-carved decoys. Zee says your father carved quite a few and that they're excellent. That was another reason for asking her to bring me down here." He put a smile on his face. I looked at him.

"What was the first reason?"

He and Zee exchanged looks. Then he took a sip of
beer. "Yesterday the chief of the Edgartown police came
out to the place and asked me whether I was absolutely
sure that I'd been with Marjorie at six A.M. the day she
drowned. I said that indeed I was sure because I'd looked
at my watch just before starting my run home. I run the
bike paths every day about then, because there aren't many
bikers up yet and I don't have to worry about being run
over by some moped." He paused and we both drank
some beer. "I asked him why he wanted to double-check
that time and he said it was because Marjorie's body
couldn't have been picked up where it was netted if she
had gone swimming at six. Something about the tides. He
mentioned that you had brought the matter to his attention." He glanced at Zee and smiled, then looked at me
again. "I hadn't the slightest idea what he was talking
about when he spoke of the tides, so after he left, I phoned
Zee because she goes fishing and I figured she'd know
about such things."

"So I told him about the east and west tides," said Zee,
looking at me over her beer, "just like you told me when
you got me started fishing down at Wasque."

I made some sort of noise that was halfway between a
sniff and a grunt. I think it was supposed to be a noncom-
mittal sign of recollection.

"So I started thinking about the situation," said Mc-
Gregor, "and the more I thought about it, the more odd
it seemed that Marjorie would have been found where the
trawler picked her up. It was clear that something unusual
must have occurred after she parked her car down there at
the end of Katama Road. But I can't figure out what it
would be other than that for some reason she went into
the water far to the west of where her car was parked and
then drowned and was washed east on the rising tide until
her body was netted by the trawler." He turned the beer
bottle in his hands. "But why would that happen? What
if somebody, some nut, was there when she parked and
made her go with him off to the west along the beach and
then . . . I don't know . . . pushed her in or something.
Or maybe she got away and swam out to escape." He gave

me a grim smile. "Crazy, huh? Probably it was nothing like that. Probably she just decided to go for a walk west along the beach, and then went swimming and drowned and washed out to where they found her. I don't know."

"What's this got to do with me?"

"Zee tells me that you were a cop. That's one thing. You're also a guy who knows the tides and knows people around here and knows the area. I'm a stranger. I'm a college professor who can crawl around in books okay, but I'm no real-life detective. I want to find out what happened to Marjorie, and I want to hire you to do it. In a week I'll be going back to the mainland to tend to the publication of the paper Marjorie and I have been working on. But between now and then I want you to investigate her death. I'll be glad to pay you for your trouble. Marjorie meant a lot to me, and I would feel even worse about her death if I were to discover later, perhaps, that it wasn't just a simple accident. I want to know everything that I can, particularly about what happened that last morning." He clenched the fist with the skinned knuckles and looked me in the eye. "I'm very serious about this. If someone caused her death, I want to know about it."

I looked at Zee. She gave a slight nod.

"I'm not a private detective," I said. "You can hire a P.I. over on the Cape. Maybe there's one right here on the island. Did you look in the Yellow Pages?"

"I have indeed looked in the Yellow Pages and found a listing for private detectives, but I think that you're a better man for the job because you know the area and the circumstances of Marjorie's death." He hesitated. "Besides, Zee thinks you're the one to do it."

I looked at Zee. She looked back and drank some beer.

"You won't lose any money by taking the job," said McGregor. "I know that may not be the most important consideration for you, but it's a considerable one. I'll pay you very well, enough to more than cover whatever losses you'll incur when you take time off from your fishing business. I want this matter investigated thoroughly, and I'm afraid the police may not have the time or the personnel to tend to it. This is important to me."

"The chances are," I said, "that she just went for a walk to the west along the beach. Maybe she did it every day before she swam. That's probably what happened. Occam's razor: The simplest explanation that covers the facts is probably the right one. Save your money."

"Please," said Zee.

I had led her up to Skye's kitchen door and left her there so she could meet McGregor. I'd hoped that she'd choose me instead of him then, but instead they'd started dating and now she wanted me to help him. "All right," I said, "I'll do it."

"I'll give you a retainer right now," said McGregor. "I really appreciate this more than I can say, Mr. Jackson."

"Make it cash," I said, hearing the coldness in my voice.

"Anything you want." He put his checkbook away. It said that he'd either been confident or very hopeful of getting me. "I'll have to go to the bank. I don't carry much money around with me."

"And I have to finish smoking my fish before I go to work for you, Doctor. When I finish here, I'll want to come over to the farm and have a look at things there— Marjorie Summerharp's papers, books, her room, anything that hasn't already been cleaned up and shipped out."

"Most of it's gone, I'm afraid. Her personal belongings were sent to her people in Maine. I do have the papers associated with the project we were doing. The work's done, but our working papers are still in John's library. You're certainly welcome to see those and, of course, anything else that might interest you."

"It's just a place to begin. Maybe she left something around that would give us a clue about what happened after she left the house that morning."

We climbed out of our lawn chairs and Zee collected the beer bottles. She came over and looked up at me. "Thanks, J. W. I'm on the night shift right now, but I'm free afternoons. If I can help, I want to."

Zee worked as a nurse at the Martha's Vineyard hospital. She was very good at her job. She was very good at everything she did.

"I'll let you know," I said. "I'll show Dr. McGregor the decoys and then throw you both out. I have to think about how I'm going to earn my salary for the next week." I turned my back to McGregor and dropped my voice. "Don't let yourself get hurt by this guy."

Her warm face cooled. "I'm not a little girl."

"I know. But watch yourself."

She walked deliberately back to McGregor and took his arm. "Why don't you show us those decoys?" she asked lightly. McGregor flashed a smile that said victory. His blue eyes glinted in the sun. I led them to the house.

When they had gone, I considered how I felt about Ian McGregor. He had seemed inclined to play handshake games and had punched out at least one man on the Vineyard. He was a bit overbearing and apparently used women until he tired of them, a common enough practice among handsome men of a certain type. Was he gentle with Zee? He could be charming, obviously, and he professed to be worried about Marjorie Summerharp's last hours. And he also professed to like my house and my father's decoys. And he was smart—even Marjorie Summerharp had agreed about that. He had his Ph.D., but said he knew he didn't know anything about what he thought of as detective work.

And he had Zee.

I had plenty of reasons to dislike and distrust him.

~7~

I SMOKE MY fish for about five hours, sometimes more, sometimes less, depending on weather conditions—air temperature and moisture affect the time it takes. The test is by eye. When the fillets look just the right color, a sleek golden brown, they're done. I turn off the smoker, take the fillets out, put them on the porch to cool, then wrap them in plastic wrap. Then it's off to my secret, illegal buyer. He takes an order every week during the summer, which helps the Jackson budget quite a bit.

After I'd delivered the smoked fish and collected my illicit payment, I drove to John Skye's farm. Zee's Jeep was there, parked beside McGregor's MG, a reconditioned sportster about twenty years old but looking rakishly brand new. It sported a roof rack upon which was the surfboard John Skye had pointed out at the cocktail party. I parked beside the MG and had a good look at my ancient Landcruiser—lots of rust, many dents, bent bumpers. It looked worse than usual. I gave a wheel a kick and went to the house as the kitchen door opened and Zee and McGregor came out. They both looked smashing, as though they had stepped out of a chamber of commerce ad to entice even more folk to the island: handsome couple, perfectly maintained old New England farmhouse, new Jeep and impeccably reconditioned English sports car parked on the fringe of a green lawn, handsome barn in the background. A perfect image of a perfect island.

And McGregor did the right thing—he handed me an envelope full of cash. "I'll show you Marjorie's room," he said.

Marjorie Summerharp's room had been on the second floor of the farmhouse, at the top of the back stairs. At the foot of the stairs was a back door leading out onto a screened porch overlooking a green swale that bent out of sight behind the barn. There was a white fence across the front of the swale, and I knew it to be a pasture for the twins' horses. The view from Marjorie Summerharp's room was a loftier perspective of the same scene, which allowed you to look over the treetops and catch a glimpse of the sea. "Ocean view," the real estate brochures would say.

The room was pretty well cleaned out, just as Ian McGregor had said it was.

"She didn't bring much down with her," he said as I opened the door of a narrow closet and looked at a few wooden coat hangers. "She had only a small suitcase and her briefcase. She was pretty sardonic about the amount of stuff I brought. I'm afraid I'm not a guy who travels light unless he has to. Since I was driving down, I brought as much as I could pack into the MG or carry on top of it. She was of the 'one is enough' school of packing and used to tell me she could travel to Europe for a month and take everything she needed in a flight bag. Why, she only had that one old bathing suit and cap even though she swam every day. Said she could only wear one at a time and didn't need any more." He had a self-deprecating smile on his face. I could see how he could be charming.

I looked under the bed and opened the drawers of the dresser and the nightstand. The bed had been remade with clean sheets, and there was no sign that Marjorie Summerharp had ever been there. I thought of something my father had sometimes said about hunting and fishing, that it was good to be in the woods and by the shore, but that we should walk so lightly that we'd leave no sign that we'd passed that way.

Ian McGregor leaned against the door frame, hands in his pockets, and Zee stood beside him, arms folded, as I worked my way around the room, finding nothing.

"I don't think there's anything here," said Zee. "I

helped Ian get her things together after the police said it was okay. We sent everything to Maine. She has kinfolk up there.''

I lifted up the mattress, saw nothing, and let it drop.

"I do have her academic papers,'' said Ian McGregor. "They're downstairs in the library.''

We went down the front stairs and entered John Skye's library—four walls covered with books, a large desk, an old globe, several leather chairs and a matching couch, reading lamps, two smaller tables, and a couple of straight wooden chairs. A large old Turkish rug covered most of the floor. It was a comfortable place, like the one I'll have in my house after I win the lottery and can remodel. John Skye had told me once that he'd read all of some of the books and some of almost all of them and that the others were books he intended to read when he had time. The desk and tables were covered with papers and folders.

McGregor gestured. "This is where we worked. Much of this is photocopied material having to do with Shakespeare and, to a lesser extend, Arthurian writings. We had to play devil's advocates because we had to be absolutely sure that the document we'd found wasn't just another forgery. The result was that we spent more time trying to prove that the manuscript is a fake than to promote it. As it turned out, the more we worked to disprove it, the more we became sure that it was genuine.''

"Let me have a look at her papers,'' I said. "Maybe there's something there that will give me a clue about something.''

"Like what?'' asked Zee.

I didn't know. "I don't know,'' I said. "Maybe a hint about suicide. Maybe a note to meet somebody at the beach. I don't know.''

What I got was several hundred pages of photographed documents, pages written in a tiny, tight hand, and other pages of scribbles in two different hands. There were lots of initials. Most, it turned out, referred to people, places, and terms I'd never heard of. McGregor leaned over my shoulder and pointed. "The small handwriting is hers, the big sprawling one is mine. When our schedules kept us apart, we'd write notes to one another and answer them. The notes in her hand alone were her reasoning and summing up of the studies we made and discussed together. When we were sure of ourselves, we'd type up that portion of our paper and proofread it together.''

"It looks like a cryptogram," I said. I pointed at the initials BNYPL.

"The stands for the *Bulletin of the New York Public Library*," he said. "That's the volume number and the year and the page reference right behind it. The New York Public Library collects literary forgeries and employs experts in the field. They lock up the forgeries so they can't escape, but allow scholars to examine them as they try to test the authenticity of other documents by comparing them with the NYPL's known fakes.

"These initials are J.P.C. They refer to one of the world's champion Shakespeare forgers, a guy named John Payne Collier who lived back in the 1800s. He was so interested in having things known about Shakespeare that he not only made a lot of stuff up and published it as fact, but he also got into libraries and tampered with books and manuscripts. A strange case, but not the only one we studied.''

He ran his finger over the page, resting it here and there upon initials or scribbled lines. "N.T., here, is Nahum Tate and here's D.G., that's David Garrick. Neither of them was a forger, really, but both of them 'improved' Shakespeare's writing until it was almost unrecognizable. Garrick was an actor, of course, so we can guess that he wanted juicier lines than Shakespeare gave him.''

I saw a familiar set of initials: W.I. I touched them. "William Ireland?"

Ian McGregor put a hand on my shoulder. "None other. I'm impressed. Zee, your old friend is more than just a fisherman. I know now that I've got the right man for this job.''

Was there condescension in his voice? I remembered Marjorie Summerharp saying that all good teachers had a bit of con in them and that a lot of them were vain, petty, sloppy, and deceiving. Feeling McGregor's hand on my shoulder and looking down at the pages of initials and scrawled writing, I thought she might be right. His hand felt heavy and I was relieved when he removed it.

According to Ian McGregor, the marquis of Halifax once said that scholarly curiosity "hath a pleasure in it like that of wrestling with a fine Woman." But after spending the remainder of that afternoon looking at Marjorie Summerharp's papers, I was not persuaded. Give me a fine woman every time. Such as Zee. But Zee had left to wash her hair, an incredibly time-consuming experience for women who, I suspect, have failed to conquer the world precisely because they don't have time to do that and wash their hair, too. McGregor expressed sympathy for my fatigue.

"Someone said that the test of a vocation is a love of the drudgery it involves. That's certainly true of this sort of work. You have to be a little wacky to do it."

He'd worked with me all that afternoon, answering questions, explaining things, once in a while scratching his head in perplexity when some scribble's meaning eluded him. But there was nothing in the papers I examined that gave me any useful information about Marjorie Summerharp's death. Everything had to do with Shakespeare, scholarly documents, and individuals I'd rarely heard of.

"Ah," Ian McGregor would say, "J.H. That's Joseph Hall. He lived back about the time Shakespeare died and kept a Commonplace Book where he wrote down excerpts from other books. Little truisms and that sort of thing. Collier, the forger I mentioned earlier, got hold of Hall's book and forged a tremendous number of ballads in the blank pages."

"How can you forge a ballad?"

"By pretending that the one you just wrote is a couple of hundred years old. Collier apparently found references to ballads that had long since been lost and then just wrote them himself. He was a funny duck."

"Who is this J.W.?"

"That's John Warburton. A sad case indeed, especially for such as Marjorie and me. Back in the 1700s he owned a book that's now in the British Museum. What's left of it includes three old plays and part of a fourth, but it also contains a listing from Warburton of fifty or sixty other plays that were originally in the book, including three that he says were Shakespeare's. One was titled *Duke Humphrey,* another was *Henry I,* and there was a third, unnamed one. At the end of the list Warburton wrote a note saying that through his own carelessness he'd entrusted the manuscripts to a servant who used them under pie bottoms!" He shook his head in what I took to be genuine rue. "Can you imagine more than fifty plays by writers like Shakespeare and Marlowe being lost that way? We don't know her real name, but we call his servant 'Betsy Baker.' If we could get hold of her neck, we'd wring it! Marjorie and I often wondered if the unnamed play could have been the same one we found. We'll never know."

By early evening, I had seen more references to sixteenth- and seventeenth-century writers and writings than I'd expected to encounter in a lifetime, and I had barely tapped the spring. But I had learned nothing except what I'd already known—that Marjorie Summerharp appreciated but loathed a fraud and had put her own discovery to every test.

I got up. My neck was stiff and my eyes were sore. No wonder the stereotyped scholar was bent over and spectacled. Ian McGregor, of course, was neither bent nor blind, but was more in the mode of an Olympic skier. How did he manage it?

"I'll come back again. I don't expect to find anything, but I'd like to look some more, just in case."

"Sure." He got up. "Just give me a call first. I keep this place locked pretty tight when I'm not here."

Outside, he shook my hand with his firm grip. No hint of a contest this time. His eyes were on a level with mine. "Keep me informed of everything, will you?"

"That's what you're paying me for."

I got in the Landcruiser and drove to Oak Bluffs. In the Fireside bar, I had a couple of beers.

The faint smell of marijuana was mixed with that of tobacco and spilled beer, and in the mirror behind the bar I once caught a glimpse of a small white packet being passed beneath a table. The bar was full of a youngish, working-stiff crowd mixed pretty much fifty-fifty with the college types who come down to the Vineyard every summer to work at the hotels, to pay exorbitant prices for rooms, and to party. The working stiffs were mostly year-rounders, people who build the endless new houses that are beginning to clutter up the island; the collegians were pure summer folk, who for the most part didn't expect to actually make any money but hoped maybe to break even before Dad and Mom financed their way back to school again in the fall. The only summer employees who really saved any money were the often-illegal Irish and other foreign workers who, with the cooperation of their employers, slaved away, lived like spartans, and kept one jump ahead of the U.S. Immigration people whose job it was to keep cardless aliens from making a buck. There were a couple of them in the bar, carefully spending their hoarded dollars.

The Fireside was the bar where the fights used to start on Martha's Vineyard. Whenever there was a brawl, it was started there. I thought of starting one now. Zee was at work across town at the hospital. If I could manage to get myself punched out a little bit, I'd have an excuse to go to the emergency ward and see her. If I was bleeding, I knew I'd get quick service, for blood on the emergency room floor is anathema to the workers there; a bloodless emergency, on the other hand, usually only lands the patient in a waiting room chair for an eternity or two while the lady at the desk takes down a folio of information.

I decided not to try it and had another beer instead. Maybe Zee would for some reason just happen to walk into the Fireside right now, and the guy sitting next to me would get up and leave just in time for her to sit down. I drank my beer slowly, but it still hadn't happened by the time I finished it, so I went home.

The next day I drove down to South Beach at five in the morning. The sky was red in the east. Sailor take warning? I had rods on the roof rack, just in case the big fish were in. You can't be too prepared; it would be a lifelong bitterness to recall being on the beach without a rod the day the really big fish came in. But I wasn't fishing; I was looking for early beach walkers.

I ignored the signs saying that no vehicles were allowed on the section of the beach south of the paved road and drove west along it anyway. The signs were to keep four-by-fours from running over the sunbathers, swimmers, and kite fliers who flocked to that most excellent beach during the day, but there were no such people out at five in the morning, so the signs deserved to be ignored and were. I drove slowly, looking for anyone I could find: early walkers or illegal overnight sleepers or daybreak swimmers or leftover beach partyers—anyone who might have been on the beach the morning that Marjorie Summerharp died. It was a long shot but one worth taking, since some people are on the beach fairly early, fairly often. But not today. Nobody. I drove west to the end of the public beach and then drove on toward the entrance to the Edgartown Great Pond. Nobody was there either, not even a fisherman trying his hand at the opening. To the west I could see the beach reach past west Tisbury and Chilmark and curve out toward Squibnocket ten miles away. I turned around and drove to Edgartown.

I drank coffee and had ham and eggs at the Dock Street Coffee Shop, where you can not only get a great meal cheap, but where the cook has magic hands and is a joy to watch, proof that when a man does anything really well, it's beautiful to see. Food and superb entertainment for less than five bucks. Who'd have thunk that you could find that on Martha's Vineyard? I am so impressed that I sometimes bring guests to have breakfast at the cafe just so they can watch the cook and eat his food.

When the time was right, I walked up the street and found the chief. He was in his office for a change, which only meant that most of the stores downtown weren't open yet, so there wasn't any traffic for him to direct.

I asked him if he'd learned anything from the coast guard or anybody else. He gave me a sour look.

"She'd had to have swum out from shore a long way to the west if her body was to wash back to where it was found in six hours. The tide's nothing like it is in Vineyard Sound, but it's pretty strong."

"Maybe somebody picked her up in a boat and took her out there."

"Maybe the moon is made of green cheese. How many small boats have you seen off that beach? Boats don't go there. It's too far from the inner harbor and the launch ramps. Oh, when the family and I have been down there for a picnic on a good day, sometimes I'll see a power-boat full of kids bouncing along. And lately people have taken to surf sailing and Sunfishing more than they used to. But that's all sunny day stuff. It was raining the night before Marjorie Summerharp died, and it was still raining that morning. She went swimming and there were some joggers out on the bike paths, but I don't think there were any pleasure boats off the beach at that time of day."

"Maybe she arranged to meet somebody."

"McGregor didn't mention seeing any boats."

"Would he have seen one from the parking lot where she left the car? I think the dune is high enough to cut off any sight of the beach."

He looked at me and shook his head. "Do you really think she hired a boat to meet her and take her out to sea so she could drown herself?"

"No. I'm just trying to think of everything. Did anyone see her on the beach that morning?"

"It was a rainy morning. I've asked around, but so far nobody's said they saw anything. A case like this, people who saw anything are usually ready and willing to talk about it. It makes them feel involved. They tell their family and friends and *they* tell other people. They like their names in the paper. But so far, nothing. I'm going to put a notice in the *Gazette* asking people to come forward if they saw her or anything else that might relate to her death."

"Anybody see anything at all?"

"A couple of people saw her driving down there that morning. They remember her because she was wearing that white bathing cap. And like I said, there were some joggers out that morning in spite of the rain—those people are too dedicated for their own good, if you ask me—and a couple of them saw McGregor running along the bike path between six and seven, headed home. But nobody saw her at the beach."

"The paper said they found her robe and towel in her car, and that she was wearing her bathing suit and cap when she was found. Is that right?"

He dug out his pipe. I wondered if he ever smoked it when I wasn't there to suffer while I watched him. He stuck it in his mouth and sucked on it. "That's right," he said. "She was a tough old lady, they say, but she had one of those robes with bright stripes. Red and yellow and purple or some such combination. Not the sort of robe you'd have expected her to wear. Women."

If Freud couldn't understand them, how could I expect the chief to? I clenched my teeth on an imaginary pipe and ran everything through my mind. Then I told the chief what I was doing for McGregor.

He raised an eyebrow slightly, as great a sign of interest as the chief ever makes. "You don't say. Well, why not? But what's it gotten you so far?"

"So far, it's gotten me nothing. But I have a few more days to nose around. I'll let you know if I find anything."

"You're very kind," said the chief. And to prove that he wasn't, he scratched a match and lit up right in front of my nose.

The bank was open, so I stuck McGregor's money in my checking account. Then, since life goes on even for ace investigators such as myself, I went home and did the laundry, using the machine I salvaged from the dump ten years ago and have kept running since using parts from the same store. I also have an equally good dryer, but I only use it in the wintertime. In the summer I use my solar-powered dryer. I string everything on a clothesline and let the Vineyard sun do the job.

As I hung things, clothespins in my teeth, I was surprised to hear a car coming down my drive. Two cars in a single week? Most unusual. A door shut and Zee came around the house.

~8~

"THE MOUNTAIN HAS come to Mohammed," she said. She was wearing summer shorts, shirt, and sandals, and there was a scarf holding her hair back out of her eyes. She looked about seventeen, which was a couple of years older than I felt. I carefully pinned a shirt on the clothesline.

"Care for a beer?"

"No, thanks. How are things going with the job?"

"Didn't the professor tell you?"

"I haven't seen him today. Are you mad at me?"

I thought I probably was. "Why should I be mad at you?"

"Because of Ian."

"You're a big girl. You get to choose your friends."

"I thought you were one of them."

I hung up a sheet. It was the last item in the clothes basket. "I am," I said, picking up the basket and the smaller basket of clothespins and starting to the house. "I'm going to have a beer. Sure you won't join me? It's Watney's Red Barrel."

" 'Gee,' she said, 'you should have said that in the first place.' Okay, I'll have a beer."

I brought two bottles and two glasses out and put them on the lawn table. I like to drink beer from a glass, especially when it's good thick English beer. I sat down and Zee took another chair.

I felt quite awkward and rather hard inside. I wrapped my feelings with my mind. "Cheers," I said and drank. The beer was cool and smooth and yeasty.

"You haven't called me once since John Skye's cocktail party." Zee's voice was neutral.

"I figured you were probably busy."

"We haven't talked together once."

"What would we talk about? Ian McGregor?"

"No! Fishing, us, the things we always talk about."

"Doesn't McGregor talk about things?"

"Not in the same way. He talks about . . . Well, he likes to talk about himself and his work. And he can be very witty and funny. He tells good stories. . . . He can make you feel very good about yourself and about him. He's quite charming."

I wondered what it would be like to be quite charming. I did not count charm among my virtues.

"And," said Zee, "he's quite bright."

"Quite," I said.

"But . . ." Her voice trailed off. My ears perked up. I felt less sour, but not yet sweet.

"Handsome, too," I said. "Quite handsome. And quite the athlete, too. Quite."

"You don't like him."

"As a matter of fact, I don't. I find him quite charming, quite handsome and fit, quite bright, and quite wealthy. He gave me quite a big sum of money, which I quite like, and I quite intend to earn it. But quite frankly, if you really want to know, I don't quite like him having you. I would probably like him quite a lot more if it wasn't for that."

Women like confessions of weakness. They make them feel somehow more secure, more in the presence of fellow human beings. Thus the popularity of gossip and confidential chats. Zee drank her beer. "You know, there is something not quite so nice about him."

"I'm quite delighted to hear it. What's his imperfection? Does he fall off his surfboard sometimes? Does he have a cracked fingernail?"

"Maybe it's nothing. It's just that he likes stories where people are shown to be stupid. I told him that I thought one of the stories he told me was cruel. He apologized. But later he told another story like it."

Much humor is cruel. All of it, maybe. I advanced this theory.

Zee shrugged. "It seemed to me that it was rooted in a kind of vanity that I didn't expect in Ian."

"Intelligent people are often vain. They're famous for it, I understand. Marjorie Summerharp was vain and cruel, too. Maybe it's an academic syndrome. Did your Professor McGregor tell you about his skinned knuckles while he was telling you other tales?"

She looked down at her beer. "He's not *my* professor. Yes. He said something about a dispute with a man. He made light of it."

"Who brought it up? You or he?"

She raised her eyes. "He did. Do you know what happened?"

"When the professor dropped the girl before you, her boyfriend decided to teach him a lesson. But the professor taught the lesson and the student flunked the test. Or so my spies inform me." She drank some beer and shook her head. "It's manly stuff," I said. "Mere women can't be expected to fathom it."

"Men. Good grief."

"Being a mushy guy myself, I naturally appreciate the subtle nuances that are manifest in bloody fists and broken faces. I'd be glad to explain them to you, but you'd probably accuse me of pontificating."

"That would bother you? Ha! You can pontificate with the best of them!"

"But I do it in a very modest way."

Her smile made me ache. Her teeth were so bright that they seemed to glitter in the sun. "How are the tides?" she asked. "I've lost track, I'm afraid."

"The fish will be waiting for you about six tomorrow morning."

"Do you want to go?"

"I thought you were on the night shift."

"I am. But I'll be off at four in the morning. Do you want to go?"

"What about Ian McGregor? Won't he feel left out?"

"Never mind Ian! Do you want to go fishing in the morning?"

I finished my beer. "Sure," I said. "Why not?"

Then I had another thought. "Why not this afternoon? We could take the dinghy over to the Cape Pogue gut."

She looked into her glass. "I'm sorry. I can't."

"Ah."

"He's teaching me how to surf sail."

"Over at Mothers' Beach."

"Yes." She looked at her watch. "I have to go home and change." She stood up. I stood up.

"Maybe I'll spy on you from my balcony. Check out just how great a teacher this guy is."

She gave me a little smile. "I'll meet you tomorrow morning in the Katama parking lot. Five o'clock?"

When she was gone, I felt both good and bad. I climbed up onto my balcony and looked across toward the beach I call Mothers' Beach. It's the state beach between Edgartown and Oak Bluffs, where the young mothers take their babies and little children. The beach is close to the road, so the mothers don't have to lug their chairs, cribs, umbrellas, and their tons of other gear too far. The wind is usually offshore, and the water is shallow and safe for young ones. The mothers can watch them and not worry too much while they get mothers' tans: tanned backs and shoulders and tops of thighs, along with white fronts and calves. This because they sit with their backs to the sun so they can watch their kids in the water and can't turn their backs on the water long enough to get their fronts tanned. The white-bellied young mothers remain two-toned until their children are grown a bit.

Zee, like me, was tanned all over.

Mothers' Beach is also a good place to practice surf sailing. The waves are small and the offshore wind makes for little or no surf. All summer long I can see the bright sails of the surf sailors racing back and forth beyond the road. Later, when they are bolder, the surf sailors take their boards to South Beach and try their hands when the wind is high and the surf is boiling. I imagine that in Hawaii they seek out the monster surf. I think I read about a guy surf sailing all the way across the Atlantic and about another one trying to surf sail to the North Pole. Everyone to his own madness, I say.

I couldn't really see the beach well enough to watch Zee or anybody else surf sail. Besides, I had other things to do.

I phoned John Skye's farm, got Ian McGregor, and told him I wanted to go over Marjorie Summerharp's papers some more. He hummed and then said sure, so I drove over.

His MG's removable hard top still held up the surfboard and sail I'd earlier seen at John Skye's cocktail party. McGregor was wearing swimming shorts and a shirt that said "You can trust me, I'm a doctor."

"I'm afraid I can't be here to help out this afternoon," he said. "I have to be someplace else."

"Zee told me," I said. "I thought I'd bring you up to date and then work here for a while." I told him about my morning drive and my talk with the chief.

McGregor listened, then nodded. "I didn't see any boat of any kind that morning, although I guess the trawlers were working offshore somewhere. I don't think you can see the beach from the parking lot, so I guess there could have been a boat."

"I don't know if there was one," I said.

"What other explanation is there?"

"None that makes sense so far. Maybe I'll find something here."

"I hope so, but I can't imagine what it might be."

We went to the library and he unlocked the door. I told him that I'd lock up again when I was through, and he said he'd see me later then. I watched through a window while he got into his snappy refabricated little car and went buzzing off. It was the perfect picture of a sophisticated vacationer: sports car, surfboard, a tanned Apollo at the wheel, heading off to meet a beautiful woman at a golden beach beneath a bright blue summer sky. Romance!

I sat down and went to work.

I found names and initials I'd seen before, along with

others that were totally new. I came across what appeared to be telephone numbers and wrote them down on a piece of paper, so I could check them out later. I studied microfilmed copies of elderly documents and pages of scribbles. A remarkable number of the documents had to do with frauds, fakes, phonies, and the people who had been taken in by them. Experts, it was clear, have been conned by slickers down through the ages, and Marjorie Summerharp had not, it seemed, proposed to be another such sucker.

And apparently had found nothing fraudulent about the play in question. As I came to her later notes, it seemed that she had become almost persuaded of the quarto's authenticity. Almost, but not quite. I remembered her craggy face and the toughness of her voice and wondered if she ever absolutely believed in anything. Likely not, I suspected. If it could be doubted, she would doubt it.

Bored, I had a perverse desire to see the final draft of the paper, but McGregor's desk drawers were locked. I knelt and looked at the drawers. Not hard to jimmy, really. I mean, how sophisticated are the locks on the desks, especially old ones like this one of John Skye's?

I left the library and went upstairs. I got a coat hanger from a bedroom closet, came back down, went to the kitchen, found the junk drawer every kitchen has, and took the pliers I knew I'd find there. Back in the library, I straightened then sharply bent the end of the coat hanger and slipped it into the keyhole of the center desk drawer.

Bingo. The lock clicked and the drawer slid open.

The third drawer I opened contained the manuscript. I sat down at the desk and began to read it.

It consisted of four parts: a narrative of the discovery of the document and the circumstances that had led up to it, a description of the document and a photocopy of three of its pages to illustrate that description, a description of the tests that had been applied to the document, and, finally, a commentary on the origin and merit of the play itself.

It appeared that the article was to be accompanied by photographs of the book in which the document had been found, of the library where it had been discovered, and of McGregor and Marjorie Summerharp.

The play, in quarto form, had been found bound with other seventeenth-century documents in a book in the library of a family named Pavier, descendants of Thomas Pavier, a bookseller in London at the time of Shakespeare's death. McGregor had gained access to the library some years before by dint of having been teacher to a Miss Genna Pavier, granddaughter of the library's owner, when she was doing graduate work in America. She had prevailed upon her grandfather to allow her teacher to examine the library in search of materials in the area of his specialization, seventeenth-century English drama. The old man, it seemed, had until then followed a family tradition of not allowing scholars into the library, the origin of this policy being unclear but presumably due to some real or imagined insult or event in the eighteenth-century or before. McGregor had charmed the old man just as he had charmed the granddaughter and had worked there a portion of each summer since, examining the books for material pertaining to his work, particularly his interest in a trio of playwrights I'd never heard of, three guys named Dekker, Marston, and Middleton.

Marjorie Summerharp had become involved almost as a fluke. She had gone to London for purely social reasons to visit friends (Ah, I thought, she *did* have some!) and had bumped into McGregor at a theater during intermission. He had not even known she was abroad. But as fate would have it, he had a day or two earlier come across a play in the Pavier library that, although its author was unnamed, seemed to McGregor to be in the style of William Ireland, the well-known forger of Shakespearean dramas. Knowing of Dr. Summerharp's interest and expertise in such matters, he had invited her to examine the document. She, having become a bit bored with socializing, accepted the invitation and thus arrived at the Pavier manor house and was in the library examining the Ireland forgery when McGregor happened to pull out a previously unexamined volume and, totally unexpectedly, found the play they were now presenting to the public.

The two scholars immediately suspected that they might have stumbled on a manuscript as authentic as Ireland's was obviously fraudulent. But Marjorie Summerharp was by inclination and experience a professional skeptic, and Ian McGregor had no wish to join the parade of scholars and experts who had been gulled in the past, so both had agreed to keep silent about their find and to subject it to the closest of scrutinies until they could be certain of its character.

I remembered McGregor saying that the love of drudgery was the test of a vocation. Cops and scholars had that much in common, at least. Both jobs took lots of patience. But my patience, unlike McGregor's, was not the literary kind. I couldn't imagine doing what he and Marjorie Summerharp had then done: spend two years testing a manuscript.

First they made long searches to see if such a play might have been mentioned in some other document, some list, some reference, some nation; then they communicated with other scholars and institutions—university libraries, the Folger, the many initials and telephone numbers I'd found.

And of course the secret was soon no secret at all. Rumors and speculation crept and then ran through the world of scholarship. Cameras and modern devices had been brought in. Photos had been taken, scientific tests had been conducted. The precious book itself had been secreted out to the laboratories of the British Museum and there had its paper, ink, typeface, and binding materials put to tests that could not prove that the work was of the proper period but could also not prove that it was not.

And now the book was again in the Pavier library, a domain closed to all entry but McGregor's and Summerharp's.

I picked up the draft of an introductory statement by McGregor telling of the untimely death of his colleague and of the invaluable contributions she had made to the project. It was quite well written, expressing affection for her in life, sadness at her death, and determination to get on with the scholarship so important to both of them. He was a smoothie, I thought. Then I wondered if I'd have thought that if he wasn't right now out on a windsurfer with Zee. So I put the smoothie thought back down in the pit whence it had come.

I put the manuscript back in the desk where I found it, relocked all the drawers, wrote some notes, locked up the library and the house, and went home. I was tired and didn't feel too smart.

~9~

BECAUSE LIFE WILL not stop for me, I kindly stop for it. One of the pleasures from such stops is food. I opened a can of artichoke hearts in water, drained them, chopped them, and mixed them up with Parmesan cheese and mayo, put everything into a baking dish and shoved it into a 350 oven. While it baked, I got the Stoli out of the freezer and poured myself a glass. To add just the right touch of nip, I added a tiny pickled chili pepper I'd canned last summer. Superior stuff to an olive or onion. I got out the crackers and put them on a tray, finished my excellent ultimate martini, and poured myself a follow-up Dos Equis. When they were nicely done, I took the baked artichoke hearts out of the oven and carried them, the crackers, and beer up onto my balcony, where I sat and ate and thought.

The sun was still warm on my shoulders, but there was a cool evening breeze moving through the trees and fussing with my hair. Beyond the garden, beyond the pond, beyond the road on the other side where the cars were moving back and forth between Edgartown and Oak Bluffs, the sailboats were walking silently across the flat blue water. Nearer to the beach, the smaller sails of the windsurfers raced brightly to and fro. Was one of them Ian McGregor's?

I dipped crackers into the baked artichoke hearts and thought of tomorrow morning's fishing date with Zee. That was better than thinking about Ian McGregor's surf sailing. Then I thought about the Marjorie Summerharp business for a while. John Skye would be getting back in a day or two. Maybe he'd know something about the dead woman that would help me figure out what had happened to her.

Man does not live on hors d'oeuvres alone, so I finally went down and thawed out a chowder I had in the freezer and had a couple of bowls of that. I love chowder. While I ate, I listened to a tape of Beverly Sills singing songs from *La Traviata*. It pleases me to know that Beverly and I both live on the same island in the summertime. Sometimes I cry when I listen to her sing.

As I was finishing up with the dishes, the phone rang. It was Ian McGregor. There was an odd note in his voice, a formal stiffness. He asked how things had gone. I told him everything except the part about reading his manuscript.

"No progress, then?" He seemed indifferent, rigid.

"Not yet. I'd like to talk to a couple of people. Maybe you know where I can find them. They were at the cocktail party."

"Who?"

"Two professional types. Bill Hooperman and Helen Barstone. They both knew Marjorie Summerharp. Maybe they know something."

"I can't imagine what."

"I'm just grabbing straws."

He had the numbers. Both of them lived up island near Menemsha.

"You should talk to Tristan Cooper, too," he said coldly. "Marjorie took a copy of our manuscript up to him just the day before she died. Maybe she mentioned something to him that might be useful."

"I thought I would do that. I want to see the Van Dams, too."

"The Van Dams?"

"Hooperman and the Van Dams crossed swords with Marjorie at John's party. Maybe they were mad enough to do something to her."

"I find that difficult to imagine. Bill Hooperman? I don't think so." There was contempt in his voice.

"He tried to take a swing at Marjorie. Didn't she mention it?"

"No. Did he really?"

"He was drunk and John said he apologized the next day, but he really did try to take a swing at her. Has Tristan Cooper returned the manuscript yet? And if so, what did he think of it?"

"I'm going to pick it up later this evening. Sunday I'm leaving for the mainland. I have an appointment with the publishers the next day."

"I'll let you know if I learn anything."

"Do," said McGregor. "Zee spoke to you, I imagine."

"Not since this morning."

"Oh. Well, I'm sure she will." His voice was without color.

"What about?" I asked, but as I did he hung up.

I called Bill Hooperman, the academic pugilist.

If you wish somebody was dead and the somebody dies, sometimes you feel guilty. Hooperman admitted that kind of guilt to me with a kind of innocence that almost charmed me. He even thanked me for having stepped between him and Marjorie. But he offered no information about her death. "I can't tell you a thing. I don't want to speak badly of the dead, but frankly I found her to be a bitter and cantankerous woman. She was cruel and spread a lot of malicious gossip about her colleagues. She herself was more petty than the people she accused of being so. It takes one to know one, I often thought."

"Can you think of anyone she might have met on the beach the day she died? Did she ever mention anybody she knew here on the island who might have been down there that morning?"

"I never heard of anyone you don't know about already, but then I wouldn't have, since she and I did not meet socially."

"You met at John Skye's cocktail party."

"That was at John's invitation only, I assure you. Marjorie and I scarcely spoke." He paused. "Of course, I was interested in the project she was working on. Several of us were interested in that."

"So that's one reason you came to the party?"

"Yes. I was also there because Tristan Cooper had been invited, but the Shakespeare document was the principal subject of interest. We were all curious for the details, but I'm afraid we didn't get much in that regard. McGregor and Marjorie were quite tight-lipped about their paper. We all went home knowing no more than before."

But filled with John Skye's booze and roast beef. To say nothing of venom.

"I understand that you and Helen Barstone have been interviewing Tristan Cooper."

"Yes. Marjorie's sarcasm notwithstanding, Tristan's work merits a wider audience than it's received, particularly in legitimate academic circles. There is increasing evidence supporting his theories of pre-Columbian Euro-American trade and explorations. Helen and I plan to publish our interview with him and hope to get a book out of it."

"Would Tristan Cooper take Marjorie's criticism seriously enough to want to harm her?"

"Harm her? Tristan? Good heavens, no! What a thought! Why, she and Tristan had argued about the matter for so many years that there was no heat left in the debate. She was absolutely sure he was wrong and he was absolutely sure he was right and never the twain did meet. Not emotionally, at least. In fact, the two of them got along famously, I thought." His voice became conspiratorial. "There are rumors, you know, that he and she were more than friends when both were at Weststock. Perhaps they remained so, in spite of their intellectual differences." Then he slid away from the joy and gossip. "No, Mr. Jackson, Tristan is too much the academician to become outraged by a difference of opinion. The only matter that fires his passion is the security of the ancient stones on his farm. A threat to them might rouse him to wrath, but certainly not Marjorie's carping."

I thanked him and rang off. Then I called Helen Barstone.

"Oh, yes," she said, "I remember you. You left the party early."

"You surprise me."

She laughed. "I keep an eye on certain men."

I asked her about Marjorie Summerharp and she stopped laughing. "She always took whatever opportunity was available to sneer at degrees in Education, especially advanced ones. Since I had my doctorate in Ed, I felt the sting more than once. Aside from that, I rather liked her. She was a tough old bird and she knew her stuff."

"You seemed pretty protective of Bill Hooperman when the two of them tangled."

"Ah, yes. Bill, you see, sometimes needs a bit of protection. He's inclined to take things too personally, and when that happens I just lead him away and distract him. His little fevers never last long, and afterwards he's always repentant in a boyish way that's actually rather charming. He was quicker than usual the other evening, and I think he might really have struck Marjorie if you hadn't stepped in."

"You don't think he stayed angry, then?"

"Bill? Still angry at Marjorie? Heavens, no. He was very embarrassed, and I ended up comforting him rather than giving him the motherly lecture I intended. Where did you learn to handle yourself so well, Mr. Jackson? I was impressed."

"I lived a misspent youth. Is Dr. Hooperman often violent?"

She seemed to smile over the phone. "He gets red in the face and sputters. And he curses and fumes. But he's a teddy bear at heart. I think he was probably one of those chubby boys who got straight A's and never had a fight. You don't strike me as the same type."

"You and Dr. Hooperman have been working with Tristan Cooper. Do you think Dr. Cooper resented Marjorie Summerharp's sarcasm about his interest in the idea of pre-Columbian contacts between America and Europe?"

"Oh, I think not. Tristan realized from the beginning that his theories were apt to be dismissed as nonsense by the traditional academicians, and no one was more Establishment than Marjorie. In her own way, of course. She was a great pooh-pooher of hacks, even if they were in total agreement with conservative scholarship, but she herself was, at the same time, on the right wing of academic theoreticians. She abhorred what she saw as revisionist scholarship, and therefore naturally held Tristan's work to be nonsense.

"You've surely observed, Mr. Jackson, that what is often called intellectual objectivity is really not that at all, but is rather a psychological predisposition to interpret evidence in one way rather than in another. I suspect that both Marjorie and Tristan knew that on some level and thus were able to remain friends even though they radically disagreed."

"Marjorie, Tristan, and Ian McGregor all worked at Weststock College, I understand."

"In Renaissance Literature. Both Marjorie and Ian did graduate work at Northern Indiana, I think. I know Northern has an outstanding program in that area. Of course they were more than a generation apart. I think she was on the committee that hired him at Weststock. Maybe because his degree was from the same place as hers."

"They were friends, then."

Again she laughed. A bit more wryly this time? "Perhaps. There are rumors about Marjorie and Tristan and there are rumors about Ian and, well, many women. Both Ian and Tristan get along with women very well. But I doubt if Marjorie was Ian's friend in the way women usually are."

"I understand that you're his friend. Or were."

She was silent for a moment. "His women rarely abandon Ian. It's a tribute to his charm. He simply slides away after achieving his little victories. There are exceptions, of course."

"One of the exceptions' boyfriend got punched out by Ian McGregor, I'm told."

"Is that a fact? I hadn't heard, but I can't say I'm really surprised. Ian is said to have done the same before. Tell me more. I love gossip!"

"I like it myself. Were you Marjorie's friend?"

"No. You can't be friends with someone who considers you a fool. But I respected her."

"Do you think she committed suicide?"

"No. I saw those hints in the papers, but I don't believe them. She was a very strong person."

"Was she honest?"

"What? What do you mean? Why do you ask that?"

"I'm not sure. I'm just trying to learn as much as I can about her. So far, I'm not having much luck."

"I think she was honest. I certainly never had any reason to think otherwise."

"And Ian McGregor?"

Her laugh was touched with ice this time. "Ian is a romancer. Are sweet nothings lies? He likes to win at the games he plays."

"The game of love?"

"That. Tennis, too. He likes to win at everything. I think he'd tell you that himself."

"How does he take losing?"

"With manly charm, of course. But it doesn't happen often. He's the kind of guy who, if he loses to you at chess, will go home and study nothing else for two weeks and then come back and beat you. And that will be done charmingly, too, so you won't be mad."

"You're not mad? You're still his friend?"

"No, I'm not mad. You can't be mad at Ian."

"I'm told that Bill Hooperman managed it."

"My, you *do* hear a lot, Mr. Jackson."

"Did Marjorie Summerharp ever mention someone she knew here on the island who might have met her at the beach that last day? Somebody with a Jeep, maybe, or a boat?"

"No. But then I scarcely saw her here. As far as I know, she used to come down here years ago, so perhaps she knew many people. I think she normally summered on the Maine coast where her family lives. Are you free about sixish the day after tomorrow?"

I was taken off guard. "I'm not sure. Why?"

"I'm having a cocktail party. I'd like it if you came. I didn't have a chance to say hello at John's place, and I simply *must* hear the details of Ian's latest brawl."

"Well . . ."

"You'll see a sign on the left between Beetlebung Corner and Menemsha. Come casual. I do hope you will."

I remembered Hooperman looking down her blouse. I remembered looking down it myself.

"Thanks for the invitation," I said.

It was a cool, gusty morning when I met Zee at the Katama parking lot at five. There was a brisk southwesterly wind blowing, and high swells in long windrows were humping in and then breaking on the sand, sending spume high into the air. A storm somewhere off to the south was sending its messengers ahead of it. The eastern sky was shot with color as the sun climbed up behind racing clouds. There was a hint of rain in the air.

"Not the best weather for fishing," said Zee, climbing into the Landcruiser after putting her rod on the roof rack. She put her tackle box on the floor between her feet. "We can try Wasque first, and if there's nothing there we can fish East Beach."

"It could be worse. It could be an east wind. I never seem to catch much with an east wind."

I drove east on the edge of Katama Bay. There were snowy egrets and oyster catchers mixed with the gulls and terns, all seemingly enjoying the change in the weather. It was too early for the quahoggers to be out in the bay working their big rakes, trying to make a day's wages. A rough way to earn a dollar any time. Worse than usual with the wind blowing up whitecaps.

"How's windsurfing?" I asked.

"Fun. I don't even know how to sail a regular boat, but after a while I got it going a little bit. Ian just whips the board around. I imagine he'd like a wind like this one."

No doubt. "I looked over toward the beach between five and six and I saw some surf sailors going up and down. I couldn't tell if any of them was you."

"No, none of them was me. We didn't stay too long."

We didn't? "Why not? It looked like a perfect day. Not too much wind."

She pointed to a blue heron standing in the shallows near the clam flats. A pretty bird. "It's hard to say, exactly," she said. "Somehow I felt like a fool. I mean I don't mind feeling like a fool sometimes because I am sometimes, but somehow I felt like Ian wanted me to know that I was a little bit foolish. It happened when I fell off the board or when I couldn't get it to turn. He'd show me how to do it right, but somehow . . . He was so good at it that maybe he couldn't really understand why I was making mistakes. He was patient and never really said anything, but . . ." She made a small gesture with her hands, and when I glanced at her she showed me a comic, rueful face. "I doubt if I know what I'm talking about. Maybe I just imagined it all. Ian never really said or did anything to make me feel that way."

"You can't be mad at Ian," I quoted.

She gave me a quizzical look. "That's right. That's absolutely right. You can't."

We came onto the Wasque Reservation. There were fresh four-by-four tracks ahead of us, and we followed them east over the bathing beach, where no bathers would be beaching today because of the weather. At Wasque Point two trucks were parked and we could see rods casting.

"Maybe there's something there!" said Zee, perking up.

We pulled alongside the nearest truck and saw fish lying on the sand. Nice eight- to ten-pounders. Zee arched her brows and opened the door. By the time I had my rod off the roof, she was down in the surf making her cast. I had time to note that she was using a red-headed Missile for a plug. Halfway in, a nice fish took her lure and she hauled back and set the hook. I watched her bring the fish in, keeping the line tight and walking to the east under the rods of the other fishermen until she had the fish in the surf and then timing the next wave just right and letting it help her bring the thrashing bluefish up onto the beach. She gave me a grin and she slipped her hand into the gills and carried the fish to the Landcruiser.

"Well, don't just stand there," she yelled over the sound of the surf. "Catch something!"

Three casts later I saw the swirl of white water and felt my first fish hit the plug. As I reeled in I glanced at Zee and saw that she had another one. Side by side we brought them in and up onto the beach.

"Not too shabby," Zee grinned as we stood together at the Landcruiser and dug the hooks out of the fish's razor-teethed mouths.

Not too shabby indeed. With the wind in our faces and the waves coming in high and noisy, we fished for two hours, and when the blues finally went away, there were a dozen four-by-fours on the beach and we had both my fish boxes piled high. We put our rods on the roof rack and broke out the coffee and doughnuts.

"I got a hundred and twenty-seven," I said. "How about you?"

"I got a hundred and twenty-eight," said Zee, "and all of them are bigger than yours."

"How do you know which ones are yours?"

"I mark mine in a special way."

"What way?"

"I'm not telling. If I tell, you'll begin to mark yours that way, too, just so you can claim that mine are really yours."

Between us we had forty-two nice fish, all a bit under ten pounds. We drank coffee and ate doughnuts.

"If this coffee was the right kind of beer, I could say it doesn't get any better than this," I said.

"You can still say it," said Zee.

We looked out through the windshield at the last few die-hard fishermen making casts into the fishless sea. The wind was rising and the spray had soaked everyone pretty well through. I turned on the radio and found the Rhode Island country and western station I can, for some reason, pick up on Wasque. Dolly Parton's voice danced like a flute's as she sang of abandonment and sorrow. C & W music, even when it's sappy, is at least intended for grown-ups, unlike the teenage orientation of rock and roll and other pop stuff. Dolly sang like a bird.

"Remember when you taught me how to fish?" asked Zee.

"Yes."

"I had my waders on and you said I looked like five pounds of shit in a ten-pound bag."

"Yes, but that was only because you thought I was after your bod and not solely interested in improving your fishing skills, and I had to prove to you that you were wrong."

"But you showed me how to cast anyway and you never once made me feel stupid."

"That's because I was after your bod and not solely interested in improving your fishing skills, and I knew that if I made you feel stupid you'd be mad at me since, my masculine intuition told me, you were, among other things, an intellectual snob."

"And you've never made me feel stupid since, either."

"No one should ever try to do that. And if they try, you come and tell me and I'll go punch out their lights."

"When I want you to go punch out somebody's lights on my behalf, I'll let you know. I can take care of myself. I want macho, I'll go see an old John Wayne movie."

"Well, don't get in a huff," I said. "We truly manly men can't help but take a protective attitude toward womenfolk. It's in our glands. It's hard for us to restrain ourselves when our little women are in peril." I took another doughnut.

"What are you going to say when you die and go to heaven and find out that God is female?"

"Tell her I'm lost and ask directions?"

"Good idea. I'm sure she'll give them to you."

"You want to drive up to Cape Pogue and see where they've moved the lighthouse?"

"Didn't we do that a couple of weeks ago?"

"Yes."

"Okay, let's do it again. But we can't be gone too long. We don't want these fish to go soft."

The drive to Cape Pogue is one of the loveliest on Martha's Vineyard. We drove past Leland's Point and up East Beach to the bathing beach outside of the Dike Bridge. There I turned in and took the road along the edge of Cape Pogue Pond. There were some giant quahogs out there in the pond, the biggest I ever saw, but you could only get to them by boat, and I hadn't tried for any for a long time.

One day I'd toss the dinghy in the back of the Landcruiser, drive over here, and take the boat across to where the quahogs are. In a day I could get enough for a year's worth of chowder.

"When we left the beach yesterday," Zee said suddenly, "I told Ian I didn't want to see him anymore."

A bit later she turned off the radio. "If you're going to whistle," she said, "you can't have the radio on. It's one or the other, but not both." I gave Zee a big smile. "Don't break your face," she said with a little smile of her own.

We drove up to see the lighthouse at its new site and then around under the cliff where it had stood before, which was now washing slowly away before winter storms and revealing old foundations of brick, once-underground pipes, and other signs of departed buildings. Then we drove back along the miles of beach to her Jeep. As we drove, the whitecaps thickened and the wind rose. I felt very good.

"I'll sell the fish and hold your split till you pick it up," I said.

"Let's spend it together on something outrageous. An expensive meal somewhere."

I ran the math through my head: forty-two fish at say nine pounds each at say forty cents a pound was . . . what? My heart was thumping and interfering with my brain. Not a difficult task. I concentrated. A hundred and twenty bucks or so, all told, half of it Zee's. Between us, we could get a couple good meals even on Martha's Vineyard. "Okay," I said. "When?"

A long strand of her hair had escaped the kerchief she wore when fishing and was blowing out straight. Along the beach the waves were building. Something was brewing down the coast and was coming this way.

Zee caught the wild strand and tucked it away. "How about Friday, I've got the night shift until then."

"I'll pick you up at six."

We drove down the windy beach. After a while, Zee said, "There's something I want you to know. Ian and I never slept together."

I felt an irrational surge of happiness and tried to think

of the right thing to say. Finally I settled on the truth: "You don't ever have to tell me such things, but I'm glad that you did this time."

"I wanted you to know. I guess you should also know that it was a pretty close thing a couple of times. He was pretty angry when I left him instead."

"He call you bad names?"

"Nothing worth repeating. I told him I preferred you. He called you some names, too."

"Nothing worth repeating, I'm sure. Ian is a jerk."

"At least. Let's not talk about Ian anymore."

"Good idea."

After leaving her at her Jeep, as I drove home, I turned on the radio again. Soon I was whistling, too. I didn't think the combination sounded too bad.

~ 10 ~

I GOT RID of the fish for the right price and drove home. There I flipped on the weather channel on the scanner and learned that a low had formed off the Jersey coast overnight and had slowed almost to a stop a hundred miles south of Nantucket while it gained strength. It was no hurricane, but it was now drifting slowly north and would give New England a very good whack if it didn't veer out to sea, which it didn't seem inclined to do. Coastal areas were advised to take precautions against flooding at high tides, and boatmen were alerted to gale warnings.

It was the sort of storm that the locals simply call a hard nor'easter and which would be forgotten by the time the real hurricane season arrived, but John Skye's catboat was on its stake between the Reading Room (where ne'er a book was opened, according to one of its gentlemen members) and the Yacht Club, and John still wasn't back, so I went down and rowed out to check her lines and make sure she was secure.

The wind was strong from the south and the harbor was choppy. Boatmen were heading out to their craft on missions like my own, putting out extra lines, putting over extra anchors, battening things down.

The *Mattie* was a fine old wooden eighteen-footer, built by Manuel Schwartz Roberts long ago and lovingly maintained by several owners before John Skye bought her and brought her up to even better snuff. It was one of my jobs to haul her and paint her bottom every spring and to keep the ice away from her during the winter. For John was of the "keep her in the water so she can't dry out and she'll last forever'' school of maritime theory, and he did not haul the *Mattie* in the fall.

She was mine to sail in the spring before John came down and in the fall after he was back at work, and I could sail her in the summertime, too, whenever he wasn't using her. But being a working stiff, I didn't have as much sailing time as I wanted. Only rich people and schoolteachers have time to sail a lot, and schoolteachers can't afford to. Working types own powerboats if they own boats at all. Most of the pleasure boats in Vineyard harbors are owned by off-islanders who only come down in the summer.

So it goes.

The *Mattie* had a stout bowline, but I added another to the stake just in case and checked below to make sure everything was screwed down tight and there was no water in her. She was tighter than a ballet dancer's pants and dry as the Gobi, as usual. Heavy and beamy, she eased slowly up and down in the gathering wind.

It was spitting a bit of rain as I rowed back to shore. I hauled the dinghy up to the back of the beach and tied the painter to a fence post just in case the tide got really high, as it well might do if the storm and high tides arrived at the same time. Other men and women were busy doing the same thing, and there was that comradely, expectant feeling in the air that you get when a town is faced with a common natural enemy—a storm, a flood, a forest fire. Under such conditions people help out other people whom they would normally actively dislike. It's odd, but consistent with the observation that a common enemy unites people as effectively as a common idol. Hitler understood the dark side of this truth and used it when he named the Jews as being responsible for all the ills of Germany. Had there not been Jews, he said, he'd have had to create them. Hatred ties tighter than love, it sometimes seems.

At home I considered my options while I made myself a smoked bluefish salad stuffed in pita bread for lunch. The wind was moaning through the trees and the water out in the Sound was gray and white under the darkening clouds. A couple of reefed-down sailboats were heading for harbor.

I got a beer and chewed my way through the sandwiches. Delish! Life wasn't bad at all, storm or no storm.

I got out the notes I'd taken yesterday at John Skye's library. Telephone numbers and some initials I didn't recognize. I could afford a few calls, considering what Ian McGregor was paying me. The first number was in area code 209 and had an extension number. I dialed and listened to the ringing at the other end and then heard the click of a connection and the smooth professional voice of a woman switchboard operator.

"Northern Indiana University. May I help you."

"Extension 172, please."

More clicks and then another voice. "Library. May I help you?"

"Could she? How? "My name is Jackson. I'm calling on behalf of the estate of Dr. Marjorie Summerharp. We're trying to clear up some loose ends following her death, and we find that she contacted you within the month. We're wondering, Do we have something of yours that should be returned? A book or books, perhaps? Can you tell me why she called you? I realize that this is perhaps an odd request, but the estate is a bit tangled and her office is a mess, so anything you might tell me could help us get things straightened out for her heirs."

"Let me put you in touch with the head librarian, Mr. Jackson. Perhaps she can be of assistance."

More clicks and then a third female voice. "Dr. Archbold. May I help you?"

I went through my spiel, adding, "I'm calling from Martha's Vineyard, where Dr. Summerharp was working when she died. We've been trying to straighten out her papers . . ."

"Ah, yes. Poor Marjorie. A great loss. I studied under her, you know."

"I never had the pleasure, I'm afraid."

She gave a small laugh. "I don't know that I'd say it was a pleasure, Mr. Jackson. Her classes were very businesslike and she brooked no nonsense."

"So I've heard."

"So when she phoned last month, I talked to her myself. She hadn't mellowed, I assure you. She has nothing belonging to us, Mr. Jackson, and we have nothing of hers. Does that help you?''

I put bewilderment into my voice. "But then why did she . . .''

"Oh, I can tell you why she called, if that's all you need to know, Mr. Jackson. She wanted copies of two doctoral theses we have in the stacks here. We sent them to her and received her check within the week. Photocopying, Mr. Jackson, photocopying. It's made life a thousand times more simple for the scholar. Our work has taken quite a modern turn, I assure you, what with microfilm, computers, and all.''

"Whose theses? Do you remember? What were they about?''

"Well, I can't be sure of the subject matter, but I can guess. Seventeenth-century drama, I should say, since both she and Dr. McGregor specialized in that area.''

"She asked for copies of both her own and Ian McGregor's theses?" I hadn't seen any sign of them among her papers. "Where did you send them, do you recall?''

"Of course I recall. We sent them to her office at Weststock College.''

I thanked her and rang off.

There were two more numbers. The first was out of state again. I dialed and listened to the rings. A man's voice answered.

"Hello.''

"My name is Jackson. I'm calling about the late Marjorie Summerharp. Perhaps you can help me. We found this telephone number in her notes and we're anxious to find out its relationship to her work.''

"I don't follow you.''

"Let me try again. Dr. Summerharp was working on a project that is of considerable importance. Unfortunately, she died before she could complete it, so now Dr. Ian McGregor is attempting to finish it alone. There are some gray areas here and there, and I'm hoping that by calling the telephone numbers we found in her notes we might clear up some of the ambiguities. Unfortunately, in your case I don't even know who I'm talking to.''

''I'm her brother, Howard. Howard Summerharp. I'm afraid I can't help you at all. I don't know a thing about Marjie's work. Never understood it at all. I'm a plumber, mister, not a college professor like Marjie.''

''If you're her brother, why do you suppose she wrote your telephone number on a pad of notes?''

''Hell, that ain't hard to figure. We just bought ourselves this new summer place down on the coast. Just got the phone in. She didn't get the number until a couple of days before she . . . died. I imagine that explains it. She was headed down this way as soon as she was done on that project. She was a Maine girl in spite of all her fancy learning, and she wanted to have a few weeks here before she went back to work at the university.'' He paused. ''Well, she got here all right. They shipped her up here in a box.''

''I'm sorry. I only met her twice, but I liked her.''

''You and not many others. But thanks.''

''Did you receive her possessions? I know they shipped them somewhere from here, but I don't know where.''

''Yeah, we got 'em. Not much. A suitcase full of clothes is about all.''

''No books? No papers or manuscripts?''

''No books. What do we need with her books? We got to go down to Weststock and clean out her apartment and her office at the college some time in the next couple of weeks, but I don't plan to bring home any books. I'll give them to the college or something, or sell 'em. Matter of fact, I don't know what we're going to do with most of her stuff. Clothes and like that, I mean. I sure don't want to haul it all back up here just to give it away.''

''They didn't send you any books or papers from Martha's Vineyard?''

''That's what I said, mister.''

''Do you know of anybody who might have had it in for your sister, Mr. Summerharp?''

''Why do you ask?''

"There are a couple of things about the way she died that don't add up."

"Well, I sure don't know what they might be. I always told her that someday she'd drown herself. Nobody in the whole rest of the family ever even wanted to swim. It's unnatural, if you ask me. As for people who had it in for her, I'd guess she had her share of them, from what she used to tell us. Mad students and deans and all. She always was bristly, even when she was a little kid."

I thanked him, hung up, and dialed the third number. Almost before the first ring was rung, a harried male voice spoke.

"Limerick Deliveries. Fastest deliveries in town. May I help you."

I went through my story.

"Sorry," said the voice, "I never heard of anybody named Summerharp. Wait a sec." The voice shouted in the distance. "Hey, Morty, Sue, either of you ever hear of some professor named Marjorie Summerharp who had a delivery made in the past couple of weeks?" Distant noises, then the voice came back. "Nope. Nobody remembers any Professor Marjorie Summerharp. Sorry."

"Could you check your records. She'd have called you from Martha's Vineyard . . ."

A light bulb went on at the end of the line. "Oh! Oh, yeah! I remember that call. She wanted us to pick something up from her office at Weststock College and deliver it to the Vineyard. But I told her we only deliver here in town, so we didn't get the job. When I told the gang about it, I nearly got my butt kicked. Everybody said they'd be glad to go to Martha's Vineyard even for no extra pay. But we didn't do it. Sorry, buddy."

I put the receiver down, then picked it up again and got the number for Weststock College. I asked for the English Department and got the head secretary. I gave my name and said I was working with Dr. Marjorie Summerharp's partner, Dr. Ian McGregor. I asked her if she could find out if the manuscripts from Northern Indiana University had arrived for Dr. Summerharp.

She was the model of efficiency and dependability. "I

took care of that myself,'' she said. ''Dr. Summerharp phoned from the Island and asked that the package be shipped down to her immediately. I sent it express mail, insured, let's see, just two weeks ago today. It must have gotten there only a day or two before she died. A terrible loss to the college, Mr. Jackson.''

Yes, a terrible loss. I hung up and poured myself a beer. Outside, the wind was roving through the trees and rain was spattering down in big drops, not too thick yet but promising more to come.

I imagined Marjorie Summerharp's office and apartment. The walls of books and files of papers. Brother Howard would have a heavy job of it when he came down from Maine to clean out her possessions. I hoped that he would give the books to the college and not just throw them into the rubbish. Surely in her long life Marjorie had picked up some books that the Weststock library would like to have. The idea of books being tossed into the trash displeased me.

On Martha's Vineyard we recycle books. We attend book sales at the libraries and buy books at yard sales and then take the ones we don't want to keep any longer up to the West Tisbury Fairgrounds for the big annual book sale. Other people buy the books we take up there and we buy the books the other people bring. And the next year we do it all over again. That's the way books should be treated. I imagined that Marjorie Summerharp's books would fit quite well in that pattern.

I went out onto the screened porch and listened to the rising wind in the trees. Nantucket Sound was getting bumpy and wet for the boaters beating their way to the sanctuary of the harbors. The waves were growing and the spume was beginning to fly. A darkening gray sky rolled above the gray and white sea. Ian McGregor had told me that he'd sent all of Marjorie's personal belongings back home to Maine but had kept all of her professional papers here. In which category did you put Marjorie's copies of his and her own thesis? And why did Marjorie want a copy of her own work? Didn't scholars keep copies of their theses? Maybe not. I remembered hearing as a child that

Edgar Rice Burroughs did not have a first-edition copy of his most famous book, *Tarzan of the Apes,* and thinking that maybe Mr. Burroughs would like to have my inexpensive edition.

I got my foul weather gear and drove to John Skye's farm. Ian McGregor's car was in the yard. I noticed that he'd taken the surfboard off the rack on the car. That was smart, since a strong wind such as that which was beginning to blow might have torn it off and done some damage.

When Ian opened the door, he did not look friendly. "I didn't expect to see you today."

I, on the other hand, felt pretty good. I gestured toward the dark wet sky. "Did you notice that it's raining and that I'm standing out in it getting soaked while you're nice and dry there in the kitchen?"

He hesitated, then stepped back. "All right, come in."

In the kitchen I stripped off my topsider and hung it on a chair. "I see you took the surfboard off your car rack. Good idea. It's going to breeze up tonight."

I smiled at him. He was wondering if I'd talked to Zee yet and if so what she'd said. He took the hardness out of his eyes. "What brings you out in weather like this?"

I saw coffee in a brewer and poured myself a cup. "I have some problems," I said, sitting down at the kitchen table. After a moment, he refilled his cup and sat down too. I told him about the telephone numbers and my telephone calls. "My problems," I concluded, "are that I didn't see the theses here and Howard Summerharp said they didn't get shipped to him along with the rest of Marjorie's personal possessions and I don't know why she wanted them in the first place." I looked at him over the rim of my coffee cup. He looked at me over his.

"I don't know what to say," he said. His face assumed an expression of bewilderment. He put down his coffee cup. "What in the world did she want with copies of our theses? And if they were forwarded to her here, where are they? I went over her things pretty carefully and I never saw them."

"She never mentioned them?"

"No. I'm sure I'd have remembered." He touched his hair with a slightly theatrical gesture. "How curious."

"You cleaned out her room?"

"Oh, yes. Quite thoroughly." He hesitated. "Zee Madieras helped me."

"And there was nothing." I thought a moment. " 'The Purloined Letter'?"

"Ah, yes. Poe. Hide in plain sight. Naked is the best disguise. The library. Hide a rock amid rocks, hide a book amid books. Do you want to have a look?"

"Yes." We stood up. "Do you think John will mind having us nosing around his library?"

"Not at all. That's what libraries are for. He's due home tomorrow, you know. If the ferries are still running, that is. Do you think this storm will stop the boats?"

We were walking down the hall to the library. "Too soon to tell," I said. "I doubt it. The storm should have blown over by then."

McGregor started at one end and I started at the other. John had several thousand books lining the walls of his library, and it was hard to get through them. Too many ordered me to stop and read. I had to force myself to move along without pausing. Still, it wasn't as slow as it might have been. If we'd been looking for something small—a letter, a hollowed place holding some secret item—we'd have had to open every book and fan through every page. But two Ph.D theses were not to be hidden within other bindings, so our work went faster.

And came to nothing. McGregor and I met about midlibrary and exchanged reports of failure.

"You take my end and I'll take yours," I said. "We'll double check."

He gave me a long look.

"Just in case one of us missed something," I said, and went right to work before he could argue. After a moment, he followed suit.

Again we found nothing.

I looked around the room. There were file cabinets behind John's big desk. I went to them and slid one open. "They're not locked. Let's have a look."

"You are a nosy fellow indeed," he said. "Did you know that Ben Franklin supposedly had a large collection of racy writings? What if John has one, too?"

But John did not have such a collection. At least not in his file cabinets. And the missing theses were not there, either.

I looked out a window and saw the rain falling in earnest. It was a dark-looking rain, and through it I could see the wind bending the trees. Leaves were beginning to tear away from the branches.

"You can search the house, if you like," said McGregor coolly. His voice made me think there was nothing to find.

"It's a big house. I would take days to do it well. When John and Mattie and the girls get here, I can ask them to do it for me. They'll know what should be where and if anything's been added or subtracted."

"You have any theories?"

"Only the obvious one."

"Which is?"

"That either Marjorie got rid of it or you got rid of it." His eyes narrowed. "I don't care for that remark."

"You're not paying me to trust people."

"I sense a certain unfriendliness about you, Mr. Jackson."

"You're not paying me to be friendly, either."

He made a large fist out of his right hand and the muscles jumped in his arm. He looked at me, smiled a dreamy smile, and relaxed the fist. "Of course you're right about the theses. Either Marjorie got rid of it or I got rid of it. That's logical."

"Unless they never arrived or unless the secretary I talked to at Weststock was lying."

"But if she did send them, then they should have arrived. And the only two people who might have gotten rid of them were Marjorie and I."

"Not the only people. Only the most likely people. Somebody we don't know about might have done it."

He raised a brow. "Who? Why?"

"I don't know. I don't even know why Marjorie wanted

the theses in the first place. If I knew that, maybe I could figure out who would have gotten rid of them.''

He was looking at me, the dreamy smile back on his lips. ''You expect people to lie, don't you? You expect to be deceived.''

''No, not really. Actually I believe almost everything I'm told. I don't think people lie all the time or even a lot of the time. But I think it's hard for them to tell the truth when they think their own lives are going to be seriously affected by what they say. Dostoevski believed that we're so intent upon creating certain perceptions of ourselves that we can't tell the truth even in our most secret journals, diaries that we never expect anyone else to read. I sometimes think I agree with him. Mostly, though, I trust people. I think it would be impossible to be happy otherwise. I can't imagine living in a world where I couldn't believe that people were more or less what they seemed. I think there are psychological terms for people who see themselves as surrounded by liars and deceivers. I know some people like that, and they all lead miserable lives. They're all afraid. All of the time. I won't live like that.''

''And what do those people think of people like you?''

''They think I'm a fool, a sucker. Maybe they're right. I don't think so. What was the subject of your thesis?''

''I don't want to bore you.'' He shaped and relaxed his fist.

''Bore me. Maybe it will mean something somewhere along the line.''

He shrugged. ''If you wish. It was a study of English drama during the reign of Charles the First, 1624 to 1642, when the theaters were closed. I was interested in showing the way drama grew increasingly dependent on the court during that period. I called it *The Curtain Falls: The Last Period of Elizabethan Drama.*''

''Was that something other people hadn't written about?''

''God, no. But I'd been in London and had gotten hold of some material that others had overlooked, so I was able to add a bit to the area. Nothing earthshaking, I assure you.''

"Do you have a copy of your dissertation?"

"I imagine so. Somewhere. I don't remember looking at it since I got my degree."

"Do you know what Marjorie Summerharp's thesis was about?"

"You *are* a curious chap. Yes. I read it while I was researching my own thesis. She wrote about the court masque in seventeenth-century British drama."

"Why did you read it?"

"I read everything I could find that might relate to my own topic. The court masque was a type of drama I had to consider, so I read her thesis. And several others, I should add."

"Can you think of anything that might tie the two theses together?"

"Only what I've told you."

"Can anyone order a copy of someone's thesis?"

"I suppose so. I really don't know." For the third time he made a large fist. "Have you talked with Zee?"

"We went fishing this morning. When we fish, we talk."

"She's a bitch."

I glanced around the library. "What will John think when he finds this place all broken up?"

"I'll report that you started it." He had become very smooth and graceful and was balanced on his feet. "Your bitch can learn to love a different face from the one you're wearing."

"You have a bad mouth," I said, putting my hands on one of John's fine old oak chairs. "I can understand why Zee would prefer me to you. For one thing, I try not to call women nasty names and for another I don't like smashing up good furniture that belongs to somebody else. I suggest that we either step outside in the rain where we can both slip and slide around like idiots or just forget this."

"So you're a coward as well as a shithead. I should have known." He leaned forward. "You aren't worth getting wet for. I'll be around here for a few days and I'll look you up when the rain stops, so don't think I'm through with you. Meanwhile, don't forget to tell your bitch how I threw you out.''

I let go of the chair, went into the kitchen and got my topsider, and then went out into the rain.

~11~

WHEN I GOT home I phoned Northern Indiana University. The librarian put me through to Dr. Archbold, who remembered me from the conversation we'd had before. I asked her to send me copies of the two dissertations as quickly as possible.

"I take it that you've developed an interest in the seventeenth-century British drama, Mr. Jackson."

"Yes, more or less."

"Are you also a teacher?"

"No."

"Ah. In theater, then?"

"In bluefish and clams, actually."

"Eh?"

"I'm a fisherman."

"Oh." There was a pause, then an unexpected chuckle. "Yours is what my father used to call honest work, I believe. Well, you'll get your dissertations as soon as I can have them copied and mailed. Good luck in your reading, Mr. Jackson."

After I rang off, I sought out my encyclopedia to look up court masques. I had no idea what they were.

Court masques, it turned out, were masques performed at or for the court. What else? I should have guessed, I guessed. Dumb me. They'd started out as dances performed by masked lords and ladies dressed as shepherds or classical gods and goddesses and the like, and had progressed to include revels, pageants, and, eventually, entertainments by professional performers, many of them allegorical, complex, and increasingly expensive. Inigo

Jones had devised scenery. Ben Johnson had written masques, as had almost every other playwright of note except Shakespeare. Why not Shakespeare? My book did not explain. My sense was that the masques, as Renaissance equivalents to modern movie special effects, had finally become so spectacular that they detracted from the drama and comedy they were initially intended to enhance.

So I now knew something about Marjorie Summerharp's doctoral thesis. Through my window the next morning I could see the wild white sea banging in from the northeast as the storm moved slowly off toward Nova Scotia. As I stood and looked through the rain-dashed windows, I thought about Marjorie. She had been fascinated by masks and deceptions all of her life. It was the core of her professional reputation.

I got into my oilskins and drove downtown. Edgartown was even more crowded than usual. All of the normal shoppers and strollers were there and all of the beachers were there, too. I finally got to Collins Beach, where I parked. From the Reading Room parking area I could see the *Mattie*. She was doing fine, rising and falling slowly in the lee of the Yacht Club. She had a self-bailing cockpit and showed no sign of taking on water. Her lines were still snug on the stake. I left the Landcruiser on the beach wan walked down South Water Street to Main. The rain was heavy and the wind was high, and I leaned into both as I walked.

The narrow streets of Edgartown were filled with rain-soaked cars groping slowly ahead in search of nonexistent parking places, and the sidewalks were crowded with vacationers wearing bright rain gear and carrying brilliant umbrellas. There was a festive air about the town as the doors of the shops opened and closed and people ducked in and out of the rain. The bars and restaurants were doing boom business, as they usually do on stormy days. People were enjoying the break in the weather and were spending their money with enthusiasm, and the merchants were happy as clams at high tide.

I found the chief standing in the lee of the drugstore, watching his summer rent-a-cops trying to keep rain-blinded cars from running over rain-blinded pedestrians. So far, they were succeeding.

"One nice thing about the rain," said the chief. "No mopeders to speak of. Here it is almost noon, and so far we haven't had to take one moped driver to the hospital. I hope it rains all summer."

I raised my eyebrows.

"All right," he said, "I hope it rains half the summer. I don't think I could stand to have this many people downtown every day."

"Your lot is not a happy one," I agreed. "Get rid of one problem, another pops up in its place."

"I think you should start writing down these original gems of wisdom before they're lost to the world," said the chief. "Did you come down here just to help me hold up this wall, or did you have something else in mind?"

"You hold up walls more often and better than anyone else in town," I said. "I do not presume to be in your league as a wall holder-upper. No, I came to ask you which of your fine officers of the law was on patrol duty the night before Marjorie Summerharp supposedly went swimming."

"Supposedly?"

"Whatever. Do you recall who it was?"

"What time?"

"Say, about two or three in the morning. Maybe between midnight and three or four. In there someplace."

"Precision is not your specialty, I take it."

"Between midnight and four, then."

"I think I remember. I can check the records. We probably had two men out that night. What do you want to know?"

"I want to know who they saw driving around that morning. If they can remember seeing anyone driving to or from Katama or if they saw anyone parked in the Katama parking lot or along South Beach."

"There's always somebody driving around or parked down that way."

"It was raining that night, remember?"

"I remember. What do you want to know?"

"I want to know if Marjorie Summerharp's car or Ian McGregor's car was seen down there that night between midnight and four."

"Why?"

"If I tell you, you'll think I have a good reason or should have a good reason to think I know what might have happened, but I don't. But if either of those cars was seen down there between those times, I won't be surprised."

The chief got out his pipe, turned it upside down in the rain, and lit it with his big Zippo lighter. The smoke floated up into my nose and I inhaled deeply. I had an terrible urge to run into the drugstore and buy myself a corncob pipe and a pack of Amphora.

But I didn't. Instead I watched the chief puff contentedly on his upside-down pipe as the rain dripped off his rain hood.

"Tell me," he said. "And give me credit for never thinking you have a good reason for thinking anything."

I considered this while I held my nose over the wafting smoke from his briar. "All right. Marjorie Summerharp had a particular interest in fakery. She wrote her dissertation on court masques, which were sophisticated entertainments involving aristocrats wearing tricky costumes and masks so nobody could be absolutely sure who they really were. And most of her research on this current paper she was writing with Ian McGregor had to do with proving this play they found wasn't another con job by a literary faker. If she didn't like scams, at least she was fascinated by them and knew a lot about them. I've been wondering if her death wasn't a scam of some kind."

The chief took his pipe from his mouth and examined it carefully. " 'What do you mean?' asked the slow-witted old chief of police."

"I mean that unless Marjorie swam out to sea a long way to the westward of where she left her car, she must have gone into the ocean between midnight and two or three o'clock instead of at six. That means she had to get there somehow, which means that she probably did it in either her own or Ian McGregor's car. I'd like to know if your patrolmen happened to see either of those cars down that way that night.''

The chief put his pipe back between his teeth. ''But Ian McGregor said he took her down there that morning at six.''

''That's right. But maybe he lied. Unless somebody took her off to the west just after he left her at the Katama parking lot, she couldn't possibly have been found out there where the trawler picked her up. So far, I haven't seen an iota of evidence that she went into the sea from out to the west someplace. You were going to ask some questions about that, too. Did you come up with anything?''

''Not yet. There's an inquiry in this week's paper asking anybody who was on the beach that morning to get in touch with me if they saw anything that might relate to her activities. Are you saying McGregor lied?''

''Maybe.''

''Why would he do that?''

''People lie for lots of reasons.''

''Name one, in this case.''

''Maybe he killed her.''

''Give me a break. Why would he kill her? What's his motive?''

''How should I know? Maybe he didn't like her writing style. What do I know about these literary scholars? Besides, there's the matter of theses that have gone missing.''

He looked interested for the first time. ''What theses?''

I told him about the theses.

''Hmmmph,'' he said, and puffed for a while. ''That might be worth looking into.''

''I plan to,'' I said. ''Gosh, maybe we'll find one of those clues you read about.''

''That would be exciting,'' said the chief. ''You can be sure of one thing. These scholarly types are about ninety-nine percent the same as everybody else. People kill each other for the same reasons, whatever they do for a living or whatever money they have.''

''Well, I don't know why anyone would kill her. I'm

not saying McGregor did. Maybe he had another reason for lying.''

"Like what?''

"Like protecting her. There were hints in the papers that she was sick and maybe suicidal. Insurance policies don't pay off on suicides, do they? Maybe she was sick and depressed and wanted to do herself in in a way that looked like an accident, and he agreed to tell everybody that she went swimming as usual that morning so everything would seem normal when actually he drove her down there at two or three in the morning so she could swim out when there'd be no chance of anybody seeing her and maybe picking her up before she could drown herself.''

The chief's pipe smoke floated up into the rain. "There are a couple of big maybes in that argument, but I'll check it out,'' he said at last. "I doubt if anybody saw anything, but I'll ask. It's hard to see much on a rainy night.''

"I know. You'll let me know?''

"Yes.'' He gave me an ironic look. "There is one small detail that sort of weakens your theory.''

"What's that?''

"Marjorie Summerharp was seen driving down to South Beach about six that morning. Aside from that little fact, your theory isn't too bad. Romantic, but not bad. Not true, of course, but not bad.''

"A petty detail that I haven't got worked out yet.''

"Sure.''

A woman appeared out of the rain. She held a sopping parking ticket under the chief's nose. "Look at this!'' she said. "A ticket! I pay taxes in this town! Look at this ticket! I'm a native, not some summer gink! I live in this town!''

"Yes, Ada,'' said the chief. He took the ticket and looked at it. "There's a half-hour parking limit on Main Street, Ada. You know that.''

"You see this street? You see these people? How am I supposed to get everything down in half an hour? I got the post office, I got the hardware store for Gus, I got the paper store, I got the bank. And now I got this ticket!''

It seemed to be a good time for me to leave, so I did.

The vanity of intellectuals has been observed by smarter people than I am, and some have argued that this vanity creates within intellectuals a state of constant frustration based largely on the fact that they are not admired, financially rewarded, or adored as much as they believe they and their brains deserve to be. Thus the intellectuals become complainers or critics or harpers and bitchers about government, for example, because of vanity. Smart politicians, knowing this, turn the intellectual venom away from themselves by embracing the brains, who then, feeling loved and appreciated at last, attack the critics of politicians who flatter them.

Intellectuals, then, could be bought off with real or feigned adoration or respect. When they didn't get it, they got mad. Like Ian McGregor when he didn't get it from Zee.

The windshield wipers on the Landcruiser were not too terrific, so I drove slowly through the rain. Creeping out of Edgartown, I thought about symbols, about how we tend to prefer symbols to reality. How we will borrow money and put ourselves in debt in order to buy expensive cars that will symbolize our financial success. How we will choose certain clothing because it is symbolic of the people we want others to think we are, how we similarly choose furniture, neighborhoods, and even food for symbolic reasons, preferring the symbols to the actualities of our lives. Particularly, I remembered the case of a brilliant college student who was caught cheating on an examination so he could attain the grade point average necessary to win a Phi Beta Kappa key. For him, as for all cheaters on exams in all the schools of all the world, the symbol of success was more important than the success itself.

I thought of John Skye's library. So many books. John lived in a scholar's world of which I knew little, though of late I'd caught a glimpse of it. The big world is made up of little worlds that most of us know nothing of.

My world was usually one of fish and fishermen, but now might again include crime and criminals. I was aware that I was enjoying the variation in my routine and linked it to the almost forgotten pleasure of police work in Boston. Occasional snooping seemed to appeal to me. I wondered if that was good or bad.

The rain beat against the windshield, and the trees shivered and swayed alongside the road. It was a better than average storm and was probably causing some damage along some coast or other. Chatham, which had lost a barrier beach in a winter gale, was probably catching it again.

Nature is violent, but only man is vile.

When I walked into my house, the phone was ringing. It was John Skye calling from Woods Hole to say that the boats weren't running, so he and his family were in a hotel waiting things out. He said it would probably take him longer to get from Woods Hole to the island than it did to get from Colorado to Woods Hole. I reminded him that he was not the first to say something like that and that some people thought it was part of the island's charm.

"Charm, schmarm," said John. "Well, at least the phones are still working. We'll probably be over tomorrow. Terrible news about Marjorie. Ian will be around until Sunday. Maybe we can all get together before he leaves."

"Ian said something about getting together with me."

"Fine. I hope you saved me a few fish."

"I think there are still a couple swimming around someplace."

The rain slashed down all afternoon. At five I put on my Vineyard cocktail party clothes and my topsider and drove up island. Between Beetlebung Corner and Menemsha was a sign saying Barstone. I turned in. There were several cars in the yard of the house. A little gale does not inhibit the island's cocktail set. There was a crowd inside the house drinking Helen Barstone's booze. I joined them.

Helen Barstone was wearing a red dress that was cut high in the front and low in the back and set her fine figure off well indeed. She saw me come in and came right to me. She had a few drinks head start. In a far corner I saw Hooperman frown as he watched her.

"I'm so glad you could come. What should I call you?

J. W.? John told me your initials, but not what they stood
for.''

"J. W. is fine.''

"And I'm Helen.'' She stood on her toes and gave me
one of those cheek-against-cheek kisses where the lips
never actually touch skin. With her mouth close to my ear,
she said, "The rest of these people are just here for drinks,
but you're invited for supper afterward. I'd like to get to
know you.''

"And I'd like to talk to you.''

"Oh, dear, nothing impersonal, I hope.''

"Not to me.''

She smiled and took my arm. "Excellent. Now, let me
escort you to the bar and then introduce you to some people.''

She did that, and I watered the small smile on my face
with glasses of vodka on ice as I listened to cocktail conversations in the up-island mode, and was introduced to
ladies in pastels and men in red trousers and boat shoes
who spoke of art galleries, New York financial doings, and
the dangers of development on the Vineyard. There was
less yachty talk than at Edgartown cocktail parties, but
otherwise not too much difference. Girls in casual party
clothes carried trays of excellent hors d'oeuvres from group
to group, and the bar was generous in its portions. I exchanged brief pleasantries with Hooperman, who put a
false smile on his face to match my own. Finally, everybody lese left and Helen Barstone and I were alone.

"I thought your husband might be here,'' I said.

"Warren? Oh, no. Warren only comes on weekends.
The rest of the time I'm a bachelor girl. Bill Hooperman
sometimes thinks I belong to him on weekdays, but as you
see, you're here and he isn't. I tell him he should bring
his wife down, but she won't leave Cambridge. Poor Bill.''

The serving girls had cleared the clutter from the party
and taken it all into the kitchen before leaving, but the
table holding the bottles was still there. Helen Barstone
went to it and poured herself a nice jolt, then took my
arm and led me to a couch. "Sit down. Let's relax before

we eat. These parties are fun, but I'm always glad when they've ended. Do you feel that way, too?''

"At my parties the guests stay as long as they please. If I don't enjoy them, I don't invite them.''

"Well, you must invite me the next time." She had a silvery laugh.

"It may be a while. I do a lot of my drinking alone.''

"Do you? Isn't that dangerous? I'm sure that's one indication of alcoholism.''

"An island ailment for sure.''

She adjusted her skirt, and when she was done she was closer. She smelled like gin and expensive perfume. Not a bad combination. My arm was across the back of the couch. My hand was near her shoulder. She took it in hers. "So scarred," she said, "so rough. But it's a strong hand.''

"All fishermen have scarred hands.''

"The men I know have soft hands.''

"Soft hands, hard hearts?''

She was amused. "Hard hands, soft heart? I see I must be wary of you, J. W." She drank half her glass, then set it on the coffee table and slid closer. "Tell me about yourself,'' she said.

"Tell me about Tristan Cooper,'' I said. "You and Dr. Hooperman have been interviewing him. What sort of guy is he? And what's this theory of his all about?''

"I'd rather talk about you.''

I put my arm around her shoulders. "I'd rather talk about Tristan Cooper. I'm going to see him and I'd like to know who I'm dealing with. I'd also like to know about Sanctuary. We can talk about me later.''

"Rats,'' she said, "you aren't as malleable as I'd hoped. All right, I'll let myself be bullied. But why do you want to know about Tristan and Sanctuary?''

"Because Marjorie Summerharp had unkind words to say about them and because they're in Chilmark and Chilmark is west of the spot where the dragger pulled in her body.''

"I don't understand.''

I told her about the problem of Marjorie Summerharp's body with respect to time and tides.

She pulled away and stared at me. "Good God, you surely don't think Tristan had anything to do with her death?"

"I don't know anything about him. But the facts are that he knew her, that they'd argued, and that he lives in a part of the island where her body might have entered the water. The same is true of the Van Dams."

"Well, as I told you, the argument between her and Tristan was purely academic and was long past the time when either of them were passionate about it. As for the Van Dams, well . . ." She settled back into the circle of my arm and took my hand again. "Well, they're hardly what I'd call the murdering sort. Religious phonies, probably. Money grubbers, absolutely. Panderers, I'd bet on it. But murderers? I doubt it."

"Panderers?"

She reached for her drink and got it. "I couldn't care less, but yes, I'd bet on it. Have you been up there?"

"No."

"I was. Once. By mistake. We were on our way to visit Tristan the first time and we took the Sanctuary road because that's where his mailbox is. As it turned out, the main houses and outbuildings on the Cooper farm are all Sanctuary places now, and Tristan is living in one of the cottages a half mile away that's reached by another road. But by the time we got that all straightened out, I had a chance to look around."

"And?"

"And the guests are all rich and the help is all young and beautiful. Beautiful boys and beautiful girls. I got the picture pretty fast. Later Tristan more or less confirmed it."

"He told you that Sanctuary was offering sex to its clients along with its other therapies?"

"No." She giggled. "A couple of weeks later, as I was driving up to see Tristan I saw one of the girls I'd seen at Sanctuary slip away from his house. She wasn't quite dressed."

"A dark-haired girl with a good tan?"

She stared up at me. "A redhead, actually. Why did you say that?"

"Jut a bad guess. I was told that he liked that type."

"Maybe he does, but Tristan's tastes are apparently catholic. It's heartening to know that being eighty-four doesn't keep some men from liking women and knowing how to please them."

"I'm told that Tristan has always had women in his life."

"Yes. He doesn't talk about them, but I've talked with old-timers at Weststock and they say he was a pistol while he was there. Two divorces, other women, a couple of fairly serious scandals . . ." Her voice was getting thicker as the drinks relaxed her.

"What kind of scandals?"

"Scandals. Fights, I think. The people I talked to were a bit fuzzy about details. Tristan had a wild streak in him, at any rate."

"But now he doesn't."

"He's eighty-four years old, for God's sake." The glass slipped in her hand and spilled on her dress before falling onto the floor. She brushed at herself, then gave it up. "Give me a kiss," she said, tilting her head back against my arm and pursing her lips.

I bent my head and kissed those wet red lips. Her fingers squeezed mine. After a while she pulled away, gasping. She got unsteadily to her feet. "Dinner can wait," she said in a slurred voice. "Give me just a minute then come in." She waved an arm toward the back of the house and wandered off in the direction she had pointed. After I finished my drink, I picked up her fallen glass, took it and my own into the kitchen, then walked back and found her bedroom. She was on her back on the bed, snoring gently. I pulled off her shoes and covered her with a blanket I found in her closet and went home and cooked my own supper.

About ten o'clock the wind began to die and the rain started to slack off. The storm had moved on.

The next morning I drove down to Katama to do some

quahogging. As I pulled onto the beach, I met George Martin coming off. He held out a hand and we stopped side by side.

"I hope you're not planning to bluefish off of Wasque this morning," he said.

"Littlenecking," I said, pointing to the rake on my roof rack.

"A good thing," said George. "The storm punched an opening through the beach down at the calm flats. Chappy's an island again. If you want to fish Wasque, you'll need a boat or you'll have to take the Chappy ferry."

~ 12 ~

MOST OF THE time the island of Chappaquiddick isn't an island at all, but a peninsula linked to the Vineyard by a spit of sand along South Beach called, on some maps, Norton's Point.

It's called Norton's Point because from time to time a storm comes along and knocks a channel through the sand spit; Chappy becomes an island and the sand spit west of the opening becomes a point named after a local fisherman of yore. Between the two, the tides flow to and fro, into Katama Bay on the rising tide and back into the sea on the ebb. Boatmen, if they can find a channel deep enough for their vessels, take advantage of the opening to save themselves the long trip around Cape Pogue; when the tidal river isn't too fast, young people ride inner tubes downstream through the opening.

When the tide is falling and the winds and surf are strong from the south, the opening is a dangerous place. The outflowing tide meets the wind-driven surf and there is a wild, swirling sea, with crashing waves, whirling currents, and a shifting of sands. Where once a channel was, there may now be shallow sandbars to seize your boat and break it under thundering surf. A sailor tossed from his boat may be knocked down again and again by the surf as he strives for shore until he cannot rise again.

Normally such openings are short lived. As the tides move along the southern shore, the sands build along the western edge of the opening and the opening moves slowly to the east until, finally, it fills and is no more. Norton's point is no longer a point and Chappaquiddick is again a peninsula. And the fishermen can once more drive their four-by-fours to Wasque to fish the rip.

But that was days or weeks away. Now, Wasque was hard to reach. I'd have to take the ferry or a boat I didn't have. My dinghy was too small for the trip, particularly at night or if the sea was rough.

I drove down the beach until I fetched the opening. The water was flowing out at a considerable rate. Outside, the spray was flying as the flow met the last swells from the passed storm. The surf smashed the beach on either side of the opening and roiled into the air in mid-channel. There would be bluefish and maybe bass there, I thought. I'd have to give it a try later.

Inside Katama Bay the clam flats had taken a real beating. The nice flat next to Chappy had been torn away in part and would be eaten away even further before the opening was closed again. At least a season of clamming would be lost there. Maybe more. Bad luck for me, since I liked to work those flats. But Nature cares nothing for clammers such as me, and I thought that was as it ought to be. I prefer the indifferent universe. The idea of it allows me to understand good and evil better than if I were to believe in a God who bends over the earth with, ah, bright wings.

Other fishermen and sightseers soon gathered on the point and examined the opening. We'd not had one for several years, and it was a phenomenon of general curiosity. Islanders have a natural interest in the power of wind and water, and so the opening was soon lined with Jeeps and pickups. We all watched the water pour out of Katama Bay and smash into the dying swells of the storm.

After a while, I drove west, parked, and waded out to rake myself a basket of littlenecks. They were selling for many pennies apiece in the grocery stores and for even more on the half-shell in the restaurants and bars, so there was a day's pay for me if I could capture them.

And I could. There is something nice about quahogging. It's a lonely, quiet, and slow-moving sort of job. You and your rake and your basket are all by yourselves, and you cannot hurry the work. The big rake can only be tugged so fast and the quahogs are only so numerous. You have to be patient and steady, but while you are working you can think about other things without any loss in efficiency, so there's a double pleasure in the business: making money in a pleasant way and having plenty of time to muse, observe the flat beauty of the pond and beach, and enjoy being alone.

Even though I was a good distance from the new opening, I could feel a difference in the tug of water against my legs. There was a definite movement toward the opening, one that had not been there before. Nothing big—just a small pull toward the east. South of the island not long ago a similar soft flow had washed Marjorie Summerharp's body finally into the fish-filled nets of the *Mary Pachico*. Where had the strong subtle currents grasped her first? Where had they discovered her lifeless form before gently carrying it, floating and turning, into those nets and the realm of men?

If I died now, if my heart stopped beating and I pitched into this shallow water, the gentle tug of the opening would take me slowly east along the beach until the stronger pull of the rapid water took me—where? Out into the sea? Or would the tide have turned by then and would my body, now the property of the world's oceans, be washed into Katama Bay and on into Edgartown Harbor to astonish some yachtsman as he leaned against the rail of his vessel, looked down, and saw me sliding by, trailing seaweed, circled by curious fishes.

I worked a long time for my bushel of littlenecks, but I didn't mind. Tonight Zee and I had a date, and I reckoned I might need the money. Ian McGregor was out of the picture, John Skye and his wife and daughters would be home, and the normalcy would have returned to Martha's Vineyard. President Harding would have been pleased. When I wasn't thinking about Zee, I thought about the things people had told me about Sanctuary and Tristan Cooper. When I finally got my bushel and had sold them, I went home, stripped, and lay in the yard sopping up sunshine and thinking some more. Then I got dressed and went to get Zee.

Zee lived up island, where Tristan Cooper lived, where the Van Dams lived, where Helen Barstone and Bill Hooperman lived. Up island consists of the Vineyard's three westernmost towns, West Tisbury, Chilmark, and Gay Head. Down island, on the other hand, consists of Edgartown, Oak Bluffs, and Vineyard Haven, the latter town actually being disputed territory, considered by some to be up island and by others to be down island.

Zee's little house was off the road between West Tisbury and Chilmark. I'd tried to talk her into living down island with me, but she had declined, saying she'd just gotten out of one man's house (that of her physician ex-husband, Dr. Jerk), and wasn't ready to move into another one's yet. I didn't blame her, but I felt sorry for me. She also declined to marry me for similar reasons. Again, I didn't blame her, but . . .

I passed the general store and the field of dancing fiberglass statues across the road. Past the fairgrounds, I soon came to Zee's driveway. I arrived at her front door at precisely six o'clock, feeling happy and wary. She came out of her door as I turned off the ignition.

She was wearing white. White sleeveless dress, white shoes, small white purse, a white ribbon in her long, jet black hair. Her dark eyes and sleek tanned skin, her red lips and golden earrings gave her the look of a gypsy princess, of a Nereid, a siren.

"You came," she said. Her teeth flashed in a grin. "And you look quite spiffy, too. I'm flattered."

"I always dress this way on a first date." I was wearing my yacht club clothes: white shirt, blue blazer, light gray slacks, a blue tie with little baby sailboats on it, a belt with whales on it, and boat shoes without socks, to show that I was, after all, on the Vineyard and not, therefore, *too* formal.

I took her arm, led her around the Landcruiser, and helped her up into the passenger seat.

"Thank you," she said.

"A pleasure," I said.

"Where are we going?"

"The Navigator. We'll sit by a window so we can look

out at the harbor and decide which yacht we'll buy when we win the lottery.''

"Excellent. And we can watch the dinghies come in from the yachts and tie up at the dock and unload the boat people so they can have a meal on shore for a change.''

"And we'll have a couple of drinks and then order whatever we want.''

"Because we're rich with bluefish money and can afford the very best.''

"And if we spend all of that money, we still don't have to worry because I have an emergency supply of littleneck money that I've been saving for just this occasion.''

"And if we spend all of that money, then what?''

"We'll wash dishes. The secret is to eat everything first and *then* worry about whether the money is enough. If you count it first, you may never get to eat.''

"You can trust me. I won't even look a prices. Maybe we can use the old restroom trick. I'll go to the ladies' and then just keep going. You go to the gents' and do the same. After we eat, of course.''

"Of course. We can meet afterwards in the parking lot.''

"They'll never catch us unless they remember that they buy fish from you sometimes.''

"It's a perfect plan, but I suspect that we have so much money that we won't need to employ it.''

"I think you're right. What are you going to have?''

"Only things prepared at the table. Flaming entrée, Caesar salad, anything that's on the spectacular side. Nothing unobtrusive. Flaming dessert, flaming cordial, flaming brandy. That sort of thing.''

"My, you must be feeling theatrical.''

"I want everyone to see that I'm with you.''

"Well, then, I'm going to have all that showy stuff, too, for the same reason. We'll impress everyone in the dining room. They'll think we just came in off one of the yachts.''

"Precisely my plan. That's why I didn't wear socks. I want to look nautical.''

"It's too bad you don't have one of those blue hats that say 'captain.' ''

"I have an old Red Sox cap in the back seat. Will that do?"

"No."

"Oh."

The restaurant served up both a beautiful view and a fine meal. And we didn't need spectacular food to capture many an eye. Zee did that all by herself. She was the most beautiful woman in the room. The women envied her and the men envied me, and I didn't blame any of them.

And afterward she told me to take her not to her place but to mine.

I waited till next morning to mention Ian McGregor. We were sitting on the porch, looking out toward Nantucket Sound. It was a sky-blue day with a few white clouds hovering over Cape Cod across the Sound. The storm was gone and the island was clean washed and shiny. Zee's hair hung loose around her shoulders and she was wearing my old bathrobe. We were eating smoked bluefish, red onion, and cream cheese on bagels, washed down with black coffee. Not a bad way to start any day.

"Did you have a date with Ian the night before Marjorie was drowned?"

She stopped chewing. "Do we have to talk about Ian?"

"Do you remember whether you had a date with him that night?"

"Why are you doing this? Let's forget Ian."

"I'll be glad to. If you don't want to tell me, that's okay. I don't want Ian standing between us."

"Good. He's ancient history." I poured her some more coffee and she took a sip.

"You want to drive down and look at the opening?" I asked. "It's the first one we've had for several years. We can take inner tubes and shoot the rapids."

She looked at me over a bagel. "If I don't tell you, you're going to nose around until you find out anyway, aren't you?"

"Let's forget Ian," I said. "We can take a lunch and something to drink and a couple of books and make a day of it. My tan needs to be reinvigorated and I can use a day off."

"Why do you want to know?"

"I just want to know if he was driving around that night between midnight and, say four A.M. I think you've still got a bathing suit here, so we won't need to go to your place first. I've got everything else we need."

"Why do you want to know if he was out driving around?"

"Because I don't think that Marjorie Summerharp went swimming at six in the morning. I think she probably went in about two or three at the latest. She had to get down there somehow, and Ian seems to be the best bet for the guy who did it."

"But he said he drove down with her at six that morning. And weren't there witnesses who saw her driving with him?"

"That story doesn't fit the fact of where her body was found." I told her the suicide theory and then, in part just to slander Ian, the murder theory.

"Murder? Nonsense. Why would he murder her? Ian is a vain, ambitious man, but he's not my idea of a murderer."

"You told me once that there's a cruel streak in him. And he did punch out that young man from up island."

"There's some meanness in me, too. And in you, too, Jefferson. But neither of us are murderers!" She took a sip of coffee. "All right, we were out that night. We had supper downtown—at the Navigator Restaurant, as I'm sure you'll want to know—and then went out to the Hot Tin Roof and danced until the place closed. Ian is a wonderful dancer, unlike you, and we had a very nice time. He took me home quite late."

"How late?"

"About two, I think."

"Did he come in for a nightcap?"

"That's none of your business."

"All right."

"No, he didn't."

"He drove off about two o'clock."

"Yes."

"Did anyone ever tell you that you're not only beautiful but brilliant, humane, compassionate, and articulate?"

"All the time. I hear almost nothing else."

"How about omnipotent, omniscient, eternal, and completely good?"

"People tell me that every Sunday."

"Do you want to talk about Ian McGregor anymore?"

"No."

"Do you want to spend the day on the beach?"

"Only if you promise never to mention what's-his-name again."

"Not today, at least."

She sighed and gave me a sideways smile. "Okay. But I have to get home in time to wash my hair."

We were at the opening by ten and played like children in our inner tubes, riding the tidal river as it flowed out from Katama Bay into the sea. The storm swells were gone, and only the normal surf beat against the south shore to give us a bumpy end to our inner-tube voyages. But we'd paddle to shore and run back upstream and do it again and again until at last, breathless and weak from laughter, we threw the tubes down and collapsed on our blanket. Being a kid is tiring work.

After a bit we took our rods and fished. It was the wrong time of day, but it was fun and we didn't mind catching nothing. Then we had lunch and lay on the warm sand and let the sun do its work on our skin while we read and listened to the Chatham radio station play classical music. At three, we packed up and drove to my place so we could change to dry clothes before I took Zee home to West Tisbury. As we pulled into my yard, I saw McGregor's pretty sports car parked there. McGregor was standing beyond the car, looking darkly toward us as the old Landcruiser rattled into his view.

Zee touched my arm as I pulled up and stopped.

"I have a bad feeling about this, Jeff."

I stared out at McGregor. He stood in the middle of the scraggly lawn between the house and the garden, where there was room for action. There was a comfortable silky quality about him. He was almost smiling.

"I want you to go into the house and stay there no matter what happens," I said to Zee. "Don't come out until this is over."

"I don't like this," she said.

"It'll be all right," I said. "But I'd rather have you in the house where I don't have to think about you for a little while."

"He's going to fight you, isn't he?"

"I think that's his plan. Please go inside."

"No."

"Have it your way." I got out of the Landcruiser and walked out to meet McGregor. "Hello, Ian," I said.

"Hello, shithead," he said. "I've been waiting for you. I don't expect your bitch will like what she's going to see."

"You have dirt in your mouth," I said. "Are you sure you want to do this?"

"I'm sure." He put up his hands. He was wearing leather gloves. Smart. No more skinned knuckles for Ian McGregor.

I walked out onto the grass and he came quickly to meet me, left arm extended, right fist cocked. It was time to learn something about him, so I led with an awkward right. He blocked it, tapped me with his left, then crossed with his own right. I slipped the worst of it but went down anyway and rolled, wondering where the kick would be coming from. But there was no kick. I looked at his shoes. Sneakers. He had stepped back. "Get up," he said.

I got up. He feigned a left, then a right, and as I ducked away kicked with his right leg. I took it on my arm but realized that the kick, too, was only another feint. He whirled and struck high with his left foot. I blocked a bit of it but went down again. Again he stepped back and waited.

"Get up, you stupid, nosy excuse for a man."

I thought I had learned enough, but was not sure. I got up. He circled, then came in quickly and jabbed three times. They were leads to set up the right he liked. He had been trained in the manly art and was now putting that training to good use. When the right came I went backward, off balance, and he came after me with a flurry of punches. I went down on my rump and sat there. He danced on his toes, then stepped back again.

"Get up," he said.

But I just sat there. I had learned what I needed to know about him and was soon to learn something about myself. I had a split lip, and I spit some blood onto the lawn. I don't think that I was really mad at Ian, and perhaps never would have been, had he not then looked across toward where I'd last seen Zee.

"You stupid whore," he said. "How did I ever get mixed up with a slut like you and an asshole like this guy?" He looked down at me, shook his head in contempt, and walked past me toward his car.

I had heard of people seeing red, but had not previously seen it myself. But when he, in his anger, called Zee by those names, a thin crimson curtain fell across my eyes. His words apparently triggered some primeval fury suppressed within my genetic codes—none too well, it turned out—by generations of civilized living by my more recent ancestors.

I don't know if I made some noise (a snarl, perhaps?), but he turned as I rose and even had time to put a small smile on his face as he prepared to meet me. But he was not facing the same person he had apparently downed so easily in the previous minutes. I was someone or something else, something too fast, too strong and feral for him. He raised his gloved hands, but I struck them aside as though they were of straw and hit him a terrible backhanded blow that knocked him flat on the ground. I was on him in a flash, like a leopard on a rat. Dazed, he tried to roll away but only succeeded in landing me on his back rather than his chest. I drove a knee into his kidney and then had a handful of his hair in my fist and was jerking his head back and driving it into the ground, once, twice, three times, four.

There was a roaring in my ears like the sound of some great waterfall, and faintly through it I heard Zee's voice telling me to stop, stop! Then I felt her hands on my arms and turned my wild eyes and saw a scarlet world centered by her crimson face. Her mouth moved, and I heard the words telling me to stop before I killed him, and slowly the red curtain dimmed and faded and I found myself atop a bloody, moaning Ian McGregor, my hand still tangled in his hair, my other hand bloody knuckled.

"Stop," said Zee's voice. A great trembling overtook me, and I realized that my teeth were clenched and my lips curled back. The fist that held Ian's hair did not want to release its grip, but I forced it open. His head fell face down into the ground.

"Get up," said Zee's voice. I looked at the voice and saw her face, tanned, beautiful, framed with her long, black hair. "Get off him," she said.

"Yes," I said, and did so. She immediately knelt and rolled him over onto his back with that brisk strength that nurses use to manhandle large patients.

Ian's bloody face did not look too good. His eyes were dull and confused.

"Get me some water," said Zee.

"Yes." I turned my body and walked it into the house. At the kitchen sink I splashed cold water on my face, then put my head under the faucet. It seemed to help. I felt more sane. I found a pan and filled it with warm water and took a cloth and towel from a rack and went back inside.

Zee took the water and cloth and began to clean Ian's face. Slowly his eyes became clearer. They looked at me with something close to horror.

I went and knelt beside him.

"Go away," said Zee.

"No." I looked down into McGregor's frightened eyes. "There's something about fighting that you should know. There are people like me who don't fight fair or for fun. Until now you just never met one. The next time you do, you may end up dead or walking crooked for the rest of your life or brain dead or castrated. Do you understand me?"

"Yes," he whispered.

"Keep that in mind the next time you decide to punch somebody out. This time you and I were both lucky. Zee was here to break up our dance." I looked at Zee. "Thank you, Zee." I looked back at McGregor. "Say 'Thank you, Zee.' "

"Thank you, Zee," he said.

"Now apologize to Zee for the names you called her."

"I apologize," he said. "I'm sorry. Jesus." He was a big, handsome guy, but he wasn't feeling that way just then.

"I have more advice for you," I said. "Don't use women so lightly in the future, be careful about the names you call people, and stay away from me. In fact, I suggest that you stay away from Martha's Vineyard altogether." I looked at Zee. "How is he?"

"He'll live, no thanks to you. Superficial damage, I think."

I stood and stepped back. "Get up," I said to McGregor. "Get in your car and drive away."

He got unsteadily to his feet, limped to his pretty little car, and drove away without another word. I watched him, then looked at Zee. She didn't look too well.

"Are you all right?" I asked.

She put a hand to her mouth, then took it away. "I don't know," she said. "I thought I knew you."

"You do know me," I said, and immediately wondered if that was only wishful talk. I was more than a little shaken myself by what had happened.

She gave me a troubled glance. "I don't know," she said. "You scared me. I've never been scared of you before."

"I'm sorry you decided to watch it. But it wasn't as bad as it looked."

"You were going to kill him."

"No, I think that if I'd wanted to kill him I would have done it. Maybe this incident will lead him to change his ways. Maybe it will be for the best."

"You hurt him. He hurt you. He knocked you down."

"McGregor is a vain man, and he was angry and worried. He was mad because you left him and came back to me, and he was worried because I've been trying to tie him to Marjorie's death and might be getting close to something. He wanted me to suffer and you to know that you were no good and had made a bad choice when you left him. He thought of himself as a macho guy and was going to prove it the way he has in the past, by punching me out.''

''And he almost did.''

''Not really. I fell down to find out what he'd do then. If he had a really savage streak in him, a murderous one, he'd have tried to kick my head in when I hit the ground. But he just stepped back and let me get up. I let him do it three times, just to be sure.''

''But then you . . . I don't know how to describe it. You knocked him down and . . . It was as though he was a toy. . . .''

''Adrenalin rush, I think they'd say nowadays.'' I put a smile on my face. ''He said something that he shouldn't have said.''

She shivered. ''I'm cold. I need some dry clothes.''

After we had showered and changed, we had a quiet trip back to her house. On her porch I held her in my arms and kissed her. Her body pressed against mine and we stood there for a long time. Later, at home in bed, I lay awake and wondered and worried about the fight with Ian. Had I been accumulating anger for so long that a casual insult to Zee had triggered that red rage? Was I, deep down, mad at the warrior who had filled my legs with shrapnel in that faraway war, long ago? With the petty criminal whose bullet even now lodged near my spine? With the wife who had left me because she could no longer bear wondering if her policeman husband would be coming home in a box? With a father and mother who had died too soon? With who knew what other insults and injuries, imagined or otherwise, I had encountered in half an alloted lifetime?

I had long since decided that outrage and anger were destructive passions and had about convinced myself that I had rid myself of them. I knew that, modern war being the impersonal, faceless thing it often is, the soldier who had wounded me had not even known I was there, that the bullet I carried in my back was deposited there by chance (since the Boston shootist was firing wildly rather than with skill), that my ex-wife had twice seen her husband brought home in bandages and merited a happier life than I was giving her, that my parents had not died on purpose. I knew all that, but now it seemed that perhaps such knowledge was not enough; that my will to lead a peaceful and rational life could not be depended upon to achieve that end; that there was a beast within me waiting to be loosed.

I didn't like that notion and swore a private oath never to be so angry again. But I was a long time getting asleep.

~13~

THE NEXT MORNING I phoned Sanctuary and got Hans Van Dam himself. He ran my name through his memory and like any good salesman or front man dug me out of his mental files. Of course, of course, Mr. Jackson, he would be delighted to welcome me and give me a tour. He told me where to find the driveway and said he would inform the gateman and gave me a hearty goodbye. The flash of his teeth glowed from the receiver as I hung up. Then I phoned Tristan Cooper but got no answer. No matter. I got into the Landcruiser and drove to Chilmark.

Two mailboxes stood beside the driveway entrance, and the dirt driveway led through one of the old stone walls that adorn Chilmark, relics of the days when the township was composed of working farms. A hundred yards farther along, out of view from the road, I came to a new metal gate. To one side was a neat little gatehouse just big enough for one or two people. Stepping from it were a small young woman and a large young man. Both were well scrubbed, tanned, and wearing T-shirts that said "Sanctuary" and bore a discreet emblem made, as near as I could tell, of some sort of conglomeration of traditional religious symbols. The couple smiled noncommittally.

I gestured toward the gate. "This is new, isn't it?"

The young man stepped forward. He looked like an iron pumper. His muscles were large and his T-shirt was tight. He had a pleasant, vague face. "Yes sir, it is. Our clients were beginning to complain about people driving in without invitations. You know how people are, sir. They'll follow a new road just to see where it goes and they don't pay much attention to signs." His voice was a pleasant brogue. He showed me his even white teeth. Were there muscles in them, too?

"My name is Jackson. I'm expected."

"Oh, yes, Mr. Jackson, Doc told us you'd be coming. Cindy, let the gentleman through."

He stepped aside and Cindy swung the gate open.

"Have a good day, sir." They were both all smiles and freckled skin.

I drove on up the road, remembering it from years ago when my father had brought me duck hunting on Cooper's Pond. Things had been fancied up a good deal. The trees had been trimmed, and there was grass where before there had been scrub brush. When I came to the buildings, the difference was even more marked. The houses and outbuildings that I remembered as shabby and old were newly painted, and the once-weary lawns and fences were well kept. There were flower beds and benches and paths leading off in various directions. A few well-dressed, mostly elderly people could be seen walking or sitting or otherwise apparently enjoying themselves. Here and there were young people in the mold and uniform of the two I'd met at the gate.

As I stopped the Landcruiser and got out, Hans Van Dam came out of the main house, his dazzling smile lighting up an already bright day, his hand outstretched, his body clothed in casual white linen. Somewhere off to my left, out of sight, I heard laughter, shouts, and the sounds of tennis balls being served and returned. I looked that way and saw white clothes and a flash of light on red hair.

"Welcome, Mr. Jackson." Van Dam's soft paw shook my hand. "How nice of you to visit us on this lovely day. It's an excellent time for a visit, since many of our guests are at church and the rest of us are generally relaxing. I have a whole hour, ha, ha, to myself with which to give you a tour. Come this way, we'll start with the main house."

The main house contained offices, the Van Dams' quarters, and two suites of rooms for counseling. A second house ("built, you know, in the days when families stayed together") contained the communal kitchen, dining room, and recreation room. "Our largest room," explained Van Dam with a generous sweep of his hand. "We have our group meetings here, and our dances. Folk dances, waltzes, whatever will give our guests pleasure. At other times there are card and game tables. Our female staff is quartered upstairs. Rather spartan rooms, I confess, but their compensation is that they're near the kitchen and cook has a kind heart, ha, ha!"

One barn had been converted to a garage and storage area for machinery, and a second had become a small gymnasium with accompanying exercise rooms, massage rooms, showers, saunas, and whirlpools. Very clean and professional. The tennis courts were behind the barn, and male staff were housed on the second floor.

"And the real beauty of the place," said a smiling Van Dam, leading me down a flower-lined walk, "is here." He made another of the grand gestures that he favored, this one encompassing everything west, including the roofs of two cottages half hidden beneath the trees in front of us. "Sometime back in the early part of the century, when the Coopers still had money but were hoping to make more, Tristan's uncle, I believe, decided to convert his farm into a haven for summer visitors. He had these little cottages built, twenty or so of them scattered over a hundred or more acres. But bad timing was his lot, and the Great Depression arrived and left Uncle Cooper with empty cottages and, ha, ha, an empty wallet as well, I fear. The family barely managed to hold out over the following years, and Tristan was about to be forced to sell his beloved farm when, I'm delighted to say, Marie and I arrived and saw here the perfect haven for which we had sought so long! It was, if I may say so, a perfect match. Tristan has saved his beloved stones and Sanctuary's guests have private cottages to themselves."

"I remember the cottages from the times my father came here to hunt years ago, but I don't remember the stones."

"Ah, I can show them to you if you wish, but Tristan is really the man for the job. The most important one for us here at Sanctuary is yonder." He pointed toward a rounded hill. "There is the great stone we call the Altar. We hold our own private religious services there from time to time. Would you like to see it?"

"I'm seeing Tristan Cooper later . . ."

"Then he's the man for the job. Fascinating, these old stones, but I'm not the scholar Tristan is. He can tell you everything about them." He glanced at his wristwatch. It was not the kind you get in a gas station. "By Jove, we have just enough time to show you the beach. Come along, we'll take a golf cart. We've no golf course, ha, ha, but we do have good use for golf carts. Some of our guests are a bit too elderly to make the trek to the beach and boats, and for the rest of us they're a bit quicker than walking if time is important. Mind you, though, we encourage our guests to walk whenever possible." He waved a finger. "Excellent exercise!"

The golf carts were in the barn, and each was fitted with a two-way radio. We took one southward along the gentle path. After a bit we met a young couple strolling with a vigorous-looking white-haired man wearing a robe and sandals. All three waved, called friendly hellos, and displayed perfect teeth. Again I caught the lilt of Ireland in the voices of the young couple.

Van Dam was quick on the uptake. "Yes, as you no doubt have guessed, our groundkeepers and aides are college students, mostly from abroad. They are well screened and absolutely dependable, unlike many young American students who came to the island to play more than to work. We're very particular about our help, but we pay well. Unlike most jobs on the island, ours allow a student to actually make and save some money. We do not allow our people to drink or use drugs on the grounds or to enter the grounds under the influence, and we demand absolute discretion from them. Our guests' lives here are not subjects for public discussion. The members of our staff sign contracts when they assume their positions here and understand that anyone violating that trust will be dismissed immediately and will also be sued. They all understand that and know that in return they will not only make good salaries but have access to all facilities when they are not being used by the guests.'' He smiled his white shining smile. ''I am happy to say that we have never had to enforce the provisions of those contracts. Our young people have been uniformly trustworthy!''

''What are those necklaces they all wear?''

''You've a keen eye, sir. Those are worn by all staff and guests. They identify our people and insure that they are not mistaken for others who might not belong on the grounds. Those Sanctuary amulets allow authorized members of our community to go wherever they wish whenever they wish. The gate you passed on your way in is new, installed with regret, I assure you, but necessary to insure the privacy that is essential to our guests' comfort. Visitors are always welcome, of course, but without an appointment they are usually delayed a few minutes at the gate while we arrange a guide for them.''

I caught the smell of salt water, and a moment later Van Dam pulled the golf cart off the path and stopped atop a sandy bluff. ''There,'' he said.

Below us was a white beach, a part of South Beach, which stretched from Gay Head to Wasque Point. On the beach and in the water were several people, old and young, enjoying the sun and surf. To our left was a small pond linked to the sea by a narrow channel. On the pond was a pontoon pier fronted by a wooden boathouse. Tied to the pier were a day sailer and a small sport-fishing boat. Beyond the beach another day sailer with the Sanctuary logo on her mainsail was beating westward. Out to the southwest I could see Nomans Land, the small island that serves curiously as a bird sanctuary and a naval target range and near which many a large bluefish has been hooked. Off to my right, at the far end of the beach, naked people were on the sand and in the water. I glanced at Van Dam.

He smiled. ''Yes, nude bathing is available for any who wish it. For the sake of guests not so inclined, we insist that the nude bathers stay at that end of our beach. We see no moral dilemma in this. Do you?''

"No. I do the same thing in my yard sometimes. Did the pier and boats come with the property?"

"The powerboat, yes. But Tristan kept it in Menemsha Pond. I installed the pier and boathouse and purchased the sailboats to give our guests yet another form of therapy. We dredge the channel several times a year so our powerboat won't get trapped inside. It needs it now, in fact, thanks to that last storm. We offer sailing lessons for those who wish them and fishing expeditions for our salt water sportsmen and women. The integration of the sensual, the spiritual, the emotional, and the mental, sir, that is what we teach at Sanctuary. We teach a centering of these modes of experience, a balancing, a knowledge of the self that our guests can carry back with them to their everyday worlds and that will make them happier, more creative people." He glanced at his watch.

"Do you ever take the fishing boat out yourself?"

"I'm sorry to say that I know nothing at all of boats. Both my dear wife and I prefer the beauties of landscape rather than seascape. We hire young people with knowledge of boats to give lessons and take our guests out in pursuit of the fruits of the sea." Again a glance at his watch. "You are free to go on down if you wish, but I fear I must get back to work."

"Thanks," I said, "I will, if you don't mind. You've got a beautiful place here."

He looked as though he wished he hadn't made the offer. "Very well. Here, you'll need one of these." From a pocket he took one of the medallions everyone was wearing. It bore the Sanctuary logo. I put the chain around my neck. "Before you leave, just drop that off at my office. Oh, Barkley!" He shouted down toward the beach and a young man turned. "Come up here, will you?" Barkley, looking lean and sun bronzed, came running and arrived without even being short of breath. Ah, youth. "Barkley, this is Mr. Jackson. He's going to be exploring the grounds. Will you be so kind as to be his guide?"

"Yes, sir," said Barkley. "How do you do, sir?" He shook my hand. He was young, but he was comfortable with older folk such as me. Van Dam gave me directions to Tristan Cooper's cottage, flashed his patented smile, and went off on his golf cart.

"What would you like to see, sir?"

"First, the boats. I didn't know this pond was here."

"It's a natural pond, and we dredge it in the spring before we put the boats overboard. The channel is partially filled now because of that last storm. We can still get the sailboats out because they draw less than a foot with the centerboards up, but the motorboat has a vee bottom, and right now we can only get her in and out at high tide. We'll have the dredges down here late next week and get everything squared away. The boats get good protection in the pond, and there's a sandbar a couple of hundred yards off the beach that breaks up the worst of the waves."

We walked down onto the dock. The day sailer was a seventeen-footer with centerboard, and the fishing boat was an older design but still well kept. The hatch was locked, and there was no key in the ignition. A rope for waterskiing was coiled neatly in the back of the cockpit. "I imagine the Van Dams like to use this baby to get away from it all now and then. She's a nice old boat."

"Oh, no, sir. The doctor and his wife never go out. They don't care much for the water. They don't even come to the beach."

"Let's have a look at the beach." I took off my sandals. A dozen young people and an equal number of older men and women were enjoying the sun and gentle surf. Barkley smiled and greeted people as we passed among them. I heard foreign accents. "You have a young Irishman working here. I don't know his name, but I'd like to meet him. About a month ago he would have been sporting tokens of valor on his face. Do you know who I mean?"

Barkley's pleasant face became wary. "I don't know if I can help you. Why do you want to meet him?"

"I'm not from Immigration, if that's what's bothering you. No, I just thought he'd like to know that McGregor, the fellow who pounded on him, has been pounded on in return. I'd like to tell him myself, but if I can't, perhaps you'll see that he gets the word. It might make him and the girl feel better."

We walked on. "All right," said Barkley. "If I see him, I'll tell him." The nude bathers were just ahead of us. I felt overdressed and turned back. "I'm glad that Mc-Gregor got his," said Barkley as we retraced our steps. "Davey Grant is a good guy." He threw me a sudden glance and lowered his voice. "If you want my opinion, Maggie Leary isn't worth getting your face bashed in."

"Different people have different tastes."

"I suppose."

"Tell me," I said. "When Maggie was dating Mc-Gregor, did the two of them ever come up here and use the powerboat for waterskiing or fishing?"

"Not that I know of. If we want to date somebody who doesn't work here, we do it off the grounds."

"Do many red-headed girls work here?"

He gave me a questioning look. "No. Just Maggie Leary."

"I'd like to talk to Maggie. Is she around?"

He wasn't sure what to do. His hesitation made me think that she was indeed around. He apparently didn't care for Maggie, but nevertheless felt a certain loyalty toward her. "I don't know where she is," he finally said.

It was a lie I could understand. I might have said the same thing myself. Maggie wasn't on the beach, so she had to be somewhere else. "Let's go up to the tennis courts," I said.

Barkley looked unhappy but nodded.

At the tennis courts a red-headed young woman was playing doubles, teamed with a vigorous middle-aged man against a similar couple. They were a happy foursome, laughing and exchanging remarks. The red-haired woman's partner had a pretty good backhand and used it to win match point, after which he kissed her with casual carnality before jumping the net and shaking hands with the losers. I hadn't known that people actually jumped the net anymore and took it that the jumper in this case was not unwilling to have others admire his vigor. He seemed the hearty sort.

As the girl was toweling her face and arms and two other couples took over the court, I left Barkley and walked to her. She smiled a dark-eyed smile and raised a brow. Her hair was thick and a deep red such as you sometimes see among the Irish. Her complexion was not the sort that tanned well. It was milky and clean and very lightly touched with freckles. "Miss Leary? May I talk with you for a few minutes?"

"Who are you?" she asked. Her tennis partner was looking at us with what seemed a possessive stare. I looked back at him and smiled. "Nice game," I said.

"Thanks." He waved a hand and rubbed his towel on his neck.

"My name is Jackson," I said. "I want to talk to you about life insurance. Is there somewhere we can speak privately? This won't take long."

She looked at me with wise eyes. There was a carefulness in them that made her seem older than her years. "Life insurance, is it? You don't look like a life insurance salesman, if I may say so." Her voice had that lovely Irish lilt that can make the commonest words sound like song.

I stepped closer and put my back to her partner. "I have a wallet in my pocket. There's a badge in it. If you insist, I'll get it out and show it to you and these other people. Personally, I'd prefer not to do that, but I'll leave it up to you."

Her face seemed to contract a bit. She touched her lips with her tongue. "All right. We can walk together. That's probably best." She smiled and waved her fingers at her tennis partner. "See you at lunch, Robert." Then she walked with me off the courts and past Barkley.

"We'll be back in a few minutes," I said to Barkley. "Just stay here and I'll be able to find you."

Maggie Leary walked beside me down a curving pathway through the rocks and trees. Similar paths wound here and there, connecting cottages and other buildings, leading to vistas of sea and countryside where comfortable benches were placed for the convenience of viewers. Pausing at one of these, I was again struck by Chilmark's wild beauty. Surely there is no lovelier township on Martha's Vineyard.

"What kind of a badge do you have?" asked Maggie Leary.

"Boston police," I said, and I was even telling the truth. My old one was in my wallet. "I'm working on a case down here and I need some information you might be able to provide. Before you decide whether to help me, I should tell you that I'm close to some people in Immigration who are concerned about aliens working over here without green cards."

We walked on a bit. "What do you want to know?" she asked tightly.

"Maybe it will make you more comfortable to know I'm not interested in green cards one way or another."

"How very consoling. What do you want from me?"

"I have reason to believe that you and perhaps some other of the young people who work here are contributing sexual favors to Sanctuary's guests. Before you comment, you should also know that I don't care one way or the other about whether you engage in such activities and that your answer will reach no other ears if it is honest. I am not interested in preventing or reporting activities between consenting adults. On the other hand, if you lie to me, I will suggest to my friends in Immigration that they investigate Sanctuary and its employees. I might have the vice people do the same."

We strolled beneath the trees. The southwest wind stirred the leaves and bent the flowers and tall grasses.

"I have five sisters and two brothers in Sligo," she said. "They don't know what I do over here. All they know is that the money comes. When they save enough, others will come over here. There's no work in Ireland."

"So that's why McGregor called you a whore. He knew."

"Women are fools. I'm a fool. I trusted him. I told him too much. I didn't want anything between us. I thought that he and I . . . ."

We paused at a turn in the path and looked westward toward Squibnocket. The sun danced on the blue water and the trees were many shades of green. The sky arched up like a blue bowl, pale at the horizon, darker at the zenith.

"Is this work of yours part of the Van Dams' offering to their guests, or is it something private between you and your clients?"

She gave an expressionless laugh. "You won't see it written in any brochures. But it's understood. Not all of us offer such services, but some do. We are allowed to keep whatever gifts we might receive, and that makes the work rather lucrative. We are very discreet."

"I take it that the Van Dams can insure that discretion by reminding you that you have no work permits."

"A simple weapon but an excellent one."

"You have attended to Tristan Cooper among others."

She flashed me an amused glance. "Ah, yes. Would you believe that was not for profit? I was curious about him, if you must know. A man more than eighty years old, after all. And would you believe that he loves well? He does indeed. It gives one hope for one's old age! He is a fine old man." We turned back toward the tennis courts. "If I pack quickly," she said, "perhaps I can be away before your Immigration friends can find me."

"They won't find you because of me," I said. "I am not the conscience of mankind. How you live is your business." We came up to Barkley and I handed him my medallion. "Give this to Dr. Van Dam," I said. Then I shook hands with Maggie Leary. "Sorry we couldn't do business," I said. "I could have given you a real deal on whole life. Maybe another time."

Her hand was small and firm. "Yes. Perhaps another time. Thank you, Mr. Jackson."

Her doubles partner crossed to her as I left. "Huh," I heard him say, just before I passed beyond his voice, "the nerve of that chap. Selling insurance here. How did he get in, I wonder? I'm going to speak to Van Dam about this. We shouldn't have to put up with fellows like that."

~14~

I GOT INTO the Landcruiser and drove out past the smiling gate guards. Two driveways back toward West Tisbury, I took an unmarked driveway. A few hundred yards along the road I passed a well-tended family cemetery full of departed Coopers. A small granite mausoleum with a padlocked metal door was built half into a low hill on the far side. Beyond the hill I came to a well-built cottage. Tristan Cooper was standing on the porch looking at the road as I drove into sight.

He recognized me immediately and came to meet me. He was wearing only old shorts and stout shoes, and his ancient skin was brown and tight over his stringy muscles. He reminded me of a film I'd seen of Picasso. His was the same sort of vital face, his shoulders and arms showed the same lean strength, and he moved with the same economy of motion.

"Jackson, it's you. Welcome. J. W., isn't it?"

"That'll do. I phoned but no one answered."

"I've been out, working. There." He pointed to the graveyard. "I keep it neat. They'll plant me there one day and I want the neighborhood to be in shape." He grinned a feral grin.

"I came to see the stones."

"Ha. Not the gravestones, but the great stones. Coopers lie beneath the gravestones, but no one lies beneath the great stones. Or perhaps they do. Excellent. Delighted to show you. Come along, then." He strode away and spoke over his shoulder as I followed. "Do you know anything about the stones of Martha's Vineyard?"

"Only what a couple of your friends have said, that you think they're evidence of pre-Columbian contacts between European and American cultures. There's a lot of controversy about it, I gather."

"For a lot of people, American history starts with 1492. Actually, almost everybody now knows that there were native civilizations here long before that and that Columbus was certainly not the first European to reach these shores and return home again. Even Marjorie Summerharp, bless her, wouldn't have denied the Scandinavian explorations, and she might even have accepted the Brendan voyages and the fishing journeys of the Azorians to the Grand Banks. You know that the Vineyard is thought by some to be the Vinland that Leif Ericson explored?"

"I thought they'd decided that Newfoundland was Vinland."

He laughed. "Yes, the site of L'Anse Aux Meadows. History is looking at the past through a picket fence. We only see part of it and we have to guess at the rest. If you want to learn about the Vineyard-Vinland theory, go down to the Historical Society in Edgartown and do some reading. Begin with Huntington's essay in the *Intelligencer*— that'll give you a start. As for me, I'm after older game. Look, you can see the Altar from here."

I looked ahead and saw a long gray stone outlined against the sky atop a small hill. A moment later we were there. Tristan Cooper was panting slightly and there was sweat on his hard brown skin.

The stone was granite of the kind seen all over Martha's Vineyard in walls, foundations, fields, and woods. It was roughly shaped into a rectangle. It was a dozen feet long, a third that wide and stood three feet above the surface of the lawn that surrounded it. A shallow channel was carved around the edge of the upper surface of the stone, outlining its perimeter.

Tristan Cooper placed his hands upon the stone and peered up at me with his bright old eyes. "A glacier brought these stones down during the last ice age. When the glacier stopped and then retreated, it left behind a pile of dirt and stone it had pushed before it. That stone and dirt became the islands off the south coast of New England—Nantucket, the Vineyard, Block Island, Long Island, and the other smaller ones. A long time later, people arrived. Still later, people from across the sea arrived. Look at this. Obviously worked by human hands, right? The groove might be intended to catch blood and funnel it down here. See, here's a drainage cut at this corner. The questions are: who did it, when, and why?

"Human sacrifice was practiced by people all over the world. The Bible is full of it—Ahaz, Manasseh, the sons of Hinnom, the Molech worshipers and others. Read it, by the way, it's a good book. The Wolf Clan of the Pawnees sacrificed a captured maiden every spring when Mars was the morning star, and there was human sacrifice and ritual cannibalism among Mississippi Valley people and among the Nootka and Kwakiutl on the north Pacific coast. So we shouldn't be surprised if it was tried on the Vineyard, too. Maybe right here." He patted the stone.

"Maybe."

"And maybe not," he said briskly. "I agree. Critics of those of us who believe Europeans contacted America long before the Vikings got here would say that this stone was shaped and positioned here either by colonialists in the seventeenth century or by archeological fakers who did it as a joke in the spirit of the Cardiff Giant hoax. I say not. There was no practical use for such a stone in colonial times, and my family's records indicate that the stone has been here since the late eighteenth century at least. Besides, look here." He bent over a corner of the stone. I joined him and looked down. Incised faintly into the side and end of the stone were roughly parallel lines leading away from the vertical corner. There were longer lines and shorter lines. I could see no pattern in them. "Ogham," he said happily. "Two thousand years old, I reckon. Celtic. No colonialist or faker carved these! They were here before scholars could even read ogham!" He slapped the stone and stood up. His face shone.

"A kind of writing," I said, remembering Marjorie

Summerharp's reference to such evidence. "Can you read it?"

"Yes, my lad, I can. But let's talk of that later. Look there. Do you see that notch in the hill? See that rock poking up out of the scrub? At the summer solstice, if you stand at this altar stone, the sun rises over that rock. I have photographs of the event. The rock has been worked with tools and it's standing upright, so it's not there by chance. And there, do you see that standing stone to the south? There on the slope. Yes? The sun of the winter solstice rises over that stone. Damned near froze when I photographed that. And look there and there and there . . ."

His voice was like an ancient parchment, and as I turned and followed his voice and pointing arm I saw a circle of stones standing around the altar stone fifty yards or so away from it. They were rough-hewn granite rocks, some half hidden in scrub brush, others leaning, others apparently fallen. I seemed to slide backwards through time. Then Cooper's voice stopped and I moved back into the present. I blinked and Cooper said, "Have you ever been to Europe, J. W.?"

"No."

"There are circles like this all over Britain and others on the Continent clear down to the African coast. Stonehenge, Avebury, Callenish, Stenness, Stanton Drew. And they're here in New England, too. Right here and in New Hampshire and Vermont. Over there, in Europe, they've got names and no one questions their antiquity or importance, but here they're nameless and the people who want to study them are cranks and crackpots. Like me." He grinned a lupine grin. "Come along and see some more."

He turned, and we went down off the hill along a slope broken by rocks and scrub, ducking under trees and dodging roots. In a swale below the Altar, dug into a cliff face, was a stone structure. Two large stones framed the doorway and another great flat stone topped the opening. Earth covered the topping stone. Cooper gestured, and we went inside. The room was stale and dark, but there was light aplenty from the door. The walls and ceiling were made of large flat stones, some, I guessed, weighing tons.

"There are dozens of these in New England," said Cooper, extending a hand to touch a wall. "Root cellars, according to our critics. Built by colonialists, just like the Altar. But why a root cellar here? Why did they move such great stones to build it? Could they have moved such stones? It makes no sense, no sense at all. And did the native people, those called 'Indians' build it, then? No, they did not. They were as ingenious as any folk, but there's no archeological evidence that they ever built such structures. Who, then? Europeans, my lad, Europeans. Chambers such as this are found throughout ancient Europe. They were temples perhaps, or perhaps ceremonial chambers of lesser stature than temples. Do you note the direction of the door? No? At the winter solstice precisely, a shaft of light enters this door and reaches back there, to the far wall. It touches the base of the wall and then withdraws and is seen no more for another year. What do you think of that?"

"Sun worship. A ceremony to bring the sun back before it's gone forever."

"Quite right. The work of a Christian colonialist? Pshaw! Look above you."

I looked, saw nothing, looked harder, and saw more parallel lines dissected by a single long line. "Ogham?"

"Indeed! When I mentioned ogham to my more traditional colleagues, they tell me the marks were made by colonial plows! Plows! How did they plow the top of this chamber, eh? I've gotten no answer to that question. Well, what do you think?"

I looked at him. He stood like a man out of ancient time, his simian head cocked to one side, his bright young eyes aglitter in the summer sunlight. "I think that someone went to an awful lot of trouble to create a hoax, if this is a hoax. But then I know of a lot of people who went to an awful lot of trouble to create hoaxes. There are con men who will sacrifice everything for a good con. A shrink could probably explain it."

He stared at me, then grinned, then laughed. "Yes, of course. Of course you're right. But who was the con man who built these structures all over New England? Who built the stone circles, the chambers, the dolmen? He was a busy chap, eh? Moving stones weighing tons, aligning stones with the solstices and equinoxes, building dolmen? And never being seen while all about him other colonialists were farming these lands, building homes and villages, keeping journals, and going about the work of colonial life. An amazing fellow, our con man. An invisible con man, eh? Come along back to the house."

He started off, and after a final look at the dolmen I followed.

His cottage was filled with books and papers, but he led me first to a shotgun hanging from two pegs on the wall of his living room. "Have a look at this. You're a gunner. Your father and I used to shoot together sometimes. Do you remember?"

"Yes." I took the gun, a Remington twelve-gauge, and opened it. It was empty. A box of shells sat on a shelf above the pegs. I threw the gun to my shoulder. It felt smooth and good. I handed it back to him and smiled.

He replaced it on the pegs. "I don't shoot much anymore, but I enjoyed it when I was doing it. I have no objection to hunters who eat what they shoot. I do disapprove of trophy shooters, though. Let me get you a drink."

"Beer will be fine."

"I have Whitbread. A luxury I cannot give up."

"A fine beer."

He brought two beers and waved me to a chair. "You asked me about ogham. Do you know anything about it?"

"No."

"I'll not bore you with details. Ogham is a kind of writing engraved in stone. It was first noted in Ireland in the early eighteenth century but not successfully translated until seventy-five years later. As you saw at the Altar, the letters of the alphabet consist of parallel lines. There are twenty or more letters, and they are represented by sets of one to five lines placed above, below or across a guideline. At the Altar, the guideline was the corner of the stone itself. Remember? That message translates 'This stone is Bel's.' Bel is the Celtic sun god. He is Baal, the god of whom you read in the Bible. The ogham on the roof of the chamber we entered says that it is a temple of Bel. There are similar chambers, writings, and monuments all over New England, all over the New World, in fact.''

''Celtic sailors did this?''

''Colonists, more likely. Traders and explorers at the very least. Celtics here, but Iberians, Phoenicians, Egyptians, Semites here and elsewhere. They came across the same way Columbus did later; they caught the trade winds and the currents that he followed and were carried right across to the Americas. And they went home again the way he did, by following the northern winds and currents. For thousands of years, I suspect. Some went south to Brazil, some to Central America and Mexico, others north. They went up the Mississippi and its tributaries, they came to New England, they brought their religions and their languages and left these monuments behind them.''

''For thousands of years. Why are there no records?''

''There are records. In Celtic writings, in Libya, here in inscribed stones. But no one read them, or if they were read they were dismissed as myth or fiction. But now, I believe, the evidence is beginning to accumulate sufficiently to persuade all but the hopelessly boneheaded. The linguistic evidence alone should be persuasive.'' He gave a crackly laugh. ''Have I converted you? Have I betrayed myself as a frustrated evangelist? Will you stay for lunch?''

''Yes. Will you tell me more?''

''Ha! Is the pope Polish? Is a professor wasting your time when his lips are moving? Of course I will tell you more. But first, some lunch. I am a poor cook, I fear. Peanut butter has kept me alive for the last forty years.''

''Peanut butter will be fine.''

We ate peanut butter sandwiches and washed them down with beer as we sat in his book-filled cottage. I asked him about Sanctuary.

"Do the Van Dams use the boats down at the beach for their personal use?"

"I've never seen them in a boat. They say they don't really like boats. They hire someone every season to give sailing lessons and take people fishing. Why do you ask?"

"Just curiosity. What do you think of them and their business?"

He emptied his glass. "They are the salvation of these ancient stones I've shown you and of others you've not yet seen. If it were not for them, I would have been forced to sell some of this land to developers, and the stones would not, I fear, have survived."

"Surely you could have included clauses in the sales agreement to keep the stones secure."

"As long as I lived to insure such clauses. But after my death I cannot imagine their survival. The site of the Altar is the finest homesite on the property, after all, and land developers are not concerned with ancient history. But now the Van Dams pay me a healthy rent. They are excellent tenants. I have been able to begin paying off my debts and still keep eating! In another year or so, I hope even to set something aside for my declining years. With the income from Sanctuary, I will be able to live out my life and will the property to a proper land preservation group and be certain that the stones are safe. As for the Van Dams' beliefs"—he shrugged—"I have read of worse and seen worse in practice. It is my impression that they do their clients no harm and might even do them some good."

"The synthesis of emotion, sensation, intellect, and spirit?"

"Stolen from Jung, I believe, who no doubt got the idea from somewhere else."

"Marjorie Summerharp considered them panderers."

His face lost expression. "Marjorie, poor child, had a bad word for almost everyone, including me. I ceased to take her criticism seriously many years ago."

"She said she might do an exposé on Sanctuary. Do you know what she was talking about?"

"You're very curious about Sanctuary."

I told him about the time and tide problems regarding Marjorie Summerharp's death. "I'm just checking out possibilities. You know the Van Dams better than most people do. Do you think they could have been angry enough at her to do her harm?"

"Do her harm? Murder her, you mean?" He stared at me. "I take it that you're serious. Yes, I see that you are. Very well, then. I have never seen any indication that the Van Dams have any violent inclinations whatsoever. They are laid back, if I may use a youthful idiom."

"And if she threatened an exposé?"

"What sort of exposé?"

"Prostitution seems to be what she had in mind. Some of those young lovelies and young Adonises are doing more than mowing grass, guarding gates, and teaching sailing. Synthesizing emotion and sensation, as it were."

His mouth worked. "How would Marjorie ever get an idea like that?"

"Another person suggested the same thing. She saw something when she was visiting the place. Since then the Van Dams have installed that gate so they won't get any more surprise callers."

"Do I know this other person?"

"You've met. A young woman I know. She seemed pretty sure of herself."

"That's a very serious accusation. Did this young woman give you details?"

"Some. Since then I've learned enough to know her suspicions are justified. Do you think the Van Dams would consider a threatened exposé sufficient motive for murder?"

He sank into his chair, thought written on his forehead. Then, "No, no, I cannot imagine it. I would guess that they would first brazen it out. Then, if that failed, I rather expect they would fault underlings and promise reform—and if that failed, I imagine they would simply disappear, no doubt to reemerge elsewhere, Palm Springs or Bar Harbor or wherever wealthy clients might be found, with the same sort of organization. Murder is too violent an act for so mellow a folk as the Van Dams." He looked up at me

and smiled. "No, my friend, even if Marjorie's threat were
known to them, I cannot see the Van Dams as motivated
to murder. That, of course, is the opinion of a totally
amateur criminologist. I see that you have finished your
lunch. Would you like me to speak of things I actually
know something about?"

I said that I would and for the next hours listened to a
brilliant zealot give an argument, rich in detail, that ancient European, African, and Asian people had indeed explored and colonized the New World. He spoke without
notes, but occasionally dove into a pile of books or papers
to extract a photograph or drawing illustrating a point. He
spoke of languages and place names, of epigraphy, symbols and art styles, of artifacts and maps, of animal and
plant dispersions, of stone monuments, and of Old World
sagas and histories mentioning the New World. Suddenly
he stopped.

"Good lord. Two hours! No one can stand two hours
of such lecturing! You've had enough!" There had been a
sort of cold fever in his face and voice, and now the fever
was forced away and replaced by a dry-lipped smile. "Off
you go, my lad. But do come again. There's more for you
to see. I believe I have a burial marker that may be Iberian."

As we shook hands outside, he put a hard old hand on
my shoulder. "It was good to see you, J. W. I've not had
so attentive an audience in years! I'm a vain old goat and
I enjoyed myself today. Do you think your young friend
Zeolinda would fancy visiting my ancient monuments?
Why don't the two of you come up together? We can ex-
plore the place and have a drink together afterward. I'd
like that very much. Nothing an old man likes more than
a beautiful young woman listening to him." He laughed.
"Or pretending to."

"I'll ask her. I think she might."

"Splendid! The sooner the better!"

As I drove away, I glanced in the rearview mirror. He
stood outlined against the sky like a creature out of time.
He lifted a long arm and waved a large brown hand slowly
back and forth until I drove out of sight.

In Edgartown I found the chief, who looked at me with the expression of a man who didn't need any more problems.

"What's the matter with you?" he asked as I came up.

"Nothing."

"Good."

"Maybe. Part of the nothing is the nothing that I've heard from you. Did your partrolmen see Ian MacGregor or Marjorie Summerharp driving around that night? You were going to let me know, remember?"

"Was I? Well, as a matter of fact, one of the men does remember seeing that little English sports car of McGregor's out on the road that night."

"What time?"

"He didn't log it. He thinks it was two or three in the morning. The car had that surfboard on the roof, otherwise he probably wouldn't have remembered it at all."

"McGregor and Zee Madieras were out dancing at the Hot Tin Roof that night. McGregor left Zee at home at about two. Your man could have seen him coming home. Anybody remember seeing that old Nova of Marjorie Summerharp's?"

"Nobody remembered seeing the Nova. It wasn't a very memorable car."

"Did you get any response from the ad in the paper?"

"Nothing useful. Several civic-minded types said they were on the beach that morning at one time or another, but nobody saw Marjorie Summerharp or a boat near the beach or anything else that might help."

"Nothing, again."

"Nothing may be bad for you, but it's good for me. I could use a little more nothing happening. It's the some-things that give me trouble." His eye roved the street. "I see that you and the beautiful Zeolinda are again keeping company before the youthful professor has even gone back to America."

"Your spies tell you true."

"Glad to hear it."

"You'll let me know if anything useful turns up?"

"Sure."

"Sure. Just like last time."

"Just like that."

I bought fishing line and leader material at the tackle shop and found a parking place at the A & P. While I pushed my carriage around, I wished the dissertations from Northern Indiana University would arrive.

~ 15 ~

ZEE'S FRAGRANCE LINGERED in the air of my house. Or
was it my imagination? What difference? I inhaled deep
into my lungs. Was it some perfume she wore? Some sort
of musk? Or was it just the way she smelled all by
herself? I envied the deer and lions with their fine noses,
I envied the sharks and barracuda with their fine noses. I
envied Tarzan of the Apes who, according to the books
about him that I'd read when a kid, had a nose as good as
any animal in the jungle. I remembered wishing then that
I had a Tarzan nose and going around sniffing the air trying to make it so. Did Cyrano have a better sense of smell
than his dish-faced associates? I, alas, did not. My ordi-
nary nose could only enjoy a normal mortal's pleasure
from the fragrance of Zee.

In my garden the weeds were gaining on my vegetables
and flowers, so I went out and disputed with them for an
hour under the late afternoon sun. Just because I struggled
with the Summerharp matter, the daily demands of life
did not stop. Weeds still grew and fish still swam. Nature
went on about her business.

At dusk I drove down to the new opening and did some
serious fishing. McGregor's meal ticket had run out and I
needed some income. There was a little point of sand
sticking out on the west side of the opening, and it was
already occupied with several fishermen casting into the
convergence of the outflowing tidal stream and the incoming surf. Bluefish like to feed at dawn and dusk and they're
smart enough to know that tidal streams such as that now
flowing out of Katama Bay often carry smaller fish, eels,

and other bait into the sea, so they come to feed when the tides are right.

I parked the Landcruiser and watched a while to see if anybody was catching anything and if so what lures were being used. Imitation is popular among fishermen. They watch to see what's working. Sometimes the fish get persnickety and will only bite a certain lure. Other times they'll take anything you throw out. Tonight they were taking metal, seeming to favor Castmasters. I got out and put one on my leader, found a place between two other fishermen, and went to work.

It's not bad fishing shoulder to shoulder as long as everybody knows what he's doing. If the casts are made straight, the lines don't get tangled and the fishermen haul their catches in with a nice collective rhythm. If there is a beginner in the crowd, everything can go bad fast. He'll (or she'll) cast sideways across lines, tangle gear, cause hooked fish to be lost, and if some fisherman gets furious enough, see his offending line cut off by a fish-knife. Once in a while he will be threatened. Once in a rarer while a fight might almost break out. More often, the real fishermen will simply curse and withdraw in disgust, leaving the beach to the amateur, who has no idea what he's done.

This evening I was with the regulars and things went well. There was a school of six- and seven-pounders out there, and they were hungry for whatever it was they thought Castmasters were. I caught one on my second cast and got him in, got a swirl on the next cast, had one on for two turns of the reel on the third, and got a second fish in a couple of casts later. I stayed there for almost three hours, until it was too dark to see and the tide had flattened out and the fish were getting scarce. Most people had gone home, and those few of us who remained gathered and had coffee and chewed the rag. I asked them if any of them had been down fishing along the beach west of Katama on the morning Marjorie Summerharp had died, but no one had.

I took the fish by a restaurant and sold all but one that I wanted for myself—a little two-pounder who would make me a nice breakfast. I took him home, filleted him, and threw the bones downwind into the oak brush. As long as the wind blew from the southwest I'd not get the smell. By the time the wind turned, the insects, birds, and varmints would have his bones picked clean.

The next morning I went down to the Dukes County Historical Society, which sits on the corner of Cooke and School streets in downtown Edgartown. As with libraries, the Historical Society is filled with information and has people around who will help you find it. I paid my fee and sought out information about ancient Vineyard stones. Someone found me the November 1973 copy of *The Dukes County Intelligencer* and told me to start there. In the *Intelligencer* I read of the Chilmark Cromlech, of the "Indian Gravestone from Gay Head," on which is carved the un-Indian name Haiki Cagnehein, and of the Black Rock of Nomans Land, which reportedly lay out on that small island's western beach. I also read of Captain Kidd's Rock, also on Nomans Land but on its north shore, upon which were inscribed markings that some took to be secret writing telling where Kidd had buried his treasure, but that others thought were runes written by lost Vikings from Iceland and that still others thought were the work of hoaxers if, indeed, they were human letterings at all. Such arguments were lately thought to be moot, thanks to the U.S. Navy, which uses the island as a target range.

I read, too, of the runic stone found in North Tisbury on the old Priester place, which has since disappeared but whose inscription was copied first by the farmhand who found it. Noting my subject matter, people not only directed me to other writings but brought forth the famous "Indian Gravestone" itself, which the Society had stored away out of sight while it decided what to do with it. Sure enough, it seemed to bear the rude inscription *Haiki Cagnehein*, whoever or whatever that might indicate. I read of the stones and chamber near the Christiantown chapel, of the "Viking tower" in Newport, and of the efforts of scholars and aficionados to place such artifacts in history and western culture.

By noon I had absorbed as much such information as I could stand. One thing was clear to me: Tristan Cooper might be living out on the end of a limb, far from the trunk of traditional historical and anthropological thought, but he was not out there alone. He had a lot of company, and there was evidence, however controversial, that somebody or other had gotten to America long before Columbus. The Society folk hoped that I would come back. I told them that I would.

I thought of how the sun grew round and new each day and the wind blew low and high from the southwest and at night the simple stars were bright in the black sky. Soon the month would turn and the pale July people would come to the island in exchange for the brown June people, who would take their dogs and memories back to the Mainland for another year. I thought of how, on the Fourth of July, Zee and I would watch the Edgartown parade, featuring the queen of something and her attendants waving from an open car, the Boys' and Girls' Club band, the scouts, several environmentally oriented floats (which would gradually disintegrate as the parade progressed), veterans, police and firemen marching in straggle step, fire engines blasting sirens, the Camp Jabberwocky marchers and bus, various dignitaries most people wouldn't seem to know, and the band of pipers skirling and drumming to hearty applause. It would be a first-class small-town parade, and afterward Zee and I would wish that Edgartown still offered fireworks after the parade, as it had in the good old days, but would agree that it had been a glorious Fourth anyway. Such thoughts suggested to me that perhaps I'd done too much sleuthing of late and needed a return to normalcy.

Such a return was not to be, however, for that day the dissertations arrived from Northern Indiana University.

I got the news via one of those yellow slips the post office leaves telling you that there's something you have to pick up at the office downtown. It's either something too big to fit in your mailbox or it's a registered letter or something that you may very well not want to get. But in order to find out whether you want the thing the yellow slip signifies, you have to go get it. Then it's too late not to get it if you don't want it. In this case, it was the dissertations, mailed in a large, firm container. As I picked it up at the post office, John Skye came in. He was one of the people who preferred to collect his mail in town rather than in an RFD box like mine. He said it made him feel more a part of the town and kept him better informed of current gossip.

"I hear that you're keeping company with Zee again."

"There are few secrets in small towns," I said.

"Ian looked a little bruised yesterday before he left. He seemed to have a broken front tooth. And it looks to me as if you have a split lip."

"You're keen eyed as always, Holmes. I imagine the twins will recover from their grief at his departure by the time school rolls around again."

"I imagine they will. Zee came over to see Mattie and Mattie told me that Zee told her that you and Ian had a disagreement. I'm glad to see you both lived through it."

"Some day when we're both drunk on South Beach waiting for the fish to come, we can exchange old war stories and I'll give you all the details and then some."

"I thought Zee looked good. Mattie says she doesn't feel as good as she looks. Something to do with you. Don't tell me you've finally revealed the truth about your character. That would shock any woman of sensibility."

"No, I told her the truth about you. I imagine she and Mattie at this very moment are packing up the twins and heading back to Mattie's mother."

"What brings you into town? I thought you hung out in the woods and on the beach until after Labor Day."

I tapped my package. "In here I have two dissertations on seventeenth-century British drama. I need somebody like you to go over them with me. What do you say?"

"I say let me pick up my mail and then take me to a bar where you can buy me a beer and explain to me what you're talking about."

We went down to the Wharf and I told him about the theses. I also offered him the theory that Ian McGregor might have lied about taking Marjorie to the beach at six that morning. "There's something in these papers that interested Marjorie Summerharp a lot. A couple of days af-

ter she got her copies, she walked into the sea and
drowned. Or so they say. I want to know what interested
her so much and whether there's some link between that
and her death.''

''Are you saying that she committed suicide because of
what she found in the dissertations? And that Ian is cov-
ering up for her for some reason?''

''Nope. All I'm saying is that maybe there's some hint
in these papers about why Marjorie's dead. I also think
that Ian is worried about what's in them. He got mad at
me when I got interested in them, and anger is a product
of fear. I think he was afraid of what I might find.''

John sipped his beer. ''Interesting. There's only one
little problem.''

''What's that?''

''I know zilch about the seventeenth century.''

''Jees, I thought you were a literature professor.''

''I am. But I only know about medieval stuff. Incunab-
ula is my game.''

''I thought you guys were supposed to know everything.''

''Usually we know a little about a lot and supposedly
we know a lot about a little. I know a good bit about pre-
1500 writings and not much about later stuff. Promise not
to tell.''

I drank my beer and ordered another round. It was almost six o'clock and the place was filling up.

''I need somebody who'll know what these papers are
about. I sure as hell won't. There might be something
right there in front of my face and I'd never recognize it.''

''Look,'' said John, ''let's do this. Let's look these over
together first. I don't know much about the seventeenth
century, but I probably know a little more than you do.
Maybe we'll spot something. If we don't, then let's bring
in some other people. I'm thinking of Bill Hooperman and
Helen Barstone, or better yet, Tristan Cooper, the old
master himself.''

''Marjorie wasn't too impressed by Hooperman and
Barstone.''

''Marjorie owned a tongue like a knife. She didn't like

very many people. Bill and Helen both know more about the seventeenth century than I do. If we don't find something, maybe they will. It'll tickle their vanity to be asked to help, and better yet, it'll not only give them a chance to feel smart and appreciated, it'll give them a chance to maybe get something on Marjorie or Ian or both. They'd love that!''

"You academic types are mean suckers. Your place or mine?''

"I've got a bigger library, in case we have to look something up.''

"Yours, then. When?''

He glanced at his watch. "How about right now? We'll have supper first and then get to work.''

"Who's cooking, you or Mattie?''

"Snobbery! Don't get snotty about my cooking or I might change my mind about reading these papers with you. The twins are tonight's cooks, if you must know. Something like hash browns and corned beef, I think. I imagine you can choke it down.''

"I imagine I can.''

Jill and Jen, it turned out, produced a boiled dinner from a pressure cooker: potatoes, carrots, cabbage, and corned beef, cooked perfectly. For dessert, apple pie with a choice of ice cream or Cheddar. I chose ice cream, much to Mattie's disgust.

"I thought you were supposed to be some sort of gourmet cook. No gourmet eats his apple pie with ice cream!''

"We manly American men eat our apple pie the way we like it, gourmet or not. You're just another stuffy cheese freak like all the other rich summer-visitor types who come down here to give the natives a hard time. I know all about your sort.''

"I'm with you, Mom,'' said Jen, sitting down to her cheese-topped slice of pie.''

"I'm with you, J. W.,'' said Jill, sitting down to her ice-cream-draped slice of pie.''

"Thanks, Jill,'' I said. "Your sister Jen is famous for her peasantlike ways, whereas you are a truly sophisticated woman. I've often remarked upon the differences between you.''

"I'm Jen," said the ice cream eater. "That's Jill with the cheese."

"Exactly," I said. "Your sister Jill is a barbarian like her mother, whereas you are highly civilized like me. I've often remarked upon the differences between you."

"Good food," said John, scarfing up the last of his pie.

I concurred with vigor, and after John and I had another piece of pie apiece, we carried the dishes into the kitchen, loaded up the dishwasher, wiped off the counters and table, thanked the twins again, and went into the library. John produced Cognac and two Cuban cigars from a box left as a gift by Ian McGregor, and we settled down to read the dissertations.

Tough going for me, but I plowed ahead, reading Ian McGregor's commentary on the increasing dependency of English drama upon the court in the first half of the seventeenth century. Allusions and footnotes abounded. I recognized names I'd encountered in my review of Marjorie Summerharp's notes and could follow the argument, but had no idea whether it was strong or weak, valid or nonsense. Strong and valid, apparently, since his review committee had given him his Ph.D. Beyond me, though. References to people and publications, playwrights and princes, players and plays I'd never heard of. Small details upon which large notions seemed to turn; accumulations of evidence, some apparently well known, other more obscure. Everything documented, everything just a bit ponderous, a bit heavy. Humor was not allowed in academic writing, apparently. At least not in dissertations upon the seventeenth century. Comedy was discussed, since it was part of the theater of that time, but the discussion was solemn.

I wore out before I finished the manuscript.

"I'm out of here," I said, getting up. "I'll have at it again tomorrow and come over tomorrow night after supper to trade books."

"I'm made of sterner stuff," said John. "I read this sort

of thing all the time, so I'm used to it. I'll hang on a little longer before I quit. See you tomorrow night.''

I left him with his face in Marjorie Summerharp's dissertation, leaned into the telly room, said good night to Mattie and the twins, and left, feeling slightly cross-eyed.

I was up early and down at the opening at dawn. Only a couple of trucks in front of me, since it was a weekday and most of the regulars were working men who didn't have time to fish before going to their jobs. The fishermen before me were retired guys and a couple of summer people who had been coming to the island as long as I could remember. A man and his son, both excellent fishermen. Side by side we stood in the rising sunlight and cast for the wily bluefish, sending silver lures arching out into the waves where incoming surf and outflowing tide met in a roil of white water.

No action for a time. We cast, reeled fast, reeled slow, changed lures, cast some more. Then a rod bent at the end of the line. A hit. We cast some more and suddenly the fish were there for all of us.

The sun rose and it got warm. We peeled down to undershirts and kept fishing. We were happy. I thought about how much Zee would have loved being here and how I would razz her for missing the show.

Then we began making casts and not catching fish every time. Then we were not catching many at all. Then they were gone. I put a four-ounce Hopkins on and threw it as far as I could but did not catch the very last fish right at the very end of my cast as the school moved off. I cranked the Hopkins in empty and felt good anyway.

''Bonanza,'' said the guy next to me as we loaded our hauls into our trucks. ''It doesn't get much better than that.''

True.

After I got rid of my fish in town, I went home and washed up and took Ian McGregor's thesis out onto the porch with a cup of coffee and picked up reading where I'd left off last night. By midafternoon I had finished and had flipped through the pages of documentation. I was exhausted and had seen nothing that meant anything to me. The only thing I had learned was that I wasn't going to try to get a Ph.D. It was not my sort of work.

After supper, I drove to John's farm. Jill or Jen was coming up from the barn.

"Hi," I said.

"Hi," she said.

"You know I really do favor you over your sister, don't you?"

"Oh, yeah. It makes a girl feel good to know an elderly man likes her best."

"You can trust old J. W."

Her sister came out of the house. "Hi," she said.

"J. W. here was just telling me how much he preferred me to you," said Jill or Jen.

"You can trust old J. W.," I said. "I never said any such thing. It's you I prefer. Everybody knows that. I like a girl who likes ice cream on her cheese, not the other way around."

"See, I told you he likes me best," said Jill or Jen. "You won't even eat cheese."

"I will, too. I just don't eat it on ice cream."

I went in through the kitchen, kissed Mattie, and went on down to the library.

"Well," said John, "did you finish? Good. So did I. Did you find anything? No? Neither did I. Let's trade, then. Maybe we'll have better luck this time."

Marjorie Summerharp's argument concerning the court masque was more arcane than Ian's, if that was possible. The pages were thickly footnoted, the references many, the argument serpentine, the documentation massive, the subject occasionally interesting anyway.

I learned that the masque had developed from a simple sort of masked entertainment for aristocrats, which allowed for amorous goings-on in disguise, or at least official disguise, into a highly sophisticated entertainment mixing professional and amateur participants in complex and convoluted symbolic theater. I read of *The Masque of the Queens, Proteus and The Adamantine Rock* (which sounded to me like an excellent name for a hard rock band), *Of Blackness*, and of other masques of the era, which ended with the overthrow of the monarchy and the rise of Oliver Cromwell, of whom I had heard no good word, but toward whom Marjorie Summerharp directed no criticism, apparently being of the opinion that Charles I deserved to be removed from the throne.

It was very late when we put the dissertations aside, lit final cigars, sipped final Cognacs, and looked at one another questioningly.

"Well?" John lifted a professional eyebrow.

"Well, indeed. I can't make head or tail of any of it."

"I did see that Ian quoted Marjorie's thesis when she wrote of *Salmancida Spolia.*"

"That sounds like a disease."

"It was William D'Avenant's last masque, 1640. King Charles and his queen were both participants. Then the civil war broke out and that was the end of court masques."

I had no recollection of the name. I was very tired. "What about it?"

"Nothing. Just that it was the only thing I saw that tied the two theses together. Ian referred to Marjorie's argument when he was making his own, that's all. He used her as a reference, which was pretty smart, since by the time he was writing his thesis she was a world-famous authority. I imagine he got points for being enterprising enough to dig out her thesis and to quote from it. Who could find fault with that?"

"Not me."

"Nor me." We puffed and sipped. There's no doubt but that the Cubans make the best cigars and the French the best brandy in the world. "Shall we scream for help?" he asked.

"From Helen Barstone and Bill Hooperman? Why not? They can't tell us less than we know already."

"Let me call them. And while they're poring over these papers, you see if Zee would like to go sailing tomorrow. Mattie and the twins and I were thinking of going down harbor, out the new opening, then around Chappy into Cape Pogue Pond for a picnic. We'd like to have you two along."

"Fine. I can use a break from all this."

He leaned over and touched a weather cube on his desk. We listened to the weather in Boston, north of Cape Cod, and finally south of Cape Cod. Sunny and mild with light southwest winds. Nothing could be finer. John punched off the cube. "Bring bathing suits," he said, smiling. "I don't want you shocking my daughters."

It was sunny that next morning, but later clouded over a bit and breezed up. We had the tide with us going down harbor and out the new opening. The *Mattie* slid slowly along, barely listing as we close-hauled across Katama Bay and rode the new river into the sea off South Beach. There were fishermen there and they were enjoying themselves, although they seemed to be having little luck. As the outflowing tide met the incoming waves, the *Mattie* pitched and rolled and spray flew. But she was a shallow-drafted, beamy old boat made for such turbulence, and she banged her way on out into smoother water.

"Wouldn't want to try that in a high wind at half tide," said John, looking appreciatively back at the wild water we'd just come through. He patted *Mattie* approvingly, slacked off his sheet, and headed east toward Wasque Point.

The south shore of Chappaquiddick was covered with walkers who had parked their cars on top of the bluff inside the sands and had walked the quarter mile to the water. Past them on the point were a few four-by-fours and some fishermen who had come over on the Chappy ferry from Edgartown to try their luck. It was a warm day, and soon most of us had shed all but bathing suits. The twins arranged themselves on the deck and painted their noses with lotion. John and I admired Mattie and Zee as they stretched out on *Mattie*'s seats.

"Browning the meat," said John. "An excellent ritual. Women do it best."

We jibed around Wasque and sailed a broad reach north along East Beach to Cape Pogue. All along the beach were four-by-fours surrounded by small packs of people preparing for picnics, playing with Frisbees, fishing for fish who were not interested in being caught. At Cape Pogue we came around onto a close haul and tacked against a rising wind down along the elbow to the gut, where, blanketed by the cliffs, we eased inside the pond against the dying tide. The sky was beginning to show some clouds.

At the south end of Cape Pogue Pond we were in the lee of the island and mostly in the sun. Thinking ahead, I'd brought my quahog rake and basket, and once we were squared away at anchor just off the beach, I went overboard with my gear.

"Giant quahogs," I explained.

So while the others swam or walked the empty white beach, I waded out chest deep amid an underwater forest of waving grasses and began raking for the big chowder clams. They were few but humongous, each one too big for fit in the rake, each feeling more like a fair-sized rock than a quahog. When I felt them, I'd dig at them with the rake until I could get it under them, then I'd turn it and bring the quahog up and drop him in the basket. Quahogging is the world's best job if you need time to think about something else while you're working. I thought about how fine Zee looked, walking with Jill or Jen along the beach, looking for shells. No matter how long you live near a beach, you never stop looking for shells. The other Jill or Jen was walking the other way with her mother and John. Also looking for shells.

When I hooked my thirtieth quahog into my basket, it sank, settling slowly toward the bottom, overloaded. I pulled it up again and towed it to shore. Chowder makings galore.

We picnicked on the beach, and afterward we snoozed and loafed and watched the Jeeps drive to and from Cape Pogue on the east side of the pond. And we watched the clouds slowly thicken overhead until the sky was pale white instead of blue. Then we got back onto the *Mattie,* put up the great, gaff-rigged sail and headed back for Edgartown. I found Zee's camera and took shots of her at the helm. Captain Madieras bringing her home. Very stylish. *Cruising World* would love it.

At home, as Zee and I were chopping up quahogs for chowder, the phone rang. It was Tristan Cooper. "I've been trying to get in touch with you," he said, "but haven't had much luck. Have you asked your young friend if she'd like to see my monuments? I'd like to have both of you come up."

"Ask her yourself. She's right here." I handed the phone to Zee and listened to her listen to him.

"We'd love it," she said after a bit. "Tomorrow evening, then. Thanks. See you there." She hung up the phone. "Cocktails and the grand tour. Tomorrow at five. Sounds like fun."

"The Vineyard is a fun place," I said. "You can ask anybody. All of us fun people have fun here all the time." I reached for her.

She dodged. "Keep your clammy hands to yourself or I'll put tomatoes in your chowder. You won't think that's so funny."

"Some things even we fun people don't joke about, lady. Tomatoes in clam chowder is one of them. Only weirdos from New York put tomatoes in clam chowder. True Americans gag at the thought."

We were finishing off bowls of fresh chowder made the true American way and washed down with cold Chablis when the phone rang again. I was suddenly a very popular fellow. It was John Skye. "The jury is in," he said. "Bill and Helen have strutted their stuff. They've just arrived and they're drinking my booze. You want to come over?"

I looked at the mess in the kitchen. "We're on our way," I said. "The mystery of the missing dissertations has been solved," I said to Zee. "Do you want to join the cast in John's library while All Is Revealed?"

"You bet."

We shoved the leftovers into the fridge and the dishes into the slave and left.

～16～

I THOUGHT THAT Professors Helen Barstone and Bill Hooperman looked pretty happy when we met them in John's library. And why not? They'd been sampling his bar for an hour at least and were, moreover, feeling smart. I soon discovered why.

"D'Avenant," said Helen Barstone, lifting a forefinger into the air and poking it at me. "D'Avenant. There's the link."

"Exactly. D'Avenant," agreed Hooperman, admiring his glass of Cognac and giving the contents a swirl under his nose.

"Who's D'Avenant?" I asked.

"William D'Avenant," said John, pouring himself a drink from the rapidly emptying Cognac bottle. "The guy who wrote *Salmancida Spolia*, the last great court masque. Remember?"

I did, barely. "The masque that sounds like a disease. Charles the First and his wife were in it. Just before Cromwell decided to take over."

Helen Barstone smiled. "Something like that."

"It's hard to believe," said Hooperman almost soberly. He shook his massive head. "Really hard to believe. I'm not sure I believe it even now. It's very hard to believe. Very hard. I'm not sure I do, really. I mean—"

"What he means," said Helen Barstone, "is that when Marjorie Summerharp wrote of D'Avenant she not only used all of the right people in her bibliography, including Maidment and Logan and Nethercot and the rest, but—"

"But she used at least one other source, too!" exclaimed Hooperman, spilling brandy on his shirt as he gestured with his glass. He looked down at his front. "Oh, dear . . ."

"Exactly," said Helen Barstone, poking her finger into the air again. "Exactly. F. X. Eastford!"

"Who's F. X. Eastford?"

Barstone and Hooperman exchanged meaningful glances and nods.

"Exactly," said Hooperman. "There you've got it. Amazing, eh?"

"How so?"

"Because," said Helen Barstone, stepping closer so that when I looked down at her face I also looked down the vee of her dress, "there is no F. X. Eastford. What do you think of that?" She tapped my chest with her finger. "Eh?"

She had very fine breasts. I admired them. She smiled up at me. I glanced at Zee, who rolled her eyes and looked disgusted.

"Nonexistent," said Hooperman. "Wrote a nonexistent manuscript, too. In Marjorie's bibliography. *Forbidden Drama*. I'm not sure I believe it even now."

"How do you know it's nonexistent?"

"Not listed. Everything's listed, but not F. X. Eastford. No F. X. Eastford, no *Forbidden Drama*, either. We went to Tristan Cooper and double-checked with him. Knows everything, that old man. Says there never was any F. X. Eastford and never any *Forbidden Drama*, either. Shocking." Hooperman drank off his Cognac. "Shocking." He looked happily into his glass.

"Supposedly it was a commentary on the theater that went on during Cromwell's rule—underground, so to speak." Helen Barstone looked up at me as I looked down at her. She was, I realized, much more sober than Hooperman. "D'Avenant staged a couple of plays then, too. F. X. Eastford supposedly was a sort of theater buff who knew D'Avenant and other playwrights and actors of that time and who kept a private journal, which he had printed after the Restoration."

"*Forbidden Drama.*"

"Yes. But there is no such book."

"But Marjorie Summerharp quoted it nevertheless."

"Yes."

"Are you sure there's no such book?"

She shrugged her shoulders, and her breasts shrugged with them. "We couldn't find it listed anywhere. And Tristan says not."

I looked over her head at John Skye. He looked at me. "If the book doesn't exist, why didn't anyone notice it before this?" I asked the room in general.

"Who checks every name in a bibliography?" asked Hooperman.

"How about the committee that approves the thesis?"

"Marjorie Summerharp's dissertation contains hundreds of references. F. X. Eastford is the only one that's not valid. It probably wouldn't be noticed unless you were looking for it. Remember, too, that Marjorie was an early product of Northern Indiana's graduate program in Renaissance Studies. Her committee might have been a bit weak."

"How did you notice it?"

"Because we were looking for something strange." Helen Barstone tapped my chest again, bringing my eyes back down to her. "And at first we didn't notice anything either. I mean how many people know that some privately printed book doesn't exist? But when we checked the listings, F. X. Eastford wasn't there, and when we talked to Tristan it turned out that there was a reason for it."

"There is no F. X. Eastford."

"Correct. Would you like to dance?"

"Not right now, thanks. Excuse me." I slipped past her and poured myself the last of John's Cognac. "So Marjorie Summerharp slipped a ringer into her bibliography."

Helen Barstone said, "Exactly," and Bill Hooperman agreed but just couldn't believe it. John nodded without expression.

"Why?"

John shrugged. "Maybe she thought she needed another source to back her argument about William D'Avenant's activities during the Commonwealth. She's not the first or last to fake a document. I imagine that one reason it got overlooked is because it's really an insignificant part of her total dissertation."

I thought about Marjorie Summerharp. It did not surprise me that she had been more than the rigid, wry old lady I'd known so briefly, for which of us is only what he seems? I remembered Hooperman's voice on the telephone speaking of Marjorie and saying "It takes one to know one." Of course that had been his pettiness speaking of her pettiness, but he had been near to another truth about her, too: She was a forger herself, which perhaps accounted for her lifelong fascination with the practice. There is no one more fanatically religious than a reformed sinner, and of course no one better at catching thieves than a former thief.

Somehow I did not think the less of her. In fact, it made her a bit more human. I thought of the crooked things I'd done during my life. The thefts during my army days when I had liberated gear I felt I deserved, the occasional peeks over a friendly shoulder during high school exams, the girl who had helped me write my papers in History.

I wondered if my own excursions into immorality had anything to do with my later becoming a cop. I didn't think of myself and of Marjorie Summerharp as fanatics, but maybe down deep somewhere we had a touch of that sort of madness within us. I remembered Dostoevski writing that there was little difference between moral and immoral men, between saints and sinners.

I suggested a motive: "Could it have been done as a joke? A fast one pulled on the scholars who were supposedly judging her scholarship? She didn't have a very high opinion of a lot of people who had high opinions of themselves."

John arched an eyebrow. "I'd love to have been able to ask her. She always had a wicked sense of humor."

"Did you find anything else?" I asked Hooperman and Barstone.

They exchanged meaningful glances.

"Indeed," said Hooperman, with an alcoholic smile. "There is a link between Ian's thesis and Marjorie's. Very

interesting. Very, um, distressing.'' His large face showed
no distress at all.

"F. X. Eastford again,'' said Helen Barstone. "Ian
quotes Marjorie's thesis in his own discussion of the last
years of Elizabethan drama. Quotes a remark Eastford
made about D'Avenant, in fact.'' She smiled and I saw a
lioness. One of Ian McGregor's cast-off women was showing her fangs. She raised her pointing finger and made
little circles with it in the air, then aimed it at me. "The
remark he quotes is not in Marjorie's dissertation.''

"Shocking,'' murmured Hooperman. He lifted the Cognac bottle and noted that it was empty. A sherry bottle
was not, so he poured himself a glass from that. "Had he
been content to quote Marjorie's thesis, he could not be
faulted. But quoting a passage from *Forbidden Drama* that
is not in Marjorie's text. Tsk, tsk . . .'' He gave a happy
sigh.

I looked at John. He spread his hands. He did not share
his colleague's joy at their discovery.

"Anything else?'' I asked. "Any other revelations?''

"None at all,'' said Helen Barstone primly. "Not that
we need anything else. We found quite enough, I think.''

"Quite enough,'' agreed Hooperman. "Yes, indeed.''
He drank down his sherry and looked at Helen Barstone's
breasts. He smiled.

"Scandal,'' said John. "Major scandal. Marjorie and
Ian both guilty of fakery. Two reputations ruined. I don't
like it. I suggest that the four of us keep this pretty quiet
until we know what to do with the information.''

"I don't see why,'' said Helen Barstone coolly. "Marjorie's dead—she can't be hurt. Besides, she never pulled
a punch when it came to others' shortcomings. The things
she's said about me! And Bill! And God knows Ian has
been hard on people when it suited him. Under all that
sleekness, he's been hard on a lot of people.''

"For one thing,'' said John carefully, "we don't know
for certain that there isn't any F. X. Eastford or a book
by him called *Forbidden Drama*. All we know is that it's
not in the lists you know of and that Tristan never heard
of Eastford or his book. I'd advise all of us to move very

cautiously in this matter. We must consult with other experts and make a very thorough study of the catalogs and listings before we can decide that Marjorie and Ian are fakers. Their reputations are all that they have, after all. Marjorie's is a major one and Ian's promises to be so. I cannot say too strongly that we must walk lightly here until we know our ground better than we do now.''

Somewhat to my surprise, Hooperman agreed. "Quite so, John. Self-interest, if nothing else. What if we cried scandal and then discovered that Eastford actually *had* written that book? Damned awkward, I can tell you. No, no, we must be cautious. Swear ourselves to secrecy until we can dig deeper. Yes, indeed. Particularly since the whole thing is so hard to believe." He poured himself more sherry.

"That's not my sort of work," I said. "I leave it to you three. How long will it take you to check it out?"

The three academics exchanged questioning looks. "Oh, months, at least, I should think," suggested Hooperman.

"Months?" exclaimed Helen Barstone. "I should think less time than that. Weeks, at best."

"Weeks, months," said John. "Something like that. It takes time and money to do this sort of thing. Money would buy us help to speed things up, but none of us is rich. The important thing is to agree among ourselves not to let this suspicion out until we're absolutely certain that *Forbidden Drama* doesn't exist. Are we agreed?"

Helen Barstone rubbed her neck with her hand, sighed, and smiled a small, tight smile. "All right, John."

"Good," said Hooperman. "I find this very exciting, I must say. Shall we also agree not to publish separately, but as one? If, that is, we discover that we actually have something to publish. . . ."

"Yes," said John. "I agree to that. It'll keep any one of us from going off at half cock."

"Very well," said Helen Barstone. "I agree. We'll publish together, if at all. I say, Bill, would you like to dance?"

John frowned at them, not really seeing them as they began to sway to music heard only by themselves. It must have been sweet music, for they looked blissful as they danced. Then I was aware that he was also frowning at me. He moved closer, glanced at the dancers, then spoke quietly. There was a note of sadness in his voice.

"This means Ian had a motive for murder. Marjorie got the theses, read them, and confronted Ian. He killed her to protect himself."

"Sounds neat," I said.

I put my back to the happy dancers. "Of course, if she squealed on him, he could squeal on her, too. What about that?"

He thought. Then, "She was at the end of her career anyhow. His was just beginning. She would retire to Maine where no one knew her reputation, or cared, but his future would be destroyed. She was quirky enough to tell all and take her chances, I think. Besides, she really didn't have to say anything; all she had to do was withdraw from this Shakespeare project. That alone would make the discovery suspect enough to dim Ian's hope of fame and fortune. It would put the whole matter in limbo even if the document is authentic, which it well may be." John did not like what he was saying. He was not one who liked to sit in judgment and was, therefore, one whose judgment I trusted.

Zee was listening. "Motive isn't enough," she said. "A killer has to have opportunity, too." We looked at her. "Marjorie was seen driving to the beach that morning. Ian was seen running the bike path shortly afterward. He couldn't have killed her. If he had, her body would have been washed farther east. You said that yourself, Jeff."

"Try this on for size," I said. "His car was seen in the vicinity between midnight and four. He went home after dropping you off, confronted Marjorie, overpowered her, dressed her in her swimming gear, drove her to South Beach, drowned her, and took her offshore on his surf-sailer so no one would find her body too soon, if at all. It sounds complicated, but he had time to do it. Then, in the morning, he puts on a pair of gloves and her white swimming cap and drives her car to the beach. In case anybody actually pays any attention, they'll think he's her. He parks the car and runs home along the bike path. What do you think?''

The dancers jostled a table and laughed. They were very happy about killing two birds with one stone. John and Zee were not happy at all.

"Or,'' I said, "maybe he didn't mean to kill her. Maybe they struggled and she fell and then the rest of it happened. She can't tell us, but he can.'' As my voice said this, it occurred to me that I should reread the *Gazette* reports of the drowning.

"He shouldn't tell us,'' said John, "he should tell the police, if he tells anybody. I guess I should give them a call.'' He walked frowning toward the kitchen.

At the far end of the library, Doctors Barstone and Hooperman had stopped dancing and were kissing. Zee and I followed John out of the room and left the victors alone. I was thinking of the tale of the serpent in Eden and wondering about its moral. Was it that in every garden there is a serpent or that for every serpent there is a garden? Both the serpent and the garden were beautiful and both were tempters, the serpent offering a nibble from the fruit of the tree of knowledge and the garden offering the sweet bliss of innocence. Which was the most dangerous? Which offered the greatest blessing?

As I drove Zee home, I told her about the Man Who Craps. The Man Who Craps is a little figure of a guy wearing a red fez who is squatting and shitting on the ground, his trousers down around his ankles. He was brought to me by a friend who had been in Barcelona during the Christmas season and who, while browsing through Catalonia's markets, had come across the figure amid other figures who were in the traditional Christmas crèches: Mary, Joseph, baby Jesus, angels, shepherds, donkeys, sheep, cattle, and so forth. In Catalonia, Christmas crèches are apparently very popular, for the figures are for sale everywhere in all sizes and for all prices. But my friend had never seen the Man Who Craps as part of the scene and had been sufficiently fascinated to purchase two, one of them for me. Curious, my friend had asked acquaintances the significance of the obscene figure being mixed in with the other more traditional figures and had in time been given the following explanation: In Catalonia there were, in fact, three figures not elsewhere found in the crèche: the Man Who Craps, a woman washing clothes, and a fisherman at work. They signified that at the moment of the birth of the only son of God, surely the most sacred and important event since the beginning of time, all of the very human activities that normally took place continued to take place. Nothing really changed. Everything that usually happened continued to happen. Clothes still needed to be washed, fish needed to be caught, and shit needed to be shat. Life went on as it always does in spite of the miracle.

Or in spite of death. Marjorie Summerharp's or anyone else's.

At Christmas, when I put up my little crèche, around in back, modestly out of sight, I always put the Man Who Craps, because I like what he stands (or squats) for: life going on in spite of doom or marvel.

I suddenly became aware of my monologue. "I am a famous babbler," I said.

Zee hooked her arm in mine. "You left-bank undergraduates pretend you're existentialists, but all the girls know you're just frustrated idealists."

"God," I said. "It's such a relief to be understood at last. Does this mean that I can go back and live with Mom and Dad again and that I don't have to wear this damned beret any longer?"

"You got it, cookie," said Zee. "You can start teaching your Sunday school classes again and join the Rotary Club."

"Oh, I'm so happy! You're an angel. Let's get married right away."

"No. I've been so inspired by your return to normalcy that I've decided to enter a nunnery just like my Aunt Sylvia always wanted. I'll pray for you daily."

"Thanks a lot."

"There, there. Just think of Warren Harding and everything will be all right."

We pulled up in front of her door. "Are you sure you have to enter the nunnery right away?" I asked.

"Actually," she said, running her tongue along her lips and looking up at me, "I thought I might put it off until tomorrow."

In the morning, the rising sun poured red light through her window and touched her sleeping face with radiance. I watched her for a long time, then slipped away and made breakfast for us both and brought it back on a tray. She was sitting up, looking as lovely as a goddess, smiling. My heart thumped.

An hour later she drove to work and I drove home. She had again declined to marry me but on the other hand had decided to give up the nunnery. Things could have been worse. As I drove east into the rising sun, clouds were building in the sky. I turned on the radio and learned that we were to have rain that night and a bit of wind. I wondered if it would wash out our date with Tristan Cooper and his standing stones.

At home I dug around and found the *Gazette* editions reporting on Marjorie Summerharp's death and reread them. I had been dumb once again. If I'd been smarter, I could have saved myself a split lip. I got into the Landcruiser and drove into Edgartown.

There I parked on Green Avenue, where the meter maids never trod, and walked down Main Street. On Dock Street I found the chief trying to fit a cup of coffee into his day. Beyond him, tall sails moved out of the harbor toward the Sound, pushed by a following wind. I watched him sip from his Styrofoam cup and move his eyes here and there, as was his habit.

"Well?" he said.

"Did John Skye call you about the dissertations?"

"Yes, he did. So what?"

"So maybe there's a motive for murder in them."

"Ian McGregor's motive for murdering Marjorie Summerharp, I take it."

"Could be."

"Do you believe it?"

"I'm just an amateur snoop. You're the professional officer of the law."

"Hereabout it's the official policy to let the state cops handle murder investigations, the theory being, apparently, that we local types aren't bright enough or well trained enough to deal with such sophisticated crime. But as even you know, so far we don't have a murder here, just an accidental death."

"I think you have more than that."

"And now you think McGregor's the guy?"

"I think that if I was a real live policeman I might rank him as a legit suspect. He had motive."

"I hate to repeat myself, although with you I should expect to. Do you think that McGregor's the guy?"

"As a matter of fact, I doubt it."

"Really? My, my. I thought you were the fellow who had him taking the victim down to the beach in the early hours and running her outside on his surfboard, then faking a six o'clock drive to the beach wearing her bathing cap. What made you change your mind, if I may ask so simple a question of so complex a thinker? Now use short words—I don't want to get out of my depth."

"You may be just a poor hick cop living off parking tickets and small-town graft, but even you can grasp this. Marjorie Summerharp only had one bathing suit and one bathing cap, and according to the *Gazette* I just reread she was wearing both when the *Mary Pachico* found her. The driver of her car was wearing a white cap that morning. Unless McGregor managed to buy himself one in the middle of the night, he couldn't have been wearing one at six that morning. Ergo, it *was* Marjorie driving her car down to the beach just when McGregor said she did. Ergo, again, he didn't do her in. He just didn't have time to do that and still be seen running on the bike path when witnesses saw him there." I touched my split lip. "Besides, McGregor isn't the killing type. I gave him a chance to try to do a real number on me and he didn't take it. I don't think he could kill somebody if he wanted to and I don't think he'd want to. Most people are like that."

"I don't know what most people are like or what a

killing type is, but then I'm just a poor hick cop going broke on local graft. But I'm glad to hear that you've finally come around to believing what everybody else knew all along."

"All I'm saying is that McGregor didn't kill her. But that still doesn't explain how she ended up where she did when she did."

He crumpled his cup and dropped it into a waste barrel. "I know. For what it's worth, I've been talking with the state cops about this whole thing for the last three weeks. I understand that they're asking some questions on the mainland, trying to get a lead on what might have happened down here. It's still an accidental death, but the D.A. knows that it might be something more. Before I trudge off to protect and serve, do you have any other tidbits you'd like to add to my collection?"

"Two. First, Sanctuary keeps a couple of sailboats and a sportfisherman on South Beach. Second, there's reason to think that some of the girls and maybe some of the boys who work up there offer sexual favors to the customers but keep their mouths shut about it because they're illegal aliens trying to make some money to send back home to the poor folks."

"So?"

"So Marjorie Summerharp talked about writing an exposé about Sanctuary, and the Van Dams, who run the place, knew about it. They own a boat they might have used to pick her up at South Beach. Motive and opportunity. Don't thank me, just make sure I get the reward."

"Hmmmm," he hmmmed thoughtfully, and actually walked off without making some sarcastic remark.

~17~

I HAD A coffee at the Dock Street Coffee Shop and watched the cook perform his graceful act at the grill, thinking again that anything done well is beautiful, then walked back through town, got the Landcruiser, and took the ferry across to Chappy. I hadn't hunted the blues between Wasque and the Cape Pogue gut for days, and I needed to get at it.

By four I was home again. The sky was overcast and the wind was brisk from the southwest. I showered and climbed into chinos and boat shoes, had a fast vodka on ice, grabbed my topsider, and went to pick up Zee.

She was waiting and climbed in beside me. "You're clouding," she said as we drove west. "When you're thinking about something, a little black cloud sits on your forehead. It's there now."

"The curse of the great intellectuals," I said. "Our mark of Cain. We're doomed to think all the time, whether we want to or not."

"Pure affectation as far as you're concerned," said Zee. "Intellectuals make lousy lovers because they're always thinking about what they're doing. The same can't be said for you, that's for sure. You're a part-time thinker at best, I'm glad to say."

"Maybe you're right. I won't do it anymore. I have a hard time doing it when you're around anyway."

"I've noticed. Why are you clouding?"

"I'm not clouding." I willed my cloud away.

"Why *were* you clouding?"

"I was clouding about the same thing I've been cloud-

189

ing about for the last month—how Marjorie Summerharp ended up dead. Here we are.'' I turned off and drove along Tristan Cooper's driveway. We passed the graveyard and came to his house. Off to the southwest beyond Nomans Land storm clouds were darkening the sky, but rain seemed far off, if it was coming at all. Plenty of time for a tour of Tristan's grounds before the first drops fell. The overcast and wind made both land and sea seem older and wilder.

Tristan Cooper met us at his door, his simian face and strong brown hands thrusting forth from a turtleneck jersey.

''So glad you could come. I propose an exploratory walk first and afterward something to warm our bones while we talk. Or would you like coffee first? No? Then come along. The wind lends charm to these sites, I think.''

For an hour we walked his land as he spoke of the ancient stones scattered across it: the Altar, the equinox and solstice stones, the temple to Bel, the dolmen, a ''gravestone'' faintly marked with what Tristan took to be Iberian writing. His voice was on the surface cool and academic, but there was no disguising his love of his subject. Such a professor, I thought, might by pure passion draw students into his subject, whatever it might be; might fire them with the fire within himself and produce a race of scholars to change the face of academe.

Zee, ever sensitive to honest feeling and new thought, was fascinated and delighted, and he, ever a man who liked women, sensed her response and spun a web of words about her, flashing me a strong-toothed smile as he did so, so I would know that he knew that I knew. I could not find it in me to be angry but instead only hoped that at eighty I would possess half his magic.

Then we were back at his house and he was showing us, Zee in particular, books, sketches, photos, and maps. ''You see,'' he said. ''Such monuments as these are actually not uncommon in America. They're to be found throughout New England, down the coast, and all along the rivers flowing into the Mississippi. There are vestiges of very early European culture in Texas, Oklahoma, New

Mexico, Colorado, you name it.'' He gestured with both hands. ''The problem, of course, is that the sites are not being protected by the government and are done so by only a few enlightened private citizens. By the time our archeological and anthropological establishments take official note of them, which they will certainly eventually do, many of the sites will have been destroyed or otherwise lost. That will not happen here!'' His eyes flashed and his smile became grim. Then the darkness left his face and he thrust a pile of photos into our hands. ''I fear I'm being a wretched host. Look at these while I prepare drinks. I have whiskey and a new coffee I haven't tried. I like a strong, bitter brew, and I'm told that this new stuff should suit my fancy. What do you prefer?''

''How about both?'' I said.

''Ha! Capital! Both it shall be. I'll join you. And you, my dear?''

''Coffee and booze will do very well, thanks.''

''Excellent. I'll bring sugar and cream in case this new coffee is too acidic to be drunk black.'' He went off to the kitchen and soon returned with a tray laden with pot, cups and glasses. He put it down on the coffee table and fetched a bottle of whiskey. ''There. Allow me to pour.'' He sat down across from us and put his cup to his lips. ''Strong stuff, all right. Just my style.'' He grinned at us.

I poured whiskey in two glasses and gave one to Zee while she poured coffee. The whiskey was smooth, but the coffee was bitter. Zee tasted hers, widened her eyes, and added sugar and cream. Something happened in the back of my mind, a niggling dissatisfaction. Tristan Cooper was speaking of the photos we'd been looking at. They had no artistic merit, he confessed, for the people interested in ancient monuments were amateur photographers at best, but their subjects, the monuments, were priceless and these records of them therefore of great value, since, without such evidence, skeptics too lazy to go see for themselves would never become convinced of the monuments' existence. His voice seemed timeless, as though it was singing some ancient song of love.

I watched Zee sip her coffee and sipped my own. A

bitter brew. I rinsed my mouth and throat with whiskey and found myself remembering Marjorie Summerharp speaking of the merits of swimming. In my memory, her ironic voice flickered at Tristan Cooper and John Skye. Across the room from me, Cooper's present voice sang a psalm to his standing stones. His keen old eyes moved from Zee to me and back again. Zee was entranced. He was a magnificent old man, full of magic and passion. I lifted my cup to my lips, inhaled its aroma, tipped it, held it in my hand. Suddenly I was afraid.

"I've got to go to the head," I said, getting up. "Point me at it."

He looked at me with raven eyes, then gestured. "Certainly. There, beyond the kitchen."

Carrying my cup, I walked past him, stumbled over a rug, and went on. Behind me, Tristan Cooper's voice spoke again to Zee. In the bathroom I poured the coffee into the toilet and rinsed the cup in the sink. Then I knelt and stuck two fingers down my throat and induced vomiting. Not enough. I repeated the operation and managed a bit more. A third effort achieved little result. Filling my cup from the faucet, I drank and then attempted more vomiting. My head was fuzzy, so I splashed my face with cold water. I felt gloved with lead, shod with cement. I was in trouble, weak as a kitten. I drank more water, flushed the toilet for sound effect, and checked for a back door. There was one, and I looked through its window. Through the gathering darkness I could faintly see a line of white surf against South Beach. Even as I looked, it seemed that the darkness grew thicker. I shook my head and walked back into the living room.

Cooper smiled at me. Zee was blinking and had settled back into the couch where she sat. She looked content and comfortable. I lifted the coffee pot, half turned from Cooper, and pretended to pour another cup.

"Good stuff," I said, clumsily putting the pot down. "It's got a bite, but it sort of grows on you." I put my cup to my lips and walked around the room, pretending to look at things, until I got to where Cooper's shotgun should have been. It was gone. I swerved into a table,

disturbing some books, which slid to the floor. "Sorry."
I pretended to empty my cup, then got down on my knees
and fumbled with the books.

"That's all right," said Tristan Cooper, who was suddenly at my side. He took my arm and helped me up.
"Why don't you sit down with Mrs. Madieras? Make
yourself comfortable."

I didn't want to get comfortable. I was surprised to see
my car keys in his hands. He must have gotten them somehow as he'd helped me to my feet. I blinked at them.

"How are you feeling?" asked Cooper, following my
glance. "Oh, don't worry about these. I'll drive you home
later. I don't think you want to try driving, do you? Sit
down and rest a bit. That's it. Have some more coffee.
You're a big fellow, and you need more than your little
friend here."

He led me to the couch and I sat down. I felt dull. I
leaned forward and pushed with my hands, but didn't make
it to my feet. Beside me, Zee's eyes were closed and her
breathing was even. Her face had that quality of childlike
innocence it assumed when she slept.

Cooper put a full cup of coffee in my hand. I lifted it
to my lips but then dropped it as I attempted to set it on
the coffee table. I stared up at Cooper, who stood back
and watched me attentively.

"Chloral hydrate," I said. "You've Mickey Finned us."
I put my hands behind me and pushed, but made no progress off the couch. I fell back and stared up at him. "You
did the same thing to Marjorie." My voice felt thick.

"It's quite painless," he said. "You'll just go to sleep."

I was thinking very slowly. "They'll find this stuff in
us when they do autopsies. People will know we were
here."

"Oh, you won't be found here," he said, his head tilted
to one side as he watched me. "I'll drive you back to your
place in your Landcruiser. That's where they'll find you.
A double suicide, as I see it. A lovers' pact? I imagine
that Mrs. Madieras got the drug from the hospital, but I
really won't be able to say, in the unlikely event anyone
should ask me. I'll pour more of my syrup down your

throats after you're asleep. Ten grams is fatal, but I'll double the dose for you since you're a big man. How are you feeling now? Getting pretty sleepy, I imagine. Your eyelids look very heavy. You and your little friend here are too dangerous. You and poor Marjorie. I can't afford to have an exposé of Sanctuary. I need their money to protect my property from developers . . ."

His voice faded off as my eyelids dropped. I lifted them again. "You picked her up in your boat while she was swimming," I said. My tongue felt thick.

"Yes. I told her I felt in a madcap mood. That we'd run to Nomans Land and nail some big bluefish just like in the old days. She was delighted. I plucked her right out of the water and wrapped her in a robe and gave her a hot cup of coffee. A half hour later we were well to the west and she was asleep. I simply slipped her overboard. I confess that I did not think of where the tides might carry her." He leaned forward and studied my face. "She and I were great friends, you know. Delightful woman. Great wit. I will miss her."

My head fell back against the couch and my eyelids dropped lower. Through my lashes I watched him studying me, his face attentive and perhaps sad. "Well, well," he said to himself after what seemed a long time. "I do believe he's finally asleep." He leaned forward. "Are you asleep, Mr. Jackson?" He put out a long fingered brown hand and slapped me across the cheek. My head rolled away. He pinched hard on the nerve center between my thumb and forefinger. It hurt but I did not respond. He stepped back, looked at me some more, took out my car keys and jangled them for a long minute and then went toward the front of the house where the Landcruiser was parked.

I waited until I heard the front door open and close, then got up. It was harder than I'd hoped. I bent and got Zee over my shoulder and lifted her. She was dead weight. I staggered across the room, through the kitchen, and out the back door. It was dark, but I wasn't sure whether the darkness was within me or outside of me. There was a glow of lightning off to the southwest, and I started away from the house. A bit later I heard distant, faint thunder. Behind me, I heard the Landcruiser start up.

Cooper was between us and the highway, and he had his shotgun and my truck. And he had no chloral hydrate in his system. I tripped on something and went down, with Zee's body landing heavily on top of me. I got up, got her across my shoulder again, and headed away from the house toward the beach. By now, Cooper knew we were gone. This was his land and he had hunted it in the old days with my father. He'd be coming with the gun, and I was crashing around making more noise than a herd of cows. I headed for the beach.

I fell a half dozen times and each time got up weaker. The chloral hydrate and whiskey had done a number on Zee. She was more than drunk, she was in a near coma. If I had drunk even one full cup of coffee, I'd be as unconscious as she. But memory had saved me. Extolling the virtues of swimming, Marjorie Summerharp had spoken to Tristan Cooper at John Skye's party. "Probably cure your insomnia," she had said. "Healthier than that chloral hydrate you take for it, certainly."

In the Boston combat zone I'd come across Mickey-Finned victims who had downed booze laced with chloral hydrate and awakened without their wallets if they had awakened at all. The drug had a strong, pungent odor and a bitter, caustic taste. It was an effective sleeping agent in small doses but a fatal drug in large ones. I had some in me, but was still operational in a fashion, thanks to my timely memory of Marjorie and judicious vomiting in Tristan Cooper's bathroom. I was worried about Zee, though, because I didn't know how much she had drunk or what dosage Tristan had used in the coffee.

I crashed through the scrub and suddenly was on a narrow road. Somewhere behind me I heard a breaking branch. I lurched away down the road toward the sound of surf and abruptly found myself looking down at a stretch of beach whitened with breaking waves. The roar of the surf drowned out any sound that might have been behind me.

I realized that I was on the bluff where Van Dam and I

had stood four days earlier looking down at the Sanctuary
beach. I looked to the left, and there was the pond and
the docked boats. Buoyed by a sudden hope, I staggered
toward the dock, feeling as I went the first scattered drops
of the rain that accompanied the rising wind.

I glanced behind me through the gathering gloom but
saw nothing. Then I was on the dock. The tide was low,
so the sportfisherman was no good to me, since it could
not clear the partially sand-filled channel to the sea. But
the shallow-drafted day sailers could make it, so I carried
Zee to the first of them and awkwardly deposited her in
the bow. She was breathing regularly, so I had hope that
she had not received a fatal dose of the drug. Then I got
to work on the sails.

The wind was from the southwest and the channel led
out due south, so I knew I should be able to sail the boat
out close hauled. Once clear of the channel I could fall
away and sail through the surf parallel to the beach, east
toward Edgartown, providing, of course, that I could avoid
a broach in the climbing waves that approached the beach.

I had the sails up and was casting off from the dock
when I glanced ashore and saw Cooper appear on the
beach. He must have seen the white sails against the darkness of the storm and come running down the road. Standing on the bluff, at far range for a shotgun, he threw the
gun to his shoulder and fired.

Fiberglass splintered from the combing inches from me.
I tossed off the final line and snatched tiller and sheets.
With her centerboard up, the boat slid sideways off toward
the channel. I looked back and saw Tristan running down
from the bluff. He ran like an ape, his legs bowed, his
body thrust forward, his long arms swinging at his sides,
the shotgun in one hand.

The boat moved slowly, as if thrice adream, and Tristan
ran awkwardly but fast, cutting off the distance between
us. Then we were in the channel, crabbing awkwardly
toward the sea, which smashed at the channel's mouth.
Another glance astern showed Tristan suddenly stopping
and again lifting the gun. I heard no shot, for the surf was
roaring in my ears, but above my head the aluminum boom

suddenly had a hole in it. He was shooting deer slugs and had only missed because he'd been running and had fired too quickly. I ducked and turned back to the boat, for we were about to meet the surf as it pounded into the mouth of the channel.

The sandbar that lay outside the beach was all that made it possible to exit the channel. The bar broke up the waves and reduced their power, and the day sailer, lightly built though she was, was able to ride over the surf that got through, take the force of the waves on her starboard bow, then ride out those same waves as I cleared the channel, got the centerboard down, and fell away downwind toward Edgartown. For a time we were dropping into deep troughs then rising on crests of waves coming right at our beam and threatening to swamp us. But the little day sailer was like a cork and rode right up the waves before dropping off on the other side, and slowly I was able to crawl away from the beach until at last we were in still wild but gentler waters. Slacking off the sheets, I headed east along the beach, feeling better. Looking back through the gathering night and increasingly heavy rain, however, I discovered that things were not yet resolved. A white sail was going up in the pond. Tristan Cooper was coming after us.

The two boats were the same design and I had a head start, but there were two of us and only one of him, and I far outweighed him by myself, so he should be a bit faster. I looked at the wounds in the boat. The shattered combing was only cosmetic damage, but the holed boom was a different matter. The shot had seriously weakened an already light spar, and I wasn't sure how the boom would hold under the strain of a rising wind. The damage was near the outer end of the boom, so if it broke I probably wouldn't lose the whole sail, but there was a good chance that the main would tear. In either case, Cooper would have an even greater sailing edge than he already had.

Along the beach the surf was boiling on empty sand. South Beach runs from east to west all along the southern edge of Martha's Vineyard and is a world-class beach by any test, including the fact that no houses are built on it.

Tonight, though, I wished it was Miami Beach, lined with hotels full of people who could phone the police or give us shelter from our pursuer. The first inhabitants fairly close to the beach were the houses and condos at Katama miles ahead, where Marjorie Summerharp had taken her last, fatal swim. I wondered if we would get that far before Cooper ran us down.

The surf would be rising with the wind and it looked bad enough now. I looked forward to where Zee lay in the bow. She was still unconscious and getting soaked and chilled. I tied the tiller, went forward, and pulled her back to me. I moved quickly, but even so the shifting weight threw the light boat out of balance and she turned into the wind and lost way. A gain for Cooper, but there was no help for it. I adjusted the line to the tiller and rushed forward again to dig two life preservers from the cuddy cabin in the bow. Before I was back, the boat had again lurched up into the wind, this time nearly coming completely about before I was able to bring her back on course.

I took off my shirt and put it on Zee, then got life jackets on both of us. I did not want to attempt to beach the boat, but if I had to I wanted Zee to have at least a chance of making it ashore alive. I was exhausted from my long flight to the beach and doubted if I could get both of us ashore without life jackets. I wasn't sure I could get us ashore *with* them. And if I could, then what? There were no houses and no people. If we could survive the surf, Cooper, for all his mighty years, could, too, and with his shotgun could make two lonely kills far from the sight of any man and afterward walk away unknown.

The wind was cold, but it was a following one, so it could have been worse. Sailing is chilliest when close hauled. I looked back and saw that Cooper was coming. His sail was dim in the dark night and the rain as he sailed our wake. If it got dark enough, I thought I might be able to slip away to sea without being seen and let him sail on down the coast alone. Once he got by me, I could head west and try to make a landing behind him. For such a plan, it would be nice to have tanbark sails instead of white ones, but such was not my fortune. Anyway, with Cooper in sight, all I could do was sail straight ahead.

I put Zee's limp body amidships alongside the centerboard box and got myself opposite her, balancing the boat as well as I could to maximize her speed. I wished for the first time in my life that I actually knew something about sailboat racing. I had heard racers talk and had read analyses of races won and lost and articles about strategies and techniques to increase speed, but not much of it had sunk in or even interested me. Now I wished I knew it all. Even the least of racing sailors could no doubt squeeze more speed out of my little boat than I was managing. I wondered if Tristan had ever done any racing. If he had, I was in even more trouble. I felt sleepy in spite of the chill of the rain and wind.

A sailboat race is not often an exciting event to watch. The boats are slow, and except when they are coming around marks or tacking, nothing seems to be happening almost all the time. So it was with this race. I was grimly aware of the irony of appearances. A watcher from the shore would have seen two small boats sailing slowly along the beach, moving comfortably before a twenty-knot following wind. There would be no way for him to know that the lazy boats, so common a sight on the Vineyard's summer waters, contained, in this case, a hound after a hare, a gunner after game.

I had time to put everything together. I thought I had failed to do it sooner because I had been distracted by the Shakespeare papers and later had been inclined to suspect people I disliked: McGregor, the Van Dams, even Helen Barstone and Bill Hooperman. I had seen through a glass darkly, but now saw face to face. Marjorie had told me how she and Tristan had liked to fish from his boat long ago and had told both me and him she'd not mind going with him again, so when he showed up that morning she was an easy victim. Tristan's powerboat, for which he surely still had keys, was moored in the pond off South Beach, and he'd had no problem getting down there, taking it out, and bringing it back long before any of the Sanctuary crew was even up and about. And even if he had been seen coming back in, he could tell a satisfactory tale of having gone fishing off Nomans land. Marjorie had threatened, however idly, to write an exposé of Sanctuary, and Tristan, fearing he might lose his precious stones if Sanctuary should be forced by scandal to close its doors, decided to kill her—motive. He also had the means—chloral hydrate. Marjorie had chided him about his use of it, in fact. He also knew of Marjorie's morning swims and had been told where she took them—opportunity. I had been pretty slow.

And then I had told him enough to make him think that I knew more than I actually did, and he had seen me, too, as a danger. And, worse yet, I had inadvertently made him think that the "young woman" who had observed the Sanctuary sexploits and told me about them was Zee, when in fact it was Helen Barstone. Poor Zee, unconscious and being hunted down because of a mistaken identity. Because of me. I felt stupidly guilty.

On the other hand, if I'd mentioned Helen's name to Tristan, Helen might now be dead. Zee, at least, was still alive, no great thanks to me. I meant to keep her that way.

"Wake up," I said to Zee. But of course she didn't. It takes several hours for a Mickey Finn to wear off. If she ever did wake up, she'd have a headache but would otherwise be fine. If Tristan caught us, she would never wake up at all.

~18~

I LOOKED OVER the stern and could see Tristan's sail leaning in the wind, a pale ghost in the darkness of night and storm. I thought he seemed closer. I brought my eyes back to my own boat and sailed on.

Suddenly there was a noisy flapping and snapping, and I woke up to find the boat turning into the wind, her sails crackling as they emptied. Dull-minded and angry, I yanked back on the tiller I'd allowed to escape me and the boat banged around back on course. But I had lost momentum, and now Tristan's dim sail was even closer. I slapped myself hard and tried to shake the swamp from my brain. I could not allow myself to sleep.

I climbed out of the cockpit and sat in the combing where the wind would hit me harder, keep me colder, and perhaps keep me awake. I was also a better target for Tristan, but I thought him still too far back to shoot effectively as our boats rose and fell and the waves passed beneath us from our starboard quarter and hurried toward their doom on the beach.

Zee moved and then was quiet again. I began to shiver and was happy for it. I hunched my shoulders and pressed my teeth together so they'd not chatter. We sailed on.

I wished for a fog and got none. On the other hand, the night was gradually growing darker, and there would be neither stars nor moon to light Tristan's hunt. I wished for heavy rain, for a curtain of rain to fall between his boat and mine, but no such rain fell, only the steady wind-driven shower that had begun when we'd first fetched the beach.

I wondered if I could tie the tiller and then go overboard with Zee and let the boat sail on. I could rope the two of us together and perhaps make shore while Tristan pursued my empty boat. Men overboard were almost impossible to see in stormy waters, and Tristan would surely miss us.

But my earlier efforts to tie the tiller had not been notably successful. Every shift of weight had changed the boat's balance and caused her to point up and stop. If that happened when we went overboard, Tristan would have easy pickings when he sailed down upon us.

I wondered if Zee would float ashore alive if I put her overboard in her life jacket. I doubted it, for she was unconscious and could do nothing to keep her face out of the sea. Many a sailor was drowned while afloat in his life jacket. If she were awake, she could do it, I thought. "Wake up!" I said to her, but she only sighed and slept.

We sailed on, Tristan's dim sail growing taller in our wake. I thought of the romance of Tristan and Isolde, of how Tristan's ship was to bear a white sail if he lived but a black one if he'd died, and how the wrong sail had been mounted and Isolde, believing her lover dead, had died herself before he could arrive and love her, and how, finding her dead, he, too, had died of grief. Tristan Cooper was not so romantic a figure. If there was any dying to be done, he did not plan it to be his.

The combing splintered, and I looked astern and thought I saw Tristan raise the shotgun above his head in a sort of salute. Not a bad shot, all things considered. At least he had hit the boat. If he got much closer, we were in real trouble. Zee stirred and rolled awkwardly onto her back, the life jacket wadded clumsily about her. "Wake up!" I said, but she only made a sleepy noise and brushed vaguely at the rain that fell on her face.

How long had we been sailing this odd slow motion race? It was now darkest night and about all I could see against the night was the white of foam, the blur of Tristan's sail and the line of surf on the dark shore. In my ears were the sounds of wind, water, and the little boat itself as her rigging strained and thrust her eastward. I was cold but my brain was fuzzy. I sang. Many verses of sea chanties.

> *"What do you do with a drunken sailor?*
> *What do you do with a drunken sailor?*
> *What do you do with a drunken sailor?*
> *Early in the morning?"*

What do you do? You put him in the scuppers with a hose pipe on him, you keelhaul him till he's sober, you shave his belly with a rusty razor, early in the morning. I sang of the *Golden Vanity,* of Henry Martin, of High Barbaree.

"Don't," said Zee's voice irritably. "I'm trying to sleep." I squinted down at her. She had pulled her knees up and was hugging herself, her eyes shut tight.

"Wake up!" I said, but she only hugged herself tighter. I sang "Blow the Man Down" and "The Maid of Amsterdam," and Zee began to squirm and mutter.

Then, ahead and to the left, I saw lights on shore. We were off Katama and those were houses! Hope. I looked behind me. Where was Tristan? He'd disappeared. Hope and disbelief surged through me. Had he broached? Had he been taken unaware by some sort of rogue wave?

But then I saw him, no longer in my wake but sailing a course between me and the beach, still behind but closer to shore so that if I headed for the beach he'd arrive there at almost the same time. Tristan's brain and vision were not clouded by drugs, and he must have seen the lights before I did. He did not intend us to fetch shore here.

How much longer could I hold a lead? A mile? Less? After that he could come alongside and at close range attempt his business. I thought of the shotguns and rifle I had at home. Even my own service revolver would be something. But those weapons were all locked away and would do me no good.

Zee was slowly waking up. Not too much longer and I could put her overboard and give her, at least, a chance at life. Thinking of this, I was surprised to see her struggle into a sitting position and gaze fuzzily around. She looked at the boat and at me and up at the sail and rubbed her eyes.

"Jeff," she said, yawning. She smiled a sleepy, confused smile. "What's going on?" She hugged herself. "I'm cold."

It was not a time for gentle introductions to reality. As soon as her eyes cleared, I told her where we were and why. She looked at me with confusion. "What? I don't understand you."

I told her again, watching Tristan's sail move through the darkness between us and the line of white surf on the beach. His boat was now just behind my port quarter and perhaps a hundred yards away. Time was running out.

Zee rubbed her face and caught up rain water from the bilge and splashed herself with it. "What are we going to do?" she asked.

"I want you to slide overboard and swim for the beach. He won't see you, and you'll have a good chance of making it since it's downwind. When you get there, find a phone and call the cops."

"What about you?"

"I'll sail on down the beach. When he gets close, I'll tie the tiller and go overboard myself. I had to tie it a couple of times while you were asleep, and it worked like a charm. This little boat holds a course quite well. With us out of the boat, it may even sail faster than Tristan's. If he does catch it, I'll be long gone."

"You're lying," she said without hesitation.

"I am not. Now you get ready to go overboard."

"No. I'm not going to leave you to get yourself killed."

"It's my fault you're here," I said, "and I'm not going to let you get killed because of me. You're going overboard if I have to throw you over, so get yourself over!"

"I will not! And if you throw me over I'll scream and make such a fuss that Tristan will find me right away. He'll come for me and you can get away."

I realized that she had given herself an idea. "Look there!" I shouted and when she turned I grabbed her and pulled her to me before she could jump into the water.

Neither one of us had much zip. She wiggled and shoved at me. "Let me go!"

"No. And you listen to me. If you jump, I'm going to jump with you. And then where'll we be, eh? You sit right here, damn it!"

"Let go!" I let her go and she slid away. We eyed each other.

"Women!" I said, trying to think.

"I'm not going to leave you," she said, "so get that idea right out of your mind. We're in this together."

"I should have thrown you over while you were still asleep."

The lights of Katama were sliding behind us, and Tristan was not between us and them. I felt a sense of doom. "Please do as I ask," I said gently.

"No."

Then, ahead in the darkness, I heard a roar different from that of the surf and the waves around us. I instantly knew what it was: the opening to Katama Bay where the storm-driven waves were crowding into the channel in a chaos of pyramiding waves, swirling currents, and flying spume. It was a faint hope, but the only one I could come up with.

I put the tiller into Zee's hand. "Take this." I went to the centerboard box and cranked up the centerboard. My little boat could sail in incredibly shallow water with her board up. I returned to the tiller and looked for Tristan. I was shocked to see how close he was, but had no choice but to get even closer to him. I hauled the tiller toward me, slacked off the mainsheet and headed downwind for the opening, holding a course that would take me across Tristan's bow.

"Get low," I said to Zee. "Stay on this side of the centerboard box. It will give you some protection when he shoots." I gave her a push and got low myself. Over the cowling I watched Tristan's boat come toward ours and then saw Tristan raise the shotgun and aim. I cowered down, and his shot came through the frail fiberglass hull and smacked the metal centerboard where it nestled in its box. A second shot tore through the combing and a third plucked at my arm.

Then we were past his bow and into the cacophony of the opening. I heard Zee cry out and saw her looking at the bleeding arm I could not feel as the tidal river absorbed us.

We were surrounded by thunder, and the air was full of water that felt like whips. Our little boat lifted and twisted and smashed down with a crash. White water poured over her side and into the cockpit. Zee washed forward, and only my grip on the tiller kept me from washing after her. The boat lifted and then dropped into a trough and hit hard sand. Something snapped up forward, and the little boat cried out as though in pain. But she lifted and swept forward through the flying spume, and Zee came washing back to me. Then we hit bottom again and the mast snapped off, carrying away the sails. Still the brave little boat would not die. She lifted herself a last time onto the waves and into the wind-driven water and sand. But her back was broken, and she turned broadside to the surf.

I picked Zee up and went overboard with her just as the boat rolled over. Awash in the wild water, we were saved by our life jackets. Bouncing off sandbars, faces full of sand and water, we clung to one another and were carried by the river of the rising tide into the waters of Katama Bay.

Afloat at last in calmer waters, we looked back into the wild darkness and watched Tristan Cooper die. His boat, like ours, was too frail for such waters. Like ours, it broke its back on the shifting sands and capsized. We saw him leap or be thrown from the boat and then perhaps saw him again on the far side of the channel, struggling toward shore in waist-deep water. A wave knocked him down, but he got up again. Then another wave came, and after that we saw no more like him. The storm and the night closed over him like the lid of a casket.

Side by side, we paddled to the shore of Chappaquiddick and pulled ourselves up on the sand. After a while we were able to get up and go find a house and a telephone.

The Chappy ferry was still running, and after the owners of the telephone had given us hot coffee and dry clothes and wrapped by bloody arm, they drove us there. The chief was waiting for us on the town dock.

"You two okay?"

"Yes, but I don't think Tristan Cooper is."

He looked at my bandaged arm. "The harbor master and some others are down in Katama Bay right now looking around with spotlights. Some other men are on the beach in case he made it ashore. Let's get you up to the hospital."

He drove us to the emergency room, where my furrowed arm was properly wrapped and I was given the required shots, then took us back to the station, where we told our tale into a tape recorder while a young cop took notes and the chief puffed his pipe and asked questions. "So it was Cooper that did Marjorie Summerharp in," he said when we were done.

"It wasn't hard. He had a fast boat, and if he ran without running lights nobody would have noticed him. He was probably only off Katama for a couple of minutes, long enough to pick Marjorie up and head west again. He could have been back on the dock in Chilmark before seven. I doubt if anybody up there even knew the boat had been out."

"I imagine the state troopers will ask. You two look done in. I'll have one of the boys take you home."

The summer rent-a-cop took us first to my place, where I got my extra set of car keys, then to Zee's, where we dropped her off, then to Tristan's, where I found my Landcruiser, keys in the ignition, backed up to the front door. I suggested that the young cop take note of its position.

"He wanted to load the two of you in the back," said the rent-a-cop, who was very excited to be a part of an investigation of both murder and attempted murder.

"You got it, kid."

I got into the Landcruiser and drove back to Zee's place. Although it was the very end of June, she had a fire going in the fireplace. I went in and wrapped my arms around her, and we sat in front of the fire for a long time looking at the flames. I made some coffee and laced it with brandy, honey, and lemon juice, and we drank that.

"I've got to go to work in the morning," she said at last, standing up.

"No, you don't."

"Yes, I do," she said. Then, "What if they don't ever find his body? What if he didn't drown but is still walking around somewhere?"

"He isn't walking around," I said, wondering if he was. "And even if he is, he's no danger to us anymore. He'd know by now that we've talked to the police and that killing us would serve no useful purpose anymore. I think I should stay with you tonight."

"No. Not tonight. I'm sorry. Do you mind?"

I did mind. "No," I said. I kissed her on the forehead and left.

The next day was bright and sunny, and there were search boats on Katama Bay and outside the beach as well. There were four-by-fours on the Chappy shore and along the bay's south shore as men looked for Tristan Cooper's body. Even as those grim crews sought a corpse, the beach was filling with sunbathers and kite fliers oblivious to the somber work being done almost beside them. It was the first day of July, and pale new vacationers were after tans under yet another beautiful Vineyard sky. Day sailers pushed by gentle breezes moved over the waters of Katama Bay, mixing innocently with the boats of searchers. Along the shore, clam diggers and amateur quahoggers ignored the four-by-fours moving slowly along the water's edge.

I watched for a while from the beach, wondering if he'd washed inside the bay or whether the tide had taken him outside when it changed. I was not in a mood to fish, so I went home and made myself do some gardening, which I was also not in a mood to do. I heard the phone ring and managed to get to it before it stopped. It was Mattie Skye inviting me to supper.

"I wasn't sure you'd be up to cooking, after all the commotion. Besides, we want to hear *everything!* Our feelings are all mixed up about Tristan. We're sad and shocked at the same time. Still, it's a wonderful scandal, far better than Ian and Marjorie being possible academic fakers. Come at six and we'll ply you with rum to loosen your tongue. I phoned Zee at the hospital and she's coming, too.''

"I have fresh green beans in my garden," I said. "I'll bring a bunch."

Mattie met me at the kitchen door and steered me right outside again. "J.W., you be good to Zee. No smart mouthing for a while. She just spent a half hour telling me that she thinks there must be something wrong with her because first she married a jerk, then she thought Ian McGregor was fascinating, then Tristan Cooper enchanted her, a murderer, no less. She needs a man she can trust who won't hurt her." She looked sternly at me.

I remembered the look on Zee's face when I'd put McGregor's face in the dirt and had my doubts that I was the man she needed. "I'm not sure I'm the guy for the job," I said, and told Mattie why.

"You men are such fools," she said. "You and your fists and your guns. Little boys, all of you. None of you deserve a woman as good as Zee."

"You're probably right," I said. "I imagine I've added to her hurt one way or another, but if so it wasn't my intent."

She touched my sleeve. "I know. That's a big difference between you and the other men who've been in her life lately. Just be patient with her. She's too strong to stay down long."

"My specialty is giving women joy."

She faked a swing at my jaw, then laughed. "You are a hopeless case, J.W. Jackson. Do be gentle, okay?"

"If you give me a kiss, I'll be anything you want, lady."

"Kiss, schmiss," said Mattie. "All right, you wretched man." She grabbed my hair and pulled my face down and gave me a good kiss. "Dr. Jerk, Ian McGregor, Tristan Cooper, and you. Maybe there *is* something wrong with that girl."

"There's nothing wrong with John Skye. That man has blue-ribbon taste in women. Maybe you should let him take care of Zee."

"John Skye has his hands full with just me and the twins. He couldn't handle another woman, too."

I imagined she was right about that and followed her into the kitchen, where I was immediately put to work preparing the beans I'd brought. Fresh garden beans are one of God's gifts to man. Later, while we ate them and an excellent sole with dill sauce, I told them the tale of our adventure with Tristan Cooper. When we got to the part when Zee was awake, I turned the story over to her. She finished it, and after we answered as many questions as we could, even the twins seemed satisfied.

"By Jove," said John. "That tale earns you both another picnic sail on the *Mattie*. What do you say to an overnight trip to Tarpaulin Cove? We can make it up there one day and be home the next evening. Zee, you and J. W. can be the official ship's tale tellers. The girls can bring their guitar and banjo. What do you say?"

Zee looked at me, "Well . . ."

"Sounds good to me," I said.

"Fine! I think you two could use a short holiday."

The next weekend we made the trip, sailing out of Edgartown, around East Chop and West Chop and catching a west tide up Vineyard Sound to the lovely little cove on Naushon Island. A half dozen boats were anchored there already, for it is a favorite stopover for cruising sailors, but we hauled up *Mattie*'s centerboard and pulled deep into shallow waters where we'd have little close company.

We took the dinghy ashore and walked the clean, empty beach out to the lighthouse and back. Then, as the others continued their explorations, I swam out to the *Mattie* and prepared supper: fried chicken with my newest secret sauce, accompanied by more fresh green beans from my garden and wild rice, all to be washed down with a Colombard chilled on ice in my cooler.

The chicken was terrific. We ate it all and everything else, too.

"Naturally you all want to know the secret of my sauce," I said, "because you still have hopes of becoming as good a cook as me. But I don't mind telling you, because I'm a manly sort of cook and have no fear of potential rivals."

"As a matter of fact, I do want to know," said Zee. "It was yummy."

"You are a woman of discriminating taste. It was indeed yummy. Peanut butter is the secret. You mix that and some oil and vinegar and soy sauce and lemon juice and ginger and garlic and chili peppers all together and blast them with your food processor if you happen to have one, which we don't. Then you smear it over your chicken or beef or pork or whatever and voilà! another masterpiece from the kitchen of J. W. Jackson.

"I take it you'll be more precise when I copy down the specifics," said Mattie.

"For you, every detail."

"Peanut butter," said Jill. "Who ever heard of cooking with peanut butter? You're not supposed to cook with peanut butter, you're supposed to eat it in sandwiches."

"You ate your share," said Jen. "I thought it was excellent." She licked a finger and gave her sister a curt nod and me a nice smile.

"I always said you were a young woman of good taste, Jen," I said. "Your sister has a long way to go to reach your level of maturity."

"I'm Jill," she said.

"No, you're not," said her mother. "Don't give poor J. W. a hard time."

I was shocked. "Good grief, do you mean I actually got them right for once?"

Mattie patted my arm. "We all knew you would do it, J. W. You're not really as dumb as you act sometimes."

Sleeping six people on an eighteen-foot catboat isn't hard if it doesn't rain. The twins got the vee births in the cabin and the grownups unrolled sleeping pads on the wide deck of the cockpit. All night long the *Mattie* moved gently upon her anchor rope and the stars swung overhead. As I was drifting asleep, I felt a hand touch mine and turned and saw Zee's face in the starlight. She was smiling. We slept hand in hand all night long, and on the long sail home the next day we were happy.

When we got back we learned that Tristan Cooper's body had been found in the nets of a trawler about a mile off South Beach, not far from where Marjorie Summerharp's body had been found. I decided that maybe there was a God after all. Zee was moody for a time, but then cheered up. She was a tender but tough woman. I asked her to marry me. She shook her head.

"No. But ask me again. As soon as I know that I can live without you, I might say yes."

"I'll keep asking. I know I can live without you," I lied, "but I don't want to. Besides, you need somebody around who can cook."

"I can cook."

"I can cook better."

"No, you can't."

"Yes, I can."

"Can't."

"Can."

"Not."

"Too."

The pale July people browned. There seemed to be more of them on the roads than ever before. The bluefish began to fade away and go north to entertain the Cape Ann and Maine fishermen. They would return in September, but until then I would have to hunt other fish and harvest the land. I did serious shellfishing, gathered blueberries, picked and preserved the bounty from my garden.

One hot afternoon as I was sweating over many jars of pickles, Zee's little Jeep came down my driveway and Zee and John and Mattie Skye got out. I gave them beer, finished the batch of pickled summer squash I was working on, and joined them on my balcony.

Beyond the garden we could see the beach with its bright umbrellas, brighter surf sails and parked cars. The Sound beyond was dark blue under a pale blue sky, and there were white sails moving through a gentle wind. A thin cloud hung high over Cape Cod, and the Cape Pogue lighthouse stood clearly against the meeting of sea and sky.

"Here," said John, handing me a small magazine. I

opened it. It was full of fine gray print. "Just off the presses," said John. "An examination copy. It won't be officially released until after Labor Day."

I looked at the table of contents. The lead article was about Shakespeare's *King Arthur,* authored by Drs. Marjorie Summerharp and Ian McGregor. It was preceded by a brief tribute to Marjorie Summerharp by Ian McGregor.

I leafed through the magazine. "I don't see anything about the two dissertations."

"No, you don't. We don't yet know for sure that F. X. Eastford didn't exist. I'm willing to cover all bets that he didn't, but it will take time to prove it. Meanwhile, the Shakespeare article will come out on schedule, as it should, since it's an important piece. In fact, this edition of the journal might even go into extra printings and make its publishers some money for a change."

"Even though Marjorie and Ian probably both faked their thesis references."

"Even though. Nobody on the mainland knows anything about those dissertations. Besides, even if they fudged before it doesn't mean they fudged this time. Nobody's dishonest all of the time, not even in the ivory tower."

"Why did Marjorie want to look at those theses, anyway?"

"Knowing her, I'd guess that when she couldn't find any fault with the play they'd found, she decided to snoop around in Ian's background to see if she could find one in him. Maybe he said something about quoting her thesis in his own, but after forty years she couldn't remember exactly what she'd faked herself. She had a nose for academic fraud, maybe because she was good at it herself. Besides, she loved to snoop."

"And so do you," said Mattie.

"Absolutely," said Skye. "It's fun. Helen Barstone, Bill Hooperman, and I are the snoopers. Three profs on the trail of fraud and murder in the groves of academe. Did the late, great Marjorie Summerharp create F. X. Eastford? Did Ian McGregor, handsome discoverer of a lost Shakespeare play, fake a quotation from the fictional

F. X. Eastford? What drove the world-famous scholar Dr. Tristan Cooper to murder? What were the sex secrets of Sanctuary? It's hot stuff, and my partners Helen and Bill have a terrific edge on everybody else because they just finished spending weeks working with Tristan.''

Mattie grinned. "It's too bad they don't have pulp magazines anymore. You could write for them instead of those dull academic rags.''

"Riches and fame shall be ours at last," said Skye. "I can see it now: fifty weeks on the *Times* bestseller list, movie contracts, interviews on the late show. I'll get tenure and we'll be able to buy a summer place on the Vineyard. Beautiful women will seek me out.''

"You already have tenure and we already have a place on the Vineyard and I've already sought you out," said Mattie.

He put his arm around her. "Well, whatever," he said.

I put my arm around Zee, and the four of us drank our beer and looked out over my green garden to where the white-sailed boats, pushed by warm winds, moved across the innocent shark-filled sea.

FOLLOW IN THE FOOTSTEPS OF
DETECTIVE J.P. BEAUMONT
WITH FAST-PACED MYSTERIES
BY J.A. JANCE

Meet Peggy O'Neill
A Campus Cop With a Ph.D. in Murder

"A 'Must Read' for fans of Sue Grafton"
Alfred Hitchcock Mystery Magazine

Exciting Mysteries by M.D. Lake

AMENDS FOR MURDER 75865-2/$4.50 US/$5.50 Can
When a distinguished professor is found murdered, campus security officer Peggy O'Neill's investigation uncovers a murderous mix of faculty orgies, poetry readings, and some very devoted female teaching assistants.

COLD COMFORT 76032-0/$3.50 US/$4.25 Can
After he was jilted by Swedish sexpot Ann-Marie Ekdahl, computer whiz Mike Parrish's death was ruled a suicide by police. But campus cop Peggy O'Neill isn't so sure and launches her own investigation.

POISONED IVY 76573-X/$3.99 US/$4.99 Can
When outspoken professor Edith Silberman is accused of murder, campus cop Peggy O'Neill's gut feeling tells her Silberman is innocent and she sets out to prove it.

A GIFT FOR MURDER 76855-0/$4.50 US/$5.50 Can